MALAFORMED
REALITIES

VOLUME 1

THOMAS M. MALAFARINA

**HELLBENDER
BOOKS**

an imprint of Sunbury Press, Inc.
Mechanicsburg, PA USA

HELLBENDER BOOKS

an imprint of Sunbury Press, Inc.
Mechanicsburg, PA USA

For information about special discounts for bulk purchases, please contact Sunbury Press Orders Dept. at (855) 338-8359 or orders@sunburypress.com.

To request one of our authors for speaking engagements or book signings, please contact Sunbury Press Publicity Dept. at publicity@sunburypress.com.

ISBN: 978-1-62006-532-7 (Trade Paperback)
ISBN: 978-1-62006-533-4 (Mobipocket)

Library of Congress Control Number: 2015932260

FIRST HELLBENDER BOOKS EDITION: November 2017

Product of the United States of America
0 1 1 2 3 5 8 13 21 34 55

Set in Bookman Old Style
Designed by Crystal Devine
Cover by Lawrence Knorr
Edited by Amanda Shrawder

Continue the Enlightenment!

For my amazing wife JoAnne:

None of my books would be possible whatsoever without her patience and loving dedication to both me as well as my very bizarre craft. I offer my eternal love and thanks to her for believing in me.

CONTENTS

INTRODUCTION

"Reality... What a Concept!" is the title of the 1979 comedy recording from the late, always great Robin Williams. Williams was also quoted as having said, "Reality is just a crutch for people who can't cope with drugs."

Edgar Allen Poe expressed, "Words have no power to impress the mind without the exquisite horror of their reality."

C. S. Lewis stated, "Literature adds to reality, it does not simply describe it. It enriches the necessary competencies that daily life requires and provides; and in this respect, it irrigates the deserts that our lives have already become."

Friedrich Nietzsche said, "Hope in reality is the worst of all evils because it prolongs the torments of man."

And finally Albert Einstein stated, "Reality is merely an illusion, albeit a very persistent one."

Although there are natural rules, which govern the world in which we exist, in truth, everyone's personal impression of their reality is somewhat different. By natural rules, I don't mean regulations made by man but factors dictated by our surroundings. For example, the existence of the force we call gravity. You may choose to not believe in the law of gravity. Nevertheless, your personal beliefs are of little consequence if you are plummeting toward the earth at full speed without a parachute.

Every one of us has a slightly different take on what we perceive our individual realities to be. You may see a busker standing on the street corner dressed in old worn clothing playing a beat up guitar and singing for a few tips tossed into a tattered open guitar case. You might feel sorry for him. You may assume he must have fallen on hard times. You might even feel guilty because you have a job, which earns you a great deal of money and allows you to afford the finer things in life. You guess that he had some sort of breakdown, which caused him to lose touch with reality and has put him in this dire situation.

On the contrary, the busker may see you rushing by in a hurry to make your first meeting of the day. He sees your fine clothing and the permanent scowl of tension creased on your face. He may feel sorry for you because you are still part of in the proverbial rat race, the same rat race he managed to escape several years earlier. He is happy now because he has shed all of the so-called trappings of the world and now feels he is freer than he has ever been in his life. He may even feel guilty because he has so much freedom while you remain chained to your false sense of reality. Same situation but seen from two different perspectives. Neither one is either correct or incorrect. Neither view changes the scene in any way. It's all just a matter of perception. I'm sure you've heard the saying "perception is reality."

However, personal interpretations aside, what would happen if reality, actual reality, those concrete natural laws somehow became so twisted and so malformed that reality as we knew it no longer could be thought of as reality at all? Such a realm is one in which we horror writers tend to exist. For a time, while we are creating our stories that unreality is our reality. Our job is to make the impossible seem possible, the unreal real, and this often takes us to places even we would prefer not to go. The trick is always to leave enough breadcrumbs so we can make it safely back from those horrifying places with our souls and minds intact.

History tells us that on October 3, 1849 the great master of the macabre, Edgar Allen Poe, was found wandering the streets of Baltimore, Maryland delirious and in grave distress. He was taken immediately to the Washington College Hospital, where he died at 5a.m. on Sunday, October 7. Poe never became coherent enough to explain how he wound up in such an abysmal condition.

There are a lot of theories about his death but no concrete evidence. Maybe he simply lost his way back from those incredibly dark places his writing took him.

I can only hope that my own numerous journeys into that land of darkness will not someday take its toll on me. I would hate to think of myself thirty years from now in some home for the aged and infirm, cowering in bed with the covers tucked tightly to my chin. Would I be too afraid to leave the safety of my covers because the demons, which once only lived inside my mind, had since become as real to me as flesh and bone in my addled condition? I suppose we will have to wait and see.

In the meantime, please enjoy yet another journey into the darkest corners of my mind. This collection is called *Malaformed Realities* not just as a clever play on my last name, but because distorting and twisting reality into something it was never intended to be is what I enjoy doing best. And if in the process, I manage to disturb and frighten you along the way then all the better.

Thomas M. Malafarina

September 2014.

WHEN THEY COME FOR YOU

Darkness surrounded him. Not the pitch-black sort of darkness where nothing at all could be seen, but more of a gloomy semi-darkness. He was having trouble focusing, unsure of where he was. He could determine he was lying on his back with his head either propped up with pillows or elevated in some other fashion, perhaps by some sort of adjustable bed. He felt a dull burning pain, which seemed to radiate out from the center of his chest in all directions. As bad as his chest might feel, the disorientation and dreamlike quality of his surroundings was even more disturbing.

He could hear the beeping and humming of electronic machinery all around him, but he couldn't recall where he was or why he was lying in this strange gloomy place accompanied only by the sounds of machines. In fact, he couldn't quite even remember his own name. His mind was clouded, feeling as though he had been given some sort of mind-altering drug.

Then he slowly began to remember: drugs. Yes, that's exactly what it was: drugs for the pain. He had been given drugs, large doses of drugs. Morphine was one of the drugs and was being dripped into his body to help with... with the pain. It was all gradually starting to come back to him in disjointed fragments of lost memories. At last he finally recalled who he was—then sadly where he was and why. He realized he probably would have been better off not remembering after all. His name was Salvador, Salvador Monroe, known to his friends as Sal or Sallie. He was in bed in a hospital—no not a hospital but a hospice center. And he was dying.

Through the drug-induced fog, which he recognized was barely doing anything to dampen the searing agony in his cancer-riddled lungs, Sal understood one thing clearer than anything else; his remaining time was short, very short. He sensed he was extremely weak now, too weak to even raise his head, but he could still manage to slowly move his eyes about to take in most of the room. He could see he was all alone. Where was his wife? Where was Charlotte? She promised she wouldn't leave him, said she would stay with him till the very end. But where was she now?

Sal suddenly began to panic. He had known he was dying for months, but now he had a feeling, an unmistakable intuition that the end was close by and yet here he was... alone. He didn't want to die alone. He wouldn't allow himself to die alone. He was determined to hang on for as long as possible despite the pain. He wanted to wait for his beloved wife to return. Where was Charlotte? He couldn't cross over without saying one last goodbye to his wife.

Across the room, beyond his ability to focus within the gloom, Sal saw something—the slightest of movements, almost imperceptible but enough motion to capture his attention. What was that moving over there? Was it his wife sitting quietly in the darkness? Lord, he hoped so. He tried to speak, tried to form the words and call out her name but found he was unable to do so. His throat and lips were parched. He wanted something to drink or perhaps some ice chips to chew on, anything to quench the thirst. And God help him, he needed more morphine to dull his ever-increasing pain.

Looking closer, Sal realized what he was seeing was not Charlotte. It was someone, no something else entirely. A faint glow seemed to be emitting from that darkest corner of the room. It was pulsating and appeared to be of no definite form, its shape changing continuously. At first Sal had no idea what to make of the strange phenomena. He was almost certain it was some sort of illusion or hallucination brought on by the drugs, yet he could see it so clearly.

Then Sal experienced an awareness, a knowing of sorts. Even though his eyes were seeing nothing more than an effervescent shapeless mass floating mid-air, his mind was experiencing a completely different picture entirely. He saw his long-dead father. Sal's dad had passed away some thirty years earlier, following a sudden, massive heart attack when Sal was about twenty-nine. Yet now his father appeared before him, smiling at him from across the room with a peaceful and content expression the likes of which Sal had never quite seen cross the man's face in life. He appeared as he had when he was still tall, strong and handsome with coal black hair only just beginning to show hints of silver. "Popa," Sal said without speaking as his lips silently formed the words. The specter across the room neither replied nor moved; it just stood staring with that strange, peaceful smile.

Sal had always loved and respected his father in life and mourned his passing for years. Since then, barely a day passed by without some recollection of his father popping into his mind. He often laughed at the way he noticed things about himself as he got older that mirrored memories of his late Popa. Sal felt tears welling up in the corners of his eyes and didn't bother trying to stop them as they overflowed and trickled down his cheeks. God, how he missed his father! He had apparently forgotten just how much.

Then he saw two more glowing objects forming on both sides of the first. Soon these illusions took shape in his mind as well and Sal immediately recognized one as his mother, who had passed on fifteen years after his father, and the other was his older brother, Anthony who had been killed in the jungles of Vietnam when Sal was entering his first year of high school, way back on September 17, 1969. It was a date Sal would never forget.

The countenance of his mother was as he remembered her from back when he was a young boy. He loved his mother with all of his heart and thought she was the most beautiful woman to ever walk the earth. And now she stood to one side of her husband, his father, looking more radiant than Sal's finest memory could possibly recall. And on the opposite side of his father stood Anthony who was still wearing his trademark mischievous grin, the one that always drove the girls in his high school wild.

Sal lay helpless in his bed, unable to determine what this vision, hallucination or whatever-it-was might mean, yet at the same time he was enjoying the feeling of seeing his departed family members once again. A realization suddenly hit him and Sal instantly understood why they were here; they had come for him. Sal had heard stories through the years of family members near death who had claimed that long lost relatives had come to guide them across to the afterlife. About twenty years ago when his father's brother, Sal's Uncle Mike had passed away, his aunt Gertrude had told him that in her husband's final moments of life she heard him speaking to someone across the room whom she couldn't see. Gert had told Sal he had identified the invisible being as his brother: Sal's father. She was certain he had come to guide Mike to the other side. She told young Sal that when his time came he should be sure do what his spirit guide instructed. She said, "Sallie, when they come for you that means it's your time to go and you should not resist."

She told him she had no idea what might happen if someone refused to go with them but it couldn't possibly be good. "You don't mess with such things, Sallie." She had said, "They come for a reason, maybe to protect you from something... something else... I don't know. But what I do know is when the time comes you just must let go." And several years later that was exactly what she had done when it was her time to pass on.

Sal had always thought his aunt Gert might have been a little bit "off" but now all these many years later he understood she had been right and that was why his family was here: to help him crossover to whatever awaited him in the afterlife. And in his heart Sal knew he should go with them; it was his time. They were his family and he missed them all so much. He understood that all he had to do was let go and he would be free to cross over to a better place to be with his loved ones. At that moment Sal wanted to go with them more than almost anything else he could imagine... but then he suddenly experienced a brief pang of doubt and realized he couldn't go with them—at least not yet. He knew the choice to leave or stay was still his to make. And yet as much as he wanted to follow them, he owed it to his loving wife to stay if just for another day or even for another few more hours or minutes. He had unfinished business on this side. He wanted to tell Charlotte how much he loved her, how grateful he had been for how she had taken care of him during his prolonged illness and most importantly, he wanted to say goodbye. Was that too much to ask? She deserved at least that much and he wouldn't leave the planet until he had done so.

Across the room his father, mother and brother's peaceful smiling expressions began to darken, replaced by looks of distress and disappointment. They somehow had sensed his intentions. They looked as though they wanted to try and persuade him but were helpless to do anything but stare at him despondently. Finally, his father appearing to be straining with all of his strength slowly lifted one of his arms and extended his hand, palm up in one last pleading gesture for Sal to come with them. As tears streamed down his face, Sal sent a thought across the room, between the two worlds. That thought was of how much he loved and missed them but he couldn't go with them. Then the three images began to dissolve and fade away along with the glowing lights from which they had appeared.

It was only then that Sal realized that during the time the spirits had been present, all of the pain from his cancer had disappeared. Now, however it was returning with a vengeance. His chest seared with agony as the disease, which had been eating him alive from the inside out, resumed it deadly feast. He also experienced something else; not something tangible or anything he could accurately explain except that it was a feeling of total loss, a sense of being left behind. He had images passing through his mind of a lone man standing in the dark at a railway station as a train pulled away. He somehow understood he had just refused what was literally a once-in-a-lifetime opportunity.

Tears still coursed down his face uncontrollably, but they were no longer tears of joy over seeing his family, but were now tears of mourning for the emptiness he felt inside now that they were gone. It was as if his family had just died all over again. But somehow it was worse than simply that. Previously he at least had some hope he might see them again someday, but now there was a real fear that he was lost to them forever.

Through his glistening tears Sal saw something else across the room, another glowing shapeless mass. For a moment he felt his heart begin to race with excitement at the possibility his family might have sensed his distress and returned for him. If so, he knew he would now go with them despite not having said goodbye to Charlotte. He was ready. However, he noticed this glow seemed somewhat different than the previous. It was not as bright and was actually yellow and crimson in color.

The image, which gradually appeared in his mind when he looked into the light, was not his father, his mother or his brother. The visage was that of a young woman. She was rail thin, with long scraggly filthy and unkempt hair. She was dressed in a pair of filthy soiled white pajamas, which appeared saturated with some type of gelatinous fluid and were practically see through. There was nothing alluring about the vision however as the woman was gaunt and her minimal breasts hung down like shriveled prunes. Her sallow cheeks were enhanced by the sunken dark-ringed eyes, which seemed to bug out of her skull. Something about the woman seemed distantly familiar, but Sal couldn't quite place her.

Her mouth hung slack-jawed and was a reddish-black hole. Her lips on the left side of the deformed opening were gone, revealing a staggered row of sporadically missing and chipped teeth. It appeared as if her face had been through some sort of explosion. As if to further solidify this impression, several wisps of black smoke seeped out of the malformed orifice making it appear like some horribly ghastly flesh-covered chimney.

The woman turned her head slowly to the left as if to display something, something on her right side, which Sal sensed she wanted him to see and which he instinctively knew he would not want to see. Sadly he was correct. The entire right side of her skull was gone. In its place was an enormous gaping hole oozing a mixture of blood, fragments of flesh and a gooey gray substance, which Sal believed must have once been brain matter. Swarms of some sort of buzzing insects, perhaps flies flew about the opening while more wisps of smoke leaked from the dripping gash.

At first Sal was still uncertain who the woman might be or why she had appeared to him, but then the shock of recognition hit him like a club to the side of his skull. "Meghan?" he thought. The specter across the room nodded slightly in acknowledgement of his realization. "Oh my sweet God in Heaven!" Sal thought, "Oh no. Please no! Not this! Don't let it be her. Not Meghan!"

There had been very few things in Sal's life for which he could honestly say he was sorry about and for which he felt guilty or ashamed. But what had happened to Meghan and his part in the horrible incident was something that had haunted him his entire life. And now the memories flooded back as if they were happening all over again.

Some thirty years earlier Sal had been dating a beautiful young woman named Meghan Reilly. She was a widow with two young pre-school children. Her husband had tragically died when struck by a drunk driver. During Sal's time with Meghan, her two little ones had become very attached to him. Since they could barely remember their late father Sal had become something of a surrogate dad to them.

The affair had been going strong for close to a year there was an apparent unspoken understanding, at least on Meghan's part that their relationship would eventually result in marriage. But then something began to change for Sal. He noticed many instances over the previous six months where Meghan had acted in a very strange unpredictable way, leading him to believe that she might be bi-polar or maybe there was just something a bit unstable about the woman. The last thing he wanted at his young age was to spend the rest of his life with a woman whose emotions had become so unpredictable. He also couldn't see himself committing to taking on her two children as his own. Thinking about the potential problems was becoming overwhelming for him.

As a result he started to become distant, unwilling to face the inevitable and perhaps hoping she would grow tired of him and break off the relationship. But she didn't. He then realized at some point in time he was going to have to be the one to end things. Sal, however was not good at confrontation and so he subtly tried to further cut the emotional ties with Meghan, spending less time with her going out at night alone to local bars. But it seemed the more he tried to pull away from her, the more Meghan attempted to draw him closer. Eventually he had no other option; he decided he had to break up with her. One night while sitting at home alone contemplating his dilemma and after a few glasses of liquid courage he called Meghan, and ended their relationship over the phone: an act Sal later would come to see as avoidance, bordering on cowardice.

Meghan was devastated and heartbroken. For her, the emotional pain became unbearable. Only having been widowed for a few years, the wound was still too fresh and Sal's leaving her was like she had lost her husband all over again. Then one night after drinking herself into a stupor she called Sal cursing him for what he had done to her and her children. She was screaming and sobbing, using profanities he had never heard her use before. He could hear her kids crying in the background over the phone.

She said she couldn't stand living with the pain he had caused and that she was going to first kill her children then herself. Then he would surely be sorry for what he had done and her suffering would be over. Sal was fairly certain her threats were nothing more than her way of trying to get him to come over to her place to discuss the situation face to face. Be he had no intention of doing that. He had made up his mind and as far as he was concerned, they were finished. However Sal still did his best to try to reason with her but found it very difficult because of her drunken state, her deteriorated mental condition and the incessant noise of her children crying in the background. Megan screamed at the top of her lungs for the kids to be quiet but the wailing continued and even louder than before. That was until Sal heard two quick shots and the crying ceased.

Sal felt his stomach clench at the realization of what Meghan had just done. He was in shock and couldn't believe what he had just heard. He hoped to God he was mistaken and Meghan had maybe just shot into the air. Then perhaps the children had fled from the room. But deep in his heart he knew this was all just wishful thinking. Meghan came back on the line screaming even more hysterically than ever, "This is all your fault Sal. You did this. YOU DID THIS! You killed my babies and now you are going to kill me too. But I swear I'll be back for you Sal. You can bet your worthless life I will." Then Sal heard the final gunshot. He stood in shock for a moment before absently placing the receiver back on its cradle.

A few minutes later, after composing himself, Sal contacted the local police, telling them the whole story including the part about his breakup with Meghan. He gave them her address and said he had not left his home and would wait there to speak to them if necessary. The deaths were eventually a ruled murder-suicide committed by a despondent woman who had experienced a psychotic break. But Sal knew he was the catalyst that drove her over the edge.

A few months later when things quieted down, Sal chose to move away and start a new life far from his unpleasant past in a part of the country where no one knew him. And although time passed and most local people had all but forgotten about the incident, Sal was never able to completely come to terms with the role he played in Meghan's death. It had haunted him for the rest of his life.

And now, all these years later Meghan was back just as she had promised him, standing in spirit, ruined and broken across the room from his deathbed while he lay helplessly suffering in his final agony. The hideous specter didn't speak but smiled knowingly at Sal with what remained of her shattered mouth. Sal wanted to scream for help or to cry out to anyone who might come and make this foul hell-spawned creature leave him to die in peace but he could not.

A moment later, as if in answer to an unspoken prayer he heard the door to his room open, and his wife Charlotte slowly entered. He could see the illumination from the hall corridor backlighting her and making Charlotte look almost angelic. As the door closed and the light receded Charlotte made her way across the room to Sal's bedside where she grabbed a tissue from the nightstand and gently dabbed the tears from his glistening cheeks. Sal could still see the Meghan creature lurking in the shadows as if waiting patiently in anticipation of something—perhaps waiting for him.

As Charlotte patted Sal's cheek, one of her fingers gently brushed against his skin. The moment her flesh met his, Sal's mind became flooded with a montage of unbelievable images. He saw numerous scenes simultaneously played out like a collections of movies, each of which featured Charlotte in a variety of beds with many of his closest friends naked, sweating and grunting like rutting beasts. How could this possibly be? How could his beloved Charlotte have done such a thing to him? And why would she have done so while he laid dying in his hospital bed with unspeakable pain and beeping machines serving as his only companions?

Sal's eyes grew large with shock and his mouth flew open as he was astounded by what he had just witnessed. He wanted to believe none of what he saw was true but he knew with certainty the images were far more than simple illusions or hallucinations brought on by the drugs. They were actually a montage of the truth of what his deceitful wife had been doing behind his back, while she was pretending to care for him. He glanced across the room and saw the hideous specter of Meghan staring back at him, grinning madly with what remained of her mangled face. She knew what he had just seen and now she was basking the pleasure of the pain it was causing him.

"Sal?" He heard a voice say from his right. "It's time Sal." His wife Charlotte said. "It OK. You can let go now." She reached over and placed her hand on his in a consolatory gesture. Once again the moment their flesh met his mind was flooded with images of Charlotte and those men and he understood why she wanted him to let go. What a ridiculous fool he had been. Sal had loved that woman with all his heart, but she apparently hadn't loved him for some time. Charlotte had been much younger than Sal when they had married. Then his cancer had caused him to become a burden to her. She had found comfort in the beds of other men. And now she was ready for him to die and get it over with so she could get on with her new life. The horrible and degrading sex scenes were the final images Sal had in his mind as a living human being when his body gave out its final gasp allowing his spirit to move on. But where would it move on to? He family was gone and all that remained was that hideous specter of Meghan.

A moment later Sal was standing across the room looking back at his deathbed. Charlotte was standing by his bedside pretending to be in mourning while taking furtive glances down at her watch, as if determining how long she might have to stand next to his body playing the dutiful wife before she could call for help and eventually leave. When the nurses who were monitoring Sal's machinery from their central station came into the room Charlotte quickly turned on the waterworks crying as if she had just lost the love of her life.

Sal felt an icy chill settle upon his shoulder as he slowly turned and looked into the mutilated face of his one-time lover Meghan. She opened her mouth sensuously and a disgusting odor of rotting meat came leaching out like the stench of garbage fermenting in a can for weeks. Sal saw her gray slime-covered tongue flitting about the cavernous orifice and noticed several worm-like creatures squirming in and out of open weeping soars on her glistening face. The hideous thing that had once been his beautiful lover reached up and entwined her bony fingers into the hair on the back of his head drawing him closer. He tried with all of his might to resist her pull but her strength was much greater than his and she pulled his lips down to meet hers.

He could smell the foul reek of her as he struggled hopelessly to keep his lips away from hers. But no matter how much he fought his mouth soon became pressed tightly against the crumbling maggot-infested flesh of her gaping maw. His stomach revolted as he felt her cold slimy tongue sliding first across his lips and then diving deep into his mouth where it flitted from side to side as if it had a mind of its own.

The Meghan thing next grabbed his hand and forced it onto to one of her withered breasts as she slowly pulled her snake-like tongue out of his mouth. Sal spat some sort of foul tasting crawling things behind her as Meghan laid her right cheek against his. From his position Sal could clearly see what remained of her demolished brain, which appeared to be undulating impossibly as dozens of white maggot-like worms skated across its slimy covered surface in a hideous ballet of revulsion. Some of the larvae would occasionally stop to bore deep into the spongy meat and creep below the outer surface of the decaying brain tissue.

The Meghan specter whispered something into Sal's ear, "I came back for you as I promised so many years ago my love, and now we will finally be joined together in our own special lover's embrace in Hell for all of eternity." Sal heard a loud maniacal ear-splitting scream reverberating throughout the room and realized with horror it was coming from himself.

A LOVE BEST SERVED COLD

The solitary young man sat silently in the shadowed blackness of his living room. The sole illumination came from the faint glow of light filtering through the open doorway of the adjacent bedroom, the source of which was a single candle burning on a nearby dresser. He always kept one burning. The blood red candle stood anchored in a puddle of hardened wax inside the inverted lid of a jar that had formerly contained his last helping of applesauce. It was his favorite kind, not the health-conscious stuff, but the type made with real sugar—lots and lots of sugar. He had no idea when he might be fortunate enough to find another jar, so he savored the delectable memory for as long as he could.

Oswald liked the dark. In fact, he loved it and always had for as long as he could remember. While most small children would scream in terror at the idea of being left alone in a dark bedroom at night, Oswald welcomed it and always longed for more. As a child, he cherished the darkness like a best friend; and now, as an adult, he embraced it like a long lost lover. And he was pleased there was now so much darkness to enjoy—now that the world had finally changed for the better.

The inhabitants of the earth as it had once been, always seemed to worship illumination and would often shun those like Oswald, who thrived in darkness. He recalled how in the old days, every summer scores of individuals would spend a substantial amount of their hard earned incomes to travel long distances and pay exorbitant fees simply to bake in the sweltering, blazing sun, like raw meat on a skillet. They thought nothing of risking the threat of skin cancer by lounging on some scalding oceanfront beach. All of that expense and aggravation just to soak in sunlight was something he could never understand, especially when there was so much more to enjoy in the dark.

He suspected light represented life to most people while darkness symbolized death. "So what was wrong with death?" Oswald thought to himself. After all, no one gets out of this world alive. So why not simply accept darkness and accept death and then learn to treasure it as simply another part of living?

Oswald J. Gorn was not what anyone would consider typical, nor had he ever been. During his high school days, he had been labeled with such disparaging terms as "creepy", "weirdo", "odd-wald", "freaky" and even "scary". He didn't mind the insults and in many ways liked the attention his perceived oddness brought to him. Oswald realized if he had been able to fit in, if he were just like everyone else, it was likely no one would have ever even taken notice him at all. It was not that he needed or wanted their attention, but he found it fascinating how the other students would go out of their way to look and act like everyone else so they could fit in and to get noticed by the so-called cool kids. He managed to accomplish the exact same thing, albeit it in a negative way, by not trying to fit in but simply by being himself.

During and even after high school Oswald didn't date, so to speak; he had absolutely no interest in building any type of relationship with any female. Some of the jocks in high school had insinuated Oswald might be gay, although he was quite certain he was not. He had nothing against people who were gay, but it was simply not the way he rolled. He did however, realize there was something out of the ordinary about his sexual desires and he didn't know exactly what that might be, but he knew it was not homosexuality. But he did suspect and was quite certain that many of those same overly-macho, locker-room-towel-snapping jock types might have some of their own homosexual issues to work out.

Most of his classmates would have been surprised to learn Oswald was not a virgin and hadn't been since the age of sixteen. He found there were quite a few girls in the school who were attracted to his idiosyncrasies, to his dark black clothing, his long wild hair and the sinister-looking jewelry consisting primarily of ornamental skulls and bones.

He never even had to leave his house to score with several different girls any time he wanted to, they simply came to him. But oddly, he was not very interested in any of those girls. They seemed to be lacking something, but he could not quite figure out what it might be.

He didn't consider himself what the other students referred to as "Goths" or "vampires" and if asked, Oswald would have stated categorically that he had no desire to be lumped into any group. He preferred to stay to himself and to do what he wanted when he wanted.

After graduation, he chose to not attend college, much to his parents' chagrin. But Oswald knew college was not the route he wanted to take in life. He wanted to spend a few years trying to discover what his true calling might be. He wanted to experiment with a number of different occupations until he hopefully found one he liked. Perhaps then he might decide to return to school to focus on furthering his education in that chosen field, but at eighteen years old, he had no idea what he wanted to do with his life.

Now looking back after several years, he realized he had made the right decision especially considering how useless all of those thousands of college degrees were now that the steaming defecation had finally hit the proverbial oscillating ventilation. Now that the world was a stinking living graveyard, a good working knowledge of carpentry and plumbing, as well as familiarity with guns, knives, self-defense or hunting were all more valuable skills than an MBA ever would be.

Oswald peered through the darkness into the adjacent bedroom and considered going in to do what he needed and wanted to do, but decided to wait a bit and savor the anticipation just a little bit longer. He could see the sheets on the bed ripple from the movement of its occupant and heard a slow moaning sound like that of someone in pain.

He smiled knowingly and looked at the battery-powered digital clock on the nightstand next to the bed and saw it was ten-fifteen. He decided to wait until ten thirty if for no other reason than simply because he could. He often played these sorts of games with himself; he felt it helped keep his life interesting.

Oswald thought back to the various part-time, full-time, permanent and temporary jobs he had tried after high school and how he never seemed to fit in well with any of them. It was not like he really cared, as these were all experimental jobs, but he quickly learned that the people hiring him, those paying his salary, were not quite as accepting of his peculiarities as he thought they might be.

Although Oswald had quit many of his jobs, he was more often than not, fired. Yet he had always managed to find employment in one form or another and was able to afford to live on his own in his apartment, although it was a far cry from luxurious by any stretch of the imagination.

After three years of hopping from one job to the next, he began to think he might never find his true calling. That was, until he answered a want ad in the local newspaper for a mortuary in his town that was looking for a general laborer/helper. Oswald had no idea what the job was or what it might pay, but for some unknown reason, the idea seemed to appeal to him. After one quick interview he was immediately hired.

And much to his surprise, he found it to be the perfect job. He did virtually anything and everything the funeral director, Mr. Wilcox, needed, from parking cars to helping set up chairs for the services to preparing the funeral parlor. After several weeks he was surprised when Mr. Wilcox asked him to help assist in preparation of a body for burial.

He had no idea what to expect. Up until that point, he had never been allowed to go into the embalming room and was thrilled at the chance to be part of the action. His first assignment was simply to watch Mr. Wilcox prepare the body and hand him whatever tools he might need to complete his work.

Oswald was shocked and pleasantly surprised to discover the body lying naked on the slab in the center of the laboratory was that of a young woman perhaps twenty-five years old, just a few years older than he was. Her face was distorted and her body badly cut and bruised as if she had been in an accident or had been beaten or perhaps had even been murdered.

As his eyes traced the contours of her naked body, Oswald felt something incredible stir inside of him. A sensation of sexual arousal the likes of which he had never experienced with any living girl before. He realized it had nothing to do with the corpse's voluptuous shape, full breasts or lovely legs, but it was her pale color and the chalky mottled condition of her dead flesh. At first, the strange sensation frightened him, but then he realized this was what he had been missing all of those years. This was the one thing that none of his past lovers could provide; this was reality; this was death.

Over the course of the next several months, when the Mr. Wilcox was not around, Oswald would sneak into the lab and check out what special treat awaited him on the slab. Most of the time, he was disappointed to discover shriveled old men or wrinkled old women. But every so often, he would be rewarded with a young or middle-aged woman laid out on the table. And if the occupant happened to tickle his fancy, he would simply drop his drawers and have his way with the chilly cadavers. He figured what the hell, they were already dead: no harm, no foul.

Oswald did however understand right from wrong as dictated by the mores of the civilized world and knew he would be chastised by society and prosecuted by the law, if caught. However, he also knew what he liked and those dead bodies, rigid with rigor, cold with death, having the slight scent of impending putrefaction were exactly what he desired. He had never experienced lovemaking with any living girl that could compare with even one of these wonderful ice princesses.

Then as he had feared, his good times soon came to an abrupt and tragic end. One night he was enjoying the pleasure of an attractive thirty-something young lady who had passed away from an aneurysm or something of that nature, when the funeral director walked in and caught him in the act. Wilcox was outraged and in his fury, he grabbed one of the implements of his trade, a long drainage tube of some sort and proceeded to whip and beat Oswald with it.

Unable to defend himself with his pants down around his ankles, the young man tripped and fell to the ground, trying to ward off the attack with flailing arms. Eventually he managed to free one of his legs and kicked out wildly and accidentally struck the mortician in the chin hard with the heel of his foot. The blow was a wild gesture of self-defense, completely unplanned, but somehow it managed to knock the man backward. He lost his balance, fell to the floor, cracked his head against the marble tile and died instantly.

Unsure of what to do next, Oswald panicked realizing his life was essentially over. Self-defense or not there wasn't a jury in the world that would accept his story. After all, Wilcox was a well-known, well-respected local businessman and he was... well a freak in the eyes of many. And if the knowledge of his illicit activities with the dearly departed ever surfaced, they would lock him up and throw away the key.

Oswald hid the man's body in a closet. Then he did his best to wipe away any trace of his ever being in the building and fled home to his apartment, unsure of what he would do next. Then to his dismay something happened, which he had never believed could have happened—something that made his problem pale in comparison.

The press called it the plague, Internet bloggers called it the long awaited Zombie Apocalypse, but Oswald thought of it as his salvation. Whatever it was and whatever had caused it to occur no one knew for certain, but for some reason, the dead had begun to leave their graves, rise up and feast on the flesh of the living.

It didn't take long for local society to break down completely; just a matter of weeks, and then the entire world was thrust into chaos and anarchy. For most people it meant the end of the world, the end of mankind's reign at the top of the food chain. But this was not necessarily the case for Oswald.

He understood survival would be a challenge and at some point in time, he would likely end up being killed or simply dying only to arise once again to join the ranks of the undead. But this thought did not trouble him. Oswald always felt death was simply a part of life and that was true now more than ever. He could only do what he could to get by until that day came and in the meantime, he planned on enjoying himself as best as he could.

He soon learned that this brave new world of walking corpses was exactly the type of world he wanted to live in. He did not flee for his life but adapted and learned quickly how not only to survive in such a world, but how to truly enjoy life for the first time and to partake of the many benefits such a world had to offer.

***

As Oswald sat in his dark living room looking out into the partially lighted bedroom he glanced once again at the clock and noticed that an hour had passed. It was now close to eleven o'clock. He was amazed at how much time had passed so quickly. From the adjacent room Oswald heard the bed squeaking once again followed by the faint moaning sound.

"Well, no time like the present," he said to no one in particular. Then he stood and walked slowly into the dimly lit bedroom.

Lying on top of the sheets was the writhing body of a naked woman. Her wrists and ankles were each secured with heavy rope to one of the four bedposts. There was a gag over her mouth. He was not concerned about her screaming, as he was quite certain no one would hear her, but he did worry about her possibly biting him. He knew that would not be good at all.

She looked at Oswald through one filmy dead eye sunken deep in a bony dark ringed socket, not with fear or hatred but with an insatiable hunger. The other eye was missing, leaving a hollow pit crawling with worms. All that was left of her once beautiful tresses were a few patches, wispy strands of wild straw-like hair.

Her mottled gray flesh was covered with the filth and grime typical of her kind and dozens of flies swarmed about her. Some of them stopped to deposit their eggs in the puss-filled weeping sores, which covered her spasmodically gyrating corpse. Maggots from earlier deposits crawled from boreholes and dropped onto the bed sheets.

The single candle, although scented, did little to mask the vile stench of decomposition, which permeated the room. To most, the aroma would be considered repulsive, but to Oswald it was the scent of love. As he made his way toward the bed he began to slowly undress, knowing once again he would have the opportunity to enjoy the fruits of the new world: a love best served cold.

MEGASYNTH RP-1

Author's Note: *In July 2014, I was asked by my friend and author Mark Slade of Williamsburg, VA to write a short story for an anthology he was preparing for Rogue Planet Press, scheduled to be released in late 2014. At the time of this writing, the tentative name of the anthology is "The Black Hand Supremacy". Mark Slade is also the publisher of Nightmare Illustrated magazine. He and fellow writer/editor Gavin Chappell had developed a number of characters and a back-story to go with them. He wanted various authors to take his basic idea and run with it in whatever direction they chose. We were also encouraged to create our own new characters and technological ideas as we saw fit. Needless to say, I was intrigued.*

The premise was the stories were to be set in an occult steampunk post WWI environment where most of the world had been destroyed and one city has taken over the world's economy. It is the city of Zenith, formerly Sarajevo ruled by a corporation known as Illusion Inc., headed by a tyrant named Ronald Pryor and his unscrupulous organization The Black Hand. Through the use of Dark Magik they have developed technology that surpasses even the technology of today.

Talbot Carruthers also known as Alastor and his group The White Lodge are archenemies of Illusion and freedom fighters/revolutionaries. Alastor also has a foe in the Illusion henchman Gavril Princip. My particular story takes place several hours after a battle between Alastor and Pryor over the Book Of Magik where Ronald Pryor was almost killed.

***

The man known as Gavril Princip looked out through the large 15th floor plate glass hospital room window overlooking the vast expanse of the great metropolis of Zenith. In the distance he could see the sun was in its final stages of setting; its amber glow severely dimmed by the smoggy haze, which served as the unbreathable atmosphere permeating the city. No humans went anywhere without appropriate protection.

The large, plain, concrete buildings stood mostly in darkness now with only a few lights on in a scattering of apartments. Outside the buildings traffic lights and signals climbed in layers from the ground upward to and past Princip's current location. It was still a few hours until lights out curfew, and everyone was hurrying to get to wherever they had to be for the night.

Dozens of flying vehicles built by Illusion Incorporated Motors flew past at almost every vertical level, each used to transport workers to and from their various jobs. Once at work the evening shift employees would have to remain there until dawn when the curfew was lifted once again. Most of the mobile units were of the mass transportation variety while a few were single passenger vehicles. All of the vehicles were being driven by Synthetic Men of the non-flying variety. There were several different levels of models of Synthetic Men. The less expensive ones to produce were called Meanies, which could not fly and were so named because they were primarily used to perform menial tasks. They were however, equally as deadly as the higher-level Synthetic Men.

These flying units also known as ATDs or (Airborne Transportation Devices) looked nothing like the earlier version of motorized vehicles from before the Great War known as horseless carriages or automobiles. These were sleek and very smooth in design and their outer shells were constructed of a combination of steel and the same rubbery material used in the creation of the Synthetic Men's skin. Brass lanterns and other such brass and chrome lighting devices were strategically placed in rows along the outside for illumination. The flying vehicles were powered by a combination of Magik and a secret fuel known as Synthozine, which was produced and its distribution controlled by Illusion Inc.

Hovering in the air outside the hospital window were two Synthetic Men of the high-end variety that were capable of flying. They could do a lot more as well, including shooting lethal red-hot rays from their fingertips. They were known as Centurions and their purpose was to protect their charges with deadly force as required. There would be no warnings for any would-be assailants. Any threat, even a wrongly perceived threat would be instantly met with deadly force. People knew when they saw these Centurions they had to keep their distance.

Like most of the Synthetic Men, also known as Synthos by the common people, these were tall—well over six feet in height. They wore the black uniforms of The Black Hand adorned with a selection of numerous silver and brass ornamentations. Once such embellishment was the bronze death's head with the ruby-red eyes—the logo of Illusion Incorporated. Slithering from the grinning mouth of the skull was a silver snake. They carried no weapons nor did they need to. They wore black gloves studded with steel spikes. The fingertips had been removed from the gloves, as always, to allow quick access to the only weapons they required: their deadly rays.

Their glass camera-lens eyes were sunken deep within the rubbery flesh of their synthetic faces and darted back and forth rhythmically scanning the area for danger, always on the lookout for potential threats from members of The White Lodge. Likewise, there were four similarly clad guards watching the hall just outside the hospital room. Princip was not the reason for all of this increased security however. He was just visiting the current patient who had summoned him there.

Princip heard the soft crinkling sounds that only hospital pillows and those found in cheap hotels tended to make. He turned to look at the man lying in the bed whose face and upper chest were completely covered in blue effervescent bandages. Yet through the eyeholes cut into the cerulean mask Princip could see two eyes filled with anger and seething with hatred staring out at him. The man in the bed was Ronald Pryor, CEO of Illusion, Inc. and essentially the ruler of Zenith.

"How are you feeling Ronald?" Princip asked.

The pink tip of Pryor's tongue slowly slid along the edge of his lips through a slit cut into the mask of bandages. With a dry and raspy voice he said, "I'm fine... I suppose... Gavril... get me some water."

Princip lifted the glass of crystal clear ice water—a luxury reserved for only the most elite of society and brought it close to Pryor's lips. A small stainless steel straw had been placed in the water, making it easier for the hospital's special patients to get to the precious liquid without wasting a drop.

"Just take small sips," Princip warned. "I know you're probably dying of thirst, but you've been out for several days, being kept alive by these machines, and you need to pace yourself and ease back into the whole eating and drinking process."

"Yes... good idea... Gavril... thank you," Pryor said as he took a few small sips of the precious liquid.

Princip said, "That stuff is probably laced with the same synthetic nutrients flowing through those tubes running into your body. If it wasn't for this technology, you'd be a dead man, Ronald."

"Yeah... I... I realize that." Then Pryor's eyes grew large with shocked recollection behind the two slits. "Alastor... it was that... that damned Alastor... and his accursed Tarot Magik. That's... that's who did this to me." Pryor reached up to touch his face, remembering how his flesh had been melted from his skull like so much tallow dripping down along the sides of a flaming candle.

Princip reached out and grabbed his hands to stop him. "Easy now Ronald. The Syntho-Doc said you have to keep your hands away from those bandages for a few more days. And you know he is right, your company made him that way."

"But... but... my face!" Pryor exclaimed, his eyes now brimming with tears.

"Your face will be fine," Princip assured then corrected himself somewhat and said, "Or at least as fine as they can make it."

Pryor remained silent for a moment then said, "What... what do you mean?" But Pryor feared he understood exactly what Princip had meant.

"Well..." Princip hesitated. "I've been told your human flesh was melted in places right down to the bone, destroying skin, nerves and muscle tissue—everything gone. So now they've done their best to replace what you once had with the synthetic skin."

"Surely... you don't mean that rubbery... grayish crap... we use on the typical Synthos?" he asked.

"Yes and no," Princip said. "You know Illusion has the best scientists in the known world. And I'm sure you're aware they've been working on a new version of the synthetic skin that not only looks, feels and breathes almost like real flesh, but it can also be tinted to whatever color best matches your original skin tone."

"But... but the nerve damage!" Pryor cried in a raspy voice. "What about my... my facial movement... and my expressions?"

Princip said directly, "That might be more of an issue. You may, at least for a time, likely have no ability to show any expression. Your face will be as blank as those of the Synthetic Men. You will, however, have your eyes, which can convey your emotions. And from what I'm told this might only be for a few years. The hope is that after future technological development and many additional surgeries... well you may be a lot closer to normal, but not immediately."

Princip could see the fire in Pryor's eyes growing right along with his anger and hatred. Then with as much venom as Pryor could muster in his current condition, he rasped with his damaged harsh vocal chords, "You... You Gavril... you must... kill Alastor for me... you must do this... can you Gavril?"

For a brief moment Princip hesitated. What Pryor was asking for, Princip had tried on many occasions unsuccessfully. He and Alastor were too evenly matched. A fight to the death would mean the death of both of them. He had tried to discover Alastor's real identity with the hopes of gaining even the slightest advantage over the man. Princip had even murdered Alastor's secretary Frida in an attempt to get her to divulge his identity—but to no avail.

He looked down at Pryor and said, "You know I too would like nothing better than to see Alastor killed as savagely and painfully as is humanly possible. But we are equals in almost every way. I cannot best him and he cannot best me."

"You two... are similar... in power," Pryor said. "But you have... one advantage... which Alastor does not. You have no one... in life that matters... to you... You are a... a solitary soul. This is a major advantage... Gavril... we can use one of Alastor's associates... to lure him to you."

"What associates?" Gavril asked. "The only associates we know about are Spider Nelson and his executive assistant Frida. And for your information, Frida is dead. I killed her myself using a garrote on her in an attempt to get her to reveal Alastor's identity, but that secret unfortunately died with her. That only leaves his enforcer Spider Nelson, and not only do we have no idea where he might be, but he is even more dangerous and deadly than Alastor."

"There... is another," Pryor explained. "You know we've been... forcing mandatory teaching of TTP... or Transcendental Thought Process... in every school... All of the young children... are being forced to learn it."

"Yes, I'm aware of that," Princip acknowledged. "But what has that to do with Alastor?"

Pryor hesitated to get his thoughts in order. Princip could see he was having difficulty forming thoughts, likely due to the effect of the drugs he was receiving. "There was... a young girl... back in the time of... the Great War... when Zenith was still called... Sarajevo. She had been saved by Alastor... during one of the many... skirmishes. Her name is Ana... Ana Alana. Alastor rescued her... and made sure she was... taken care of... Ana is part of one of the classes... studying TTP. She was practicing one day... at the school... and mentally called out to Alastor... He immediately replied... and scolded her... reminding her she should never... use TTP to contact him. The conversation was... immediately cut off... Alastor knows we can... monitor and intercept such communications."

"I see," Princip said. "But how did you find out about her past association with Alastor?"

"Her mind was only left open for a few seconds... during the time she was attempting... to contact Alastor." Pryor said, "But during that time... my mental scanners were able... to probe her mind and... they got a wealth of information. We know... where the girl is... and we know we can use her... to lure Alastor to us... just as I used The Book Of Magik... to lure him into that cave. Unfortunately... the book was torn asunder... and its pages ripped out one by one... and sucked into the Ring Of Truth... probably never to be seen again... and after that... well...that was when Alastor did this to me... with his damnable Tarot Magik. But now we... now you Gavril... have another chance... to get him for me."

Princip hesitated for a moment then said, "Suppose I do use the girl to lure him to me. What then? I told you, he and I are equals. I cannot defeat him one-on-one."

"But Gavril, my friend... it will not be one-on-one... you will not be alone."

"Ronald, we've tried that before," Princip said. "I've gone up against him with a small army of Synthetic Men at my side and still he defeated them quickly leaving only he and I to do battle."

Pryor looked knowingly at Princip, his eyes glassy red orbs against the cobalt blue facemask. "I have something... no one knows about... not even you, Gavril. I have... a weapon in development... it has never been tested... but when perfected... it might be able to destroy Alastor... by itself... but at this time might... and I stress might... need your assistance."

"What?" Princip said in astonishment. "What sort of weapon can you possibly have that would be of any help if Alastor can destroy dozens of Synthetic Men with the flick of a Tarot card?"

"All... in good time, Gavril... my friend... all in good time," Pryor said. "I want you... to go to the development center... at Illusion ... see Dr. Zorn, the head of new product development... as soon as you leave here... I'll have him contacted... and make him aware of your arrival... he will show you... what you need to see... then we can plan for the death of Alastor."

Princip asked, "But can't you just tell me now what this thing might be?"

"No," Pryor replied. "This is something... you have to see... to believe."

***

Dr. Damien Zorn was a genius: a short, thin man of about fifty-three with thick glasses and a head shaved completely bald. One might accurately argue that Zorn quite possibly had more hair growing out of his ears than could be found anywhere on his head. Zorn was a typical absent-minded professor who it seemed was only able to function at his best within the confines of his laboratory. He was in the constant company of two Synthetic Men who were responsible for his wellbeing. This was not necessarily because Dr. Zorn was in any danger from Alastor or The White Lodge, but simply because without his guards Zorn couldn't find his way home. The Synthetic Men stayed with him at all times to make sure he woke up on time, shaved, showered, ate and even brushed his teeth. They were programmed to take care of all of the typical things most people did naturally but Zorn couldn't seem to accomplish of his own volition.

There was an alert at the lab door indicating someone was waiting to gain access. One of Zorn's Synthetic Men looked up at the video display then called over in its mechanically monotone voice, "Dr. Damien Zorn. Gavril Princip is here to see you. Shall I grant him admittance Sir?"

Zorn was busy at a bank of computer monitors studying scrolling data and typing frantically on several keyboards simultaneously, moving from one to the other then back again. He said absently, waving a free hand in a gesture of agreement, "Yes... yes... Jondo, by all means send him in."

"As you wish Sir, however I am Rondo," the Synthetic Man corrected. This confusion would be understandable if he and his Synthetic counterpart, Jondo were identical, as most Synthetic Men were. But Ronald Pryor had deliberately made them look different so that it might be easier for the doctor to tell them apart. But this apparently had been a wasted effort because Zorn was far too absent-minded for even such a gesture to prove beneficial.

"Whatever! Whatever!" Dr. Zorn said, still waving his free hand, "Just send him in please, Jondo."

Shaking his head in mock-frustration because these Synthos couldn't feel actual emotion but did an excellent job of mimicking real human emotional behaviors; the Synthetic Man called Rondo turned and disengaging the door lock, signaled for Gavril Princip to enter.

"Welcome Mr. Princip. Long time, no see," Zorn said stopping what he was doing immediately and doing his best to try to sound friendly. In reality, he was aware of Princip's reputation and was terrified of the man.

"Let's dispense with the small talk Dr. shall we?" Princip replied. "Show me what Mr. Pryor wanted you to show me and let me get on with my business."

Zorn looked a bit put out as well as confused and said apologetically, "Oh... oh... yes... well... um."

"Stop stammering Zorn!" Princip demanded, shouting at the scientist, causing him to tremble with fear. At the sound of Princip's angry raised voice, the two Synthetic bodyguards moved with the speed of light, forming a wall between them and Dr. Zorn.

Princip looked at them disbelievingly, giving a sinister chuckle as he stared at the two Synthos with fire burning in his eyes. Zorn was hiding behind the pair, occasionally peering out around the side of Jondo. Or was it Rondo? The two Synthetic Centurions had both of their hands extended palms down ready to deliver their deadly payload if necessary to protect their charge.

"Surely you are joking," Princip said. "Right? Don't you two idiots realize you finger rays are useless against my form of Magik? I could destroy you both with the blink of an eye."

Jondo and Rondo simultaneously replied in their simulated form of speech, "Yes Gavril Princip, we realize any violent encounter with you would result in our immediate destruction. However, we are programmed to protect Dr. Damien Zorn from any and all assumed threats no matter what the consequences. We are expendable, but Dr. Damien Zorn is not."

Princip suddenly realized just how ridiculous the situation had become. He had no desire to harm either Zorn or his two Syntho-flunkies. And most certainly didn't want to have to explain such a disaster to Ronald Pryor. Not that Princip had anything to fear from Pryor, but Princip was being compensated generously by Pryor and business was business.

Then after a pause, Princip regained his composure and said, "Just show me this new experimental weapon... and please... do it quickly."

Sensing the atmosphere returning to a non-volatile state the two Synthos lowered their arms, spread out again and returned to their duties of watching Zorn. Princip always found it incredible how these synthetic creatures could go from calm to alert and potentially deadly then back to calm again within the space of a few seconds. But that's how they were designed to perform, completely without emotion.

"If you will please follow me back this way Mr. Princip I will be happy to show you what you came to see," Zorn said.

Princip followed Zorn, flanked by his two floating Synthos to the back of the lab where they stopped in front of a large set of heavy iron doors, each about six feet wide and over twelve feet tall. Six-inch wide metal bands with brass bolts surrounded the periphery of the doors and six huge platinum hinges held the doors in place. At the center, about five feet off the floor where the two doors met was a large metal box with a set of round glass lenses in the center.

Zorn bent down and appeared to look through the glass. A moment later Princip heard a clunking sound and realized the locking mechanism had been disengaged. Then the two massive doors began to slowly open outward.

"Rondo? Jondo?" Zorn said. "Will you be so kind as to guard this entrance while I show Mr. Princip what waits inside?"

The two instantly turned and faced away from the open doors watching as instructed for any potential threats. As

Princip watched them he noticed on the back of each of their necks a round lens appeared. Apparently they were not going to stop watching the good doctor just because they were given an alternate assignment. The two Synthetic Men replied in unison, "Very good, Dr. Damien Zorn. But we will be watching you as well and can be at your side in a millisecond if required."

"Fine. Fine," Zorn replied dismissively as he led Princip into the adjacent room.

The room was hemispherical in shape and enormous. Although the room was dark and cast in shadows, Princip estimated it to be at least fifty feet high at the center of the hemisphere, which made it more than one hundred feet in diameter. As he looked around he could see the place seemed deserted. There was a scattering of small twinkly lights spread all around the domed ceiling, reminding Princip of stars. Although the only time he was able to see stars anymore was during those rare times when he was permitted outside of the city limits.

"Lights please," Zorn said, and the entire room was suddenly awash with incandescent illumination. For a moment he had to blink his eyes from the glare. When they finally did adjust, however, Princip was uncertain he was actually seeing what he thought he was seeing. He stood, mouth agape, staring at the sight before him.

In the center of the room was a large circular hole cut into the metal floor about fifty feet across and surrounded by a bronze two-rail fence of sorts. It glistened in the room's light. From the hole, heading straight to the ceiling was a cylindrical vaporous cloud appearing to be made of billions of tiny sparkling, floating, moving particles. Some were white while others were shades of blue, purple, gold, silver and red. It was one of the most wondrous sights Princip had ever seen.

Deep in the center of the cloud was an indiscernible black shadow that practically reached to the ceiling. Instinctively, Princip knew this was what he had come to see. Yet he still was unaware of what it was. The silhouette appeared to be in the shape of the upper half of an enormous man with massive shoulders below its huge head. Princip suddenly realized that below the floor where he now stood was the lower half of the spherical room. This meant the rest of this thing was submerged in the floor fifty feet below.

"Curtain down," Dr. Zorn commanded to the empty room, and in a flash Princip saw the miraculous cylindrical curtain seem to be sucked downward into the floor, revealing its contents.

"What... what the hell!" Princip said, appearing both alarmed and perhaps even a little frightened.

"His official name is RP-1," Zorn explained. "But we call him MegaSynth. He is the first of his kind: a prototype."

Princip stood silently staring in amazement and in the matter of a few seconds he took in as much of the creature before him as was possible. It was beyond incredible. Standing in the pit was an almost one hundred foot tall naked version of Ronald Pryor—that is, Pryor before his injury. Its eyes were closed, but its hair and face were identical, only much, much larger. Also unlike the man upon whom it was modeled, this creature was rippling and bulging with synthetic muscles. It also had no genitalia, a fact for which Pryor was very grateful.

Princip said, "What in the name of all that is unholy is this abomination?"

"I told you, it's RP-1 also known as MegaSynth," Zorn repeated. "He's the latest and greatest version of what we hope will become a new army of ultimate Synthetic Warriors. He is designed to be virtually indestructible."

Princip asked, "But what do we need even one such gargantuan creation for, let alone an army of them? We already control all of Zenith."

"Yes, but there is a whole world out there, Mr. Princip, and Mr. Pryor intends to expand Illusion out into that world and make it part of his empire."

Princip said, "Most of what I've seen of the world is nothing but mass destruction and uninhabitable lands."

Zorn said, "At one time Zenith was uninhabitable. The air is still unfit to breath except through a respirator. Mr. Pryor has brought Zenith back from the dead and he can do that with the rest of the world as well."

"But we already have armies of Synthetic Men. What chance could small pockets of civilization outside of Zenith have against such a force?"

Zorn explained, "Probably none. But Mr. Pryor is always thinking five steps ahead of most people and he must know of some threat out there that might prove greater than our armies, or else he would not have created this masterpiece. But, unfortunately, the unit has yet to be field tested. So I'm not sure what it actually is or is not capable of when placed in a real-world situation. I mean, I do know what RP-1 was designed and programmed to do, but as I said, it's never been tested in a live application. It might very well surpass our performance expectations or it might fail miserably with the unpredictability of real-world battle. What does Mr. Pryor want you do to while you are here? Does he wish for you to be part of the testing and evaluation?"

"No," Princip said. "What he wants is for me to use this monstrosity in an actual field operation."

Zorn looked astonished, his face reddening. "Why... it's... not possible... I mean... this thing... it's not even close to being ready for a live mission. What in the world is Mr. Pryor thinking? Has he gone mad?"

"Whether he has or if he has not gone mad is none of your concern. What is of importance to you is that Mr. Pryor has bestowed me with the power to determine whether you live five more years or five more minutes," Princip said sternly. He could hear the two Synthos in the doorway stirring and coming to attention. He was certain if he turned around he would see the two walking zombies standing with their fingers pointed at him once again.

Zorn waved his hand in the direction of the door indicating to the two Synthetic Men that everything was OK and they should stand down. Then he nodded reluctantly at Princip and said, "Well then, if that's the case, we had better get started."

During the next several hours Zorn did all he could to debrief Princip on the various features of the MegaSynth unit. Princip was amazed at the power built into the creature including many weapons that were designed to both repel and destroy various aspects of Tarot Magik. By the time the orientation was over, an astonished Princip felt confident he would actually be, for the first time in his life, able to destroy the traitorous Alastor.

***

Talbot Carruthers, also known as Alastor, was sitting in his favorite chair in his oak-lined study, relaxing with an evening cocktail. During these times, he often sank into a melancholy mood as he sat thinking about his late wife who had been murdered by Ronald Pryor's Synthetic Men. She had not been killed because she was his wife, since Pryor had no idea what his real identity was. She simply had suffered the same fate as so many others who had run afoul of the Synthetic Men. Regardless, her death was directly tied back to Pryor and was the driving force that caused Talbot to become Alastor and lead his rebellious White Lodge in pursuit of the destruction of Ronald Pryor and Illusion Incorporated.

Alastor was now staring into his fireplace, staring at his simulated flame, and was thinking about how close he had come earlier today to dying during his struggle for the Book of Magik against Ronald Pryor. Alastor didn't fear death but knew any future good he and The White Lodge might accomplish would be severely damaged with the death of its founder and leader. He had a responsibility to the rebellion to stay alive.

He wondered about Pryor. Had the man died from his horrific injuries? Alastor didn't know but he most certainly hoped so. After all, Alastor had seen the man's flesh melting from his white exposed skull. Surly he couldn't have survived that, could he? Yet at the same time, Alastor was well aware of the superior level of technology that Illusion Incorporated possessed, and it wouldn't have surprised him if somehow they had managed to save Pryor.

Suddenly he became alert. He realized he was receiving a Transcendental Thought Process message from Ana Alana. Inside his head he heard, "Alastor? Alastor? It's me, Ana."

At first Alastor was going to scold Ana for contacting him again in a manor he had warned her about but the feelings he was receiving accompanying the transmission were those of absolute terror, and Alastor instinctively knew she was in trouble.

"Ana, what's wrong?" Alastor replied using his own TPT skills.

Suddenly a dark, menacing and unfortunately familiar voice entered his mind. "Nothing is wrong Alastor, at least not yet." It was a voice he knew all too well: the voice of his archenemy Gavril Princip.

"Princip you swine!" Alastor thought. "If you harm a hair on that innocent girl's head, I'll..."

"You'll what?" Princip countered. "You are powerless to do anything to me from where you now are, Alastor, and I am free to do whatever sick and depraved thing I choose to do with this sweet little baby doll. That is of course, unless you are willing to meet me on the field of battle for one final showdown... to the death Alastor."

Not even hesitating for a moment Alastor demanded, "Any time, any place you worthless scum-sucking pig! And this time only one of us will leave alive. And I promise you it won't be you."

"All big talk my boastful foe. But it's time to put up or shut up. Meet me outside the city at the abandoned football stadium ruins. And come alone. If I see any sign of Spider Nelson, or anyone else that I might suspect is along to assist you, I will kill the girl. Be there in one hour."

With that the mental transmission ended just as suddenly as it had started. Alastor checked the time and saw it was one in the morning. He had to get to the stadium by two. It would be difficult with the curfew, and he might be cutting it close, but he had managed to traverse the city after curfew before using his Tarot Magik and was certain he could do it again. He had to, for Ana's sake. But first, despite what Princip had said, Alastor had to contact someone he needed—Spider Nelson.

***

Alastor stood alone in the center of the abandoned football stadium. It stood in ruins looking much like photos he had seen of Roman Coliseum as it looked before the Great War. Now he doubted the original coliseum even still stood. It had survived centuries of weather but could not survive the destruction of man.

He shouted at the top of his lungs, "Gavril Princip! It is I, Alastor. I've come to kill you. Show yourself coward."

A moment later he saw a lone figure casually strolling in a carefree surly manor from a darkened entrance several hundred feet away. He knew it was Princip. He could feel the force of his Dark Magik even at this distance.

"Where is the girl, Princip?" Alastor shouted from across the distance. He was holding some of his most powerful Tarot Cards in his hand ready for anything; or so he thought.

"She is here and she is safe for now," Princip shouted. Then he waved his hand in the direction of a nearby metal pole, one that was likely used to hold a flag in the time before the Great War. High near the top, wrapped in glittering chains of gold and black fashioned of Magik, was Ana.

Princip said, "As you can see Alastor Ana is safe. She is being held in place by my Magik. If I die the spell will break and she will plummet to her death. So even if you do manage to kill me you will both win and lose at the same time."

Alastor realized the severity of his predicament. The chances of his success had just become severely compromised. He would have to find a way to protect Ana so he could focus on Princip. But before he even had a chance to react he heard the whining sound like that of a hurricane approaching from somewhere up in the sky above him. Then he saw an enormous mass of something crashing downward toward the ground. It impacted with a tremendous, earth shuddering blast that caused such a quake as to almost knock Alastor off his feet. A cloud of dust and debris rose thirty feet into the air and fell back to earth like a shower of grime. Alastor noticed that in the distance, Princip had surrounded himself with some type of spell to keep the particles off of him. Unfortunately, Alastor had not been quick enough and was splattered with the dust and dirt.

As he stood brushing himself off and trying to regain his composure, he looked up at the now settling cloud of dust, unable to believe what he was seeing. It was a one hundred foot tall version of Ronald Pryor, garbed in some sort of armor and wearing the helmets of The Black Hand's Synthetic Men. In fact, the creature looked a lot like one of the Synthos, only much, much bigger—and much more dangerous he was certain.

Doing his best to hide his concern, Alastor shouted across the stadium, "I thought you said we would come alone. I held up my half of the bargain. What is this thing doing here?"

"Just to keep the record straight Alastor," Princip said. "I told you to come alone. I never said anything about my being alone. I'd like you to meet my new friend, RP-1. I like to call him MegaSynth."

"This is just the kind of cowardly act I've grown to expect from you Princip," Alastor chided.

"That might be true and if so, I apologize for my actions," Princip said with a smirk. "But then again, there really is no need for me to apologize, is there? Soon you won't have to worry about my actions any longer, since you will be dead."

Suddenly the enormous MegaSynth began to run across the field toward Alastor, his massive feet leaving two-foot deep prints in the dirt and raising clouds of dust ten feet high. It lifted its foot for the final step with the intention of driving Alastor down into the dirt. At the last moment, Alastor jumped and sidestepped the creature's deadly stomp. As he flew through the air he pulled out one of his Tarot Cards and shot a bolt of bright white light upward toward the thing's head. The creature quickly drew its head back in time to dodge the worst of the blast but its helmet was blown completely off of its head. The huge helmet flew through the air, landing on the roof of a nearby abandoned home outside the stadium and crushed the building flat.

Alastor was looking up into the face of the horrible thing. The site of an enormous version of Ronald Pryor staring down at him was quite disconcerting to Alastor, and he was momentarily caught off guard. Before Alastor realized it, Princip was on him, attacking with a flurry of kicks and punches born of a lifetime of intense martial arts training. Alastor had barely recovered from the MegaSynth's initial attack and was now struggling to maintain his concentration among the barrage of punches. Knowing he needed a few seconds to regroup, Alastor pulled another Tarot Card and began mentally casting his incantation.

A second later a blue white light exploded around him and Princip was thrown fifty yards through the air where he slammed, stunned, into the base of the flagpole that held Ana Captive. In his disoriented state, the spell Princip had cast on Ana weakened, and she began to slide slowly down the pole.

Regaining his alertness once again Princip looked upward at Ana and her descent immediately stopped. Now it was time for him to get back into the battle. Princip looked across the field and saw Alastor and the MegaSynth locked in a stalemate of power. Alastor was on the ground, his entire body surrounded by a glowing sphere of illumination. It also extended upward, halfway up the MegaSynth's body, where it met a barrage of eight glowing red death rays each about a foot in diameter. Alastor's blue white light was slowly making progress, inching higher, indicating his power was going to surpass that of the MegaSynth. Princip knew if he didn't intervene soon the creature might be destroyed.

Alastor was using every ounce of strength and Magik he could muster to push back the shower of deadly beams shooting from the fingertips of the synthetic monster above him. He had no idea how long he could keep this up but he also knew if he stopped he would die. Just when he was beginning to feel his strength waning, he felt the impact of something coming from behind him. It was Princip casting one of his own spells and pummeling Alastor. The MegaSynth's rays began to inch downward toward Alastor.

With resignation, Alastor knew his strength was almost depleted and in a few moments it would all be over. He would be dead and poor Ana would be sent to one of Ronald Pryor's work camps where she would be forced to slave in the darkness of his ore mines until she dropped. Alastor couldn't allow that to happen.

He reached down into his innermost reserve of strength and could feel his Magik power growing. Just then he heard a scream of pain and turned for a moment to see Princip gripping his right wrist, which was spewing blood through the stump where his hand had apparently been blown to pieces. Standing off in the distance holding an Ulron Rifle was Spider Nelson, grinning from ear to ear and giving Alastor the thumbs up signal. Princip suddenly shot away in a flash, obviously abandoning the battle to save himself and tend to his wounds.

Alastor shouted, "Get Ana!" and Spider turned and raced toward the flagpole where Ana was falling to her death. The MegaSynth's rays were taking advantage of Alastor's distraction and had made progress toward him. Risking another brief glance Alastor saw Spider Nelson arrive at the base of the pole just in time to catch Ana. Now with Princip out of the picture and Ana safe, Alastor could focus all of his powers of Tarot Magik and soon his blue white beams were pushing back the crimson rays toward the MegaSynth.

Alastor looked up and saw the creature open its gargantuan mouth in a roar revealing rows of razor sharp shark-like metallic teeth. In its frustration, the thing began to grit those fangs so tightly that several of them broke off and others bit into his synthetic gums. A trickle of green goo, which apparently passed for blood in this creature, oozed down its chin as it squinted its eyes and strained with every ounce of strength to defeat Alastor.

But with its handler now gone, the MegaSynth was unsure of how to defend itself against such a powerful opponent. Nothing in its programming could have prepared it for the level of fury which Alastor was now sending its way.

A moment later the MegaSynth began to glow as its synthetic flesh reddened like that of a lobster in a pot. Soon like the man it was modeled after the creature's synthetic flesh began to bubble then liquefy as it sloughed off the thing's metallic skeleton. Then the skeleton itself began to glow a bright crimson before it turned black and began to crack then break up and crumble. Soon the shattered remnants of what was supposed to be an indestructible weapon of destruction fell in a shower of debris to the ground.

Alastor collapsed to the dirt more exhausted then he had ever been in his life. He blinked his eyes in an attempt to remain conscious. The last thing he saw before blacking out was Ana and Spider walking hand in hand toward him through a landscape of smoldering debris.

***

Alastor awoke in a state of confusion not knowing if he were alive or if he had crossed over into the Land Of Those Who've Passed. He slowly looked around the room and saw he was back in the secret lair of The White Lodge. Standing next to his bed were Spider Nelson and Ana both beaming with pleasure at the sight of his awakening.

"You're gonna be alright boss," Spider said. "And thanks to you, Ana will be too."

Alastor said weakly, "Ana... I'm sorry... it was wrong of me... to put you there... in the public... in the schools... forgive me."

Ana smiled without speaking as tears of happiness streamed down her beautiful face. Then Spider said, "No Alastor, you were right to originally put her there. Remember we decided hiding her in plain site was the best alternative at that time."

"But not now," Alastor said.

"No," Spider agreed. "Now she must stay with us here in the caves below the city. We'll take care of her and see that she is properly educated. But we cannot allow those swine, Pryor or Princip to get their grubby mitts on her. They'll use her in a heartbeat to get to you my friend."

"Yes." Alastor agreed. But whatever they come up with we'll be ready for them."

BRASS

"I'm telling you this is a foolproof way to score cash," Joey said excitedly.

Ace said, "I don't know Joey, it all sounds kinda unbelievable to me and creepy too."

It was night and the pair was sitting in Joey's car in the dark on a dirt road, near Heavenly Rest Cemetery, dressed in black and each holding a hacksaw.

"I'm tellin' ya Ace, it's a sure thing. In fact I already have a buyer lined up. He'll pay us $30 per unit."

Earlier that week while working a new temporary landscaping job at the cemetery, Joey noticed an old couple stopping by to put flowers on the grave of a loved one. Heavenly Rest was a high-price exclusive cemetery where the wealthiest of the community could experience an eternal rest as pampered as their lives had been. There were no headstones at Heavenly Rest just etched marble markers sunk in the ground each with a round latch of sorts at the center. The old couple turned the round latch on one of the markers, which caused a tall brass tube to rise up to be used as a vase to hold the flowers. "Brass," Joey thought, and the idea grew from there.

So now he and his friend Ace were removing as many of the brass vases as they could, as quickly as possible. The process went surprisingly faster than they had originally anticipated, and they quickly had a bag full. As Ace was sawing off one of the units, he heard a gasping sound and turned to see a horrifying scene unfolding.

His friend Joey was standing, slightly bent over, chalk-white and paralyzed with fear, his eyes bugging out of his skull. Joey apparently couldn't speak but only made terrible raspy gasping noises as if the air was being sucked from his lungs. Surrounding him was a host of a dozen or more translucent floating figures, all swarming around him, touching and grabbing at him as if in torment. As Ace looked on in horror, Joey's flesh began to turn a dusky blue and seemed to whither on his skeleton. In a matter of seconds, the body collapsed to the ground where it broke down and disintegrated into a mound of dust. A cold wind, which seemed to come out of nowhere scattered the dust until there was no sign of what had been Joey.

Ace was about to turn and run when he felt his wrist, the one holding the brass tube grow icy cold. He looked down and saw the luminous form of a decomposing hand gripping it tightly. Soon he too was surrounded by ghostly creatures. The last thing he was aware of was his own final, futile gasps of terror.

INSPECTOR 17

"He who steals a little steals with the same wish as he who steals much, but with less power." – Plato

"What goes around comes around, and karma kicks us all in the butt in the end of the day." – Angie Stone

Bob Jenkins drove up the hilly grade of Centre Street looking for a decent spot close to McKinley's Hardware Store. Bob was a man on a mission. After two trips around the block he noticed a car pulling from a parking space directly in front of the store and Bob managed to back right in, much to the chagrin of the driver of car behind him who was similarly looking for such a choice spot.

The store was owned by Charley McKinley, a life-long resident of Ashton, Pennsylvania and last living son of the late Emma and Walter McKinley, original owners of the store. Emma McKinley's first born son, Jimmy, had been tragically killed back in 1965 when he was twelve years old while playing with friends outside of an abandoned mine. The mine had been owned by the Coogan Oil Company and rumor said that the McKinley's had gotten a nice settlement from the company as a result of the tragedy. Charley was only about six when his brother was killed.

"Mornin' Charley," Bob Jenkins said as he walked through the front door of the store, hearing the all-too-familiar jingle of the welcome bell that hung over the door.

"Bob," Charley returned, nodding in his direction. "What can I do you outta today?"

"Well," Bob said with noticeable frustration. "I'm in a bit of a pickle. It's that cordless drill you sold me yesterday. It don't work for squat and it even looks like it might be a bit damaged."

"Are you sure Bob?" Charley asked. "That drill wasn't no rebuilt; it was brand-new right outta the box from the Wamaha Tool Company up in Franksville."

"Maybe so," Bob insisted. "But it don't work worth a damn."

"Did you charge it over night?" Charley asked. "Remember I told you it had to charge overnight."

"Of course I did," Bob said with a tinge of anger in his voice. Then Bob explained how he had charged it overnight and the fully charged light was lit when he woke up this morning. However, what Bob had neglected tell Charley was how he had put a drill bit into the chuck and then accidently dropped the drill. It fell straight down to his cement garage floor, and as luck would have it the thing hit right on the bit, driving the tool up into the chuck obviously damaging something deep inside the drill. Bob knew it was his own fault, but he wasn't going to miss a chance to dodge this bullet.

"Here see for yourself," Bob said. Charley checked out the condition of the drill and if he had suspected Bob might be lying about what happened he didn't bother to confront him about it. Instead wanting to keep a much-needed customer, Charley apologized for the faulty product and immediately gave Bob another new drill in exchange. He also swapped out the battery so Bob wouldn't have to wait another 24 hours for the new battery to recharge.

"I'm terribly sorry about this Bob," Charley offered. "I'm as frustrated about this as you are. I'll tell you what I'm gonna do. I'm gonna complain to the Wamaha Tool Company as soon as you leave. I believe I'll send an email expressing my dissatisfaction."

Bob hesitated for a minute, perhaps feeling guilty about deceiving the storeowner perhaps not. But what was done was done and he felt pretty sure Charley would get fully refunded by the Wamaha Tool Company, which he knew was located only a few towns away. "Y... yeah... that's probably a good idea."

Then Bob thought of something else. "Oh yeah. This might be helpful. I found this inside the box." He handed a small square white piece of paper with the message "Inspected by 17" typed in bold letters.

As soon as Bob left the store Charley sat down at his computer and drafted a very nasty email to the attention of his local sales representative from the Wamaha Tool Company. He made a point of mentioning that the tool was supposed to have been properly inspected before leaving the facility and he noted the tag from Inspector #17 that was inside the box.

When the salesman at Wamaha received the email he too was quite unhappy. His company had a reputation for impeccable quality, but for some unknown reason a bad product had ended up in the hands of a customer. And this was simply unacceptable. He assured Charley he would take care of the situation and immediately issued McKinley Hardware a credit for the damaged drill. He then decided to take it up with his supervisor, who then suggested he address the problem with the manager of quality control since in his opinion they had to have been the ones who dropped the ball.

So the sales representative wrote his own nasty email to the head of quality control and also attached a copy of the email from Charley McKinley. When the head of QC saw the email he was fuming. He immediately fired off an email to the shop floor QC supervisor, a man by the name of George Lee, and insisted that something be done about this problem. He noted the problem had been caused by one of George's employees, Inspector 17, whoever that might happen to be. He indicated that George should consider firing the employee if at all possible. George assured him the problem would be resolved immediately.

The clock on the shop wall read 3:28. Just two more minutes until the workday was finally over. As his eyes moved from the clock to the large window of the office overlooking the shop floor, Al Girard saw his boss George watching him anxiously. He was always watching someone or something. And at the moment Al noticed he happened to be the target of George's icy stare.

At one time George had been close friends with Al, his Inspector 17, but that was before they had their falling out. And so for the past several months George had been gathering paper against Al, creating a file of as many infractions as he could find, until one day when he would finally have enough to fire him. His boss had just given him the last piece of what he needed to satisfy the labor union's requirements for dismissal. And earlier that day his boss had practically ordered him to fire Al; and what better time to drop such a bombshell than the very end of the day?

As Al stood at the time clock, punching out for the day, he saw George calling him to his office. He wondered, "What does this idiot want with me now?" He walked over to George's office and could instantly tell something was wrong. George was standing behind his desk looking very serious as he indicated Al should close the door behind him. Despite his concern, or perhaps because of it, Al said with a noticeable amount of frustration in his voice, "Yes George? What's so all-fired important that you had to call me over here; and on my own time after I punched out for the day?"

George couldn't help feeling a bit smug about Al's surly attitude. The man obviously had no idea he was about to lose his job. George had originally been prepared to ease into the dismissal and try to keep things as civil as possible, but after Al's response he decided to simply let him have it.

"Al. You're fired," George said curtly. "I want you to bring your tool box over here for me to inspect and then Sam from security will be here to escort you out of the building."

"W... wa... what?" Al said confused. Then he began to grow angry. "What the hell are you talking about George? You... you can't just fire me like that. I want to see my union rep."

George looked at him with confidence and said, "I've already spoken with Jimmy, your shop steward, as well as Frank, the union president. They are backing me one hundred percent."

"That doesn't make any damn sense," Al shouted. "You have no grounds to fire me George. What the hell are you talking about?"

"Actually I do Al," George insisted. "Ever since that run-in we had a few months back you've developed a very bad attitude and have created a hostile work environment situation. I've been keeping track of every insolent and insubordinate comment you've made since then. Every time you deliberately disobeyed one of my orders. And I've kept the union informed all along the way, as well. In addition, I've documented every time you've screwed up lately, which even before today's final straw has been quite a bit."

Al looked at him questioningly wondering what he meant by final straw. He asked, "Final straw? What are you talking about George? What final straw?"

George showed Al the emails from the sales manager and the storeowner, as well as one from his boss ordering him to take care of the problem. Suddenly Al began to lose all of his bluster, perhaps realizing for the first time that he truly was about to lose his job.

"B... but... but I've worked here for over twenty-five years. I'm almost sixty years old George. Where the hell am I going to find another job?" Al asked, feeling somewhat weak and finding it necessary to support himself by leaning on the top of George's desk. "What... what am I supposed to do? Please George, you can't let me go. I have a house, a wife and son in his third year of college. I can't tell them I've lost my job."

George looked at Al with no sympathy. Now he was the one wearing the smug and defiant look saying, "Look Al, I have no time for this. Just leave now, get your tool box and wait for Sam to arrive to escort you out." George extended his hand out, palm up finger pointing at the door.

Suddenly a fury arose up in Al, one he never would have thought possible. He reached out and, grabbing George's extended hand, he pulled him forward; the boss's overweight body fell across the top of the desk. Al looked to his right and saw a trophy of some sort—something George must have won for some ridiculous company promotion. It appeared to be a metal replica of a large drill bit mounted to a circular base. Al grabbed the base and without thinking drove the tip of the trophy drill down hard and right through the back of George's neck. Blood gushed upward from the wound shooting through the spiral flutes of the drill bit. George cried out momentarily then his body twitched once, then twice before it went still and the spurting shower of blood became a trickle of pooling gore, which was slowly absorbed by the green felt desk blotter.

Realizing with horror what he had done, Al turned and ran from the office, slamming the door behind him blood dripping from his right hand. He raced out to the parking lot when he got into his bright red sedan and sped away from the terrible scene. He drove like a madman down the highway thinking at first of nothing but getting as far away from the Wamaha Tool Company as quickly as possible.

As he got further from the factory he slowed down slightly not wanting to attract the attention of local police who might already have been called if anyone happened to find George's body. He had to come up with some plan to escape but had no idea what he should do. He found himself going over everything George had told him and had showed him. He recalled the series of emails starting with some store owner named McKinley whose customer Bob somebody had returned a drill that Al had apparently let slip through his quality check.

This infuriated Al even more because he was always very conscientious and careful about his job responsibilities and had been proud of his work for many years. He was certain there was no way he would have let a damaged unit leave the factory. He suddenly broke down in tears crying and screaming hysterically at how unfair everything that had just happened to him had been: how unfair life was. He began slamming his left fist against the steering wheel then both, never noticing that his car was veering back and forth crossing the double-yellow line in the middle of the road.

Bob Jenkins drove home from the grocery store after picking up a few items for his wife for dinner. He was feeling pretty good about himself and how his luck had been. He had managed to cover up his mistake and his careless handling of his new drill by blaming the entire thing on some unknown Inspector 17 and was even given a brand new drill at no cost to himself. He was just thinking how good life was when he saw the bright red sedan swerving over onto his side of the road. Bob understood he was a dead man a millisecond before the two cars collided head on and burst into flames.

HEAR NO EVIL

To say the man was apprehensive was an understatement. It wasn't that he was exactly nervous or even worried but he was most definitely uneasy. In fact, the only reason Simon was sitting in the audiologist's office in the first place was because his wife had asked him—no, cajoled, harassed and practically begged him to make the appointment.

For several years Simon Baxter had been noticing his hearing getting progressively worse. He really didn't mind this loss other than certain times when he had to ask someone to repeat what they had said, often multiple times. His wife however was another story. She had noticed the symptoms early on when she had accused him of not paying attention to her or not listening to what she said. Then as the years progressed his hearing loss became worse and now at the age of fifty-eight Simon finally had no choice but to admit his wife was right and his ability to hear normal conversations had greatly diminished.

He had been noticing that he was turning his right ear more toward people when they spoke. He didn't know if this was because he was able to hear better with that ear or because he could hear less; it just was something his body seemed to do naturally. All he knew for certain was, if he turned in that direction it was easier to make out what they said. He especially had trouble distinguishing the difference between the sounds of consonant such as "S" and "F" or "T" and "D". Most recently, after months of having his poor wife complain about the volume at which he played their television, she had reluctantly agreed to activate the close caption option, even though she found the text on the screen incredibly annoying.

And so now here he was sitting in the office of an audiologist, having just had his hearing tested and having just been given the bad news. That bad news wasn't that he couldn't hear well; he already knew that coming in the door. The bad news was just how expensive it was going to be to attempt to correct that hearing loss. He had originally agreed to make the appointment after he and his wife had seen an advertisement in the local newspaper for hearing aids. The ad proclaimed high tech units could be purchased for as low as six hundred dollars a pair. He knew from talking with friends who already wore them that the average cost for good hearing aids could be anywhere between two thousand and eight thousand dollars a set. And even the best medical plans didn't cover even a small portion of the cost.

The audiologist was a man who liked to call himself "Skip," which Simon thought was a ridiculous nickname for a grown man. From the moment Simon set eyes on Skip, he sensed the man's honesty might be in question. The man also seemed to be a bit of slimy sort of character, and Simon couldn't help had but feel distrustful toward the man.

Skip informed him, "Unfortunately, due to the nature of your particular hearing loss, the six hundred dollar units will not even come close to helping you."

"Ah." Simon had shot back accusingly, "So that's your game: the old bait and switch. I get how all of this works. You lure me in here with the advertised cheap hearing aids knowing full-well they won't work for almost anyone and then you try to sell me something, which might possibly help but will cost me a fortune. Right?"

"I assure you, it's not like that," Skip tried to explain. "Here, let me show you.

Then Skip went into a detailed explanation of how, based on his test results, his hearing loss was unbalanced within the spectrum of sounds and his problem wasn't based on a lack of volume but was based on a lack of clarity. This was apparently why he couldn't wear the less expensive inside-the-ear-canal model but needed the more expensive programmable outside the ear type.

"Look Skip," Simon said. "It doesn't matter what the tests say or what you might think I need. The simple fact is I can't afford four grand for a set of hearing aids. Hell, if it weren't for my wife insisting I come here I wouldn't even be here in the first place. And to tell you the truth, other than hearing what my wife has to say I really don't mind not being able to hear anyone else. Most of the time I welcome it since most people have nothing worthwhile to say anyway."

"I have to agree with you there, Simon," Skip said, now fully immersed in his salesman role. "But still wouldn't it be better to be able to pick and choose when you want to hear someone and when you don't? Right now you have no choice."

Simon said, "Well... that may be so, but the bottom line still is I don't have the cash for expensive hearing aids and I'll be damned if I'm going to put them on a credit card."

"We do offer an excellent one year, interest free payment plan if you're interested."

"No thanks!"

"Then what if I told you I could get you a pair of state-of-the-art computerized reconditioned hearing aids, which originally sold for over five thousand dollars for just under two grand cash?" Skip asked, "Would you be interested then?"

Simon thought for a few seconds then replied, "Well... maybe. I suppose it would depend on what you can tell me about them... you know what reconditioning means and what sort of warranty I would get and so on."

Skip explained, "Leave me answer the warranty question first; you'll get the same one year warranty as you would get with a brand new pair."

Simon said, "So what's the catch?"

"There's no catch," Skip told him. "It's like this. As you might imagine most of my clientele are old timers. I'm talking about really old people, you know, folks much older than you, people in their eighties and nineties. We often sell them brand new units like the ones I was telling you about. The thing is these folks usually have absolutely no interest in getting hearing aids, but their rich yuppie kids feel that Mom and Dad deserve the best. So that's what they buy for them: the best. And often what happens is the old folks hardly, if ever, even wear them and usually they just leave them sitting in a drawer. Then as fate would have it the old people pass on, leaving behind a set of brand new high-end hearing aids that were almost never used."

"You're saying they 'pass on' like your trying to sugar coat it, but what you really mean to say is they die." Simon said with a noticeable uncertainty in his voice. "So what you're suggesting is that I wear some dead guy's hearing aids? Man, that's really kinda gross and more than a little creepy don't you think?"

"No. No. Not really," Skip said, continuing with his sales pitch, "It's like this. After Mom or Dad pass on... OK die, their survivors discover the hearing aids in some drawer somewhere. Most of the time, the kids have already forgotten about ever even buying the darned things for their parents in the first place. And then they have no idea what they're supposed to do with them. As a result they sometimes end up bringing them back to me. They figure it would be better if someone else got a chance to use them rather than throwing out something they paid five grand for. And at the same time they figure if they could manage to recoup some of the money they forked out initially, well then all the better.

"So to be perfectly honest with you, what I do is offer them pennies on the dollar for the units. And most of the time they just take the money and run. Then I invest a bit of my own money and send them out to be completely reconditioned. After that, I offer them to people like you who want more than they can afford. I manage to make a small profit but not nearly as much as when I sell a new set. And even though they're essentially brand new, I can't legally resell them as new units, but if I inform you of their reconditioned status I can sell them to you as such. No harm, no foul."

Simon thought about it for a moment and then said, "Hum. Makes good business sense I suppose. I think I see what you mean. I really wouldn't be wearing some dead guys hearing aids I would be wearing a brand new reconditioned set but I'd be getting them for a fraction of the cost."

"Now you get it." Skip was quick to reply, fairly certain he had this fish securely on his hook. "I can also assure you that the units will be completely sanitized and sterilized in a special laboratory I use and any perishable components such as the small cup which goes inside the ear as well as the sound tube will all be replaced with brand new apparatuses. Then the hearing aids will be personally fitted and reprogrammed by me right here in this office and right in front of you to your specific requirements. And I'll tell you what. This is an unbeatable deal for sure. I'll let you wear them to get used to them for a month at absolutely no cost to you. If you like them, then you can pay me at the end of that time. If you don't then you simply return them and walk away. It's a no risk, no cost trial offer."

Simon thought for another moment then said, "OK, Skip. That sounds like a reasonable deal to me." He especially liked the idea of being able to bring the infernal things back in a month if they weren't everything Skip said they were.

After taking some measurements of Simon's ears, Skip said, "Today's Tuesday. If you come back next Monday, I'll have your hearing aids ready to be programmed and all set for you to try. Can you stop back around this same time next Monday afternoon?"

"Yeah," Simon said standing to leave. "Let's make it Monday after work at five. See you then."

Simon left the office with a spring in his step, knowing he had just made a great deal and couldn't wait to tell his wife. He realized if he had pressed Skip harder for price he might have been able to get the cost down a bit more, but he figured what the hell; he was already getting a high end set of hearing aids for a rock bottom price. And besides, poor old Skip needed to make a buck or two. It was the American way.

The days flew by quickly and before Simon knew it he was once again walking out of Skip's office and heading toward his car. But this time he was wearing his own personally programmed set of hearing aids. Although Simon was not a vain sort of person by nature, he did nonetheless appreciate how you could barely notice the transparent tubes running from the hearing aid receivers to the tiny cups deep inside each of his ears.

And the clarity of what he was able to hear was incredible. He had lived for so long with his hearing loss that he had no idea what he had been missing. As he approached his car he heard a man and a woman speaking. And although he couldn't make out what they were saying he could tell they were arguing. He looked around and was surprised to see a young couple standing far away across two parking lots in an adjacent shopping center. And the most amazing thing was they weren't even shouting but simply arguing in a tone slightly louder than normal. Simon was certain that only a day earlier he wouldn't have even noticed them. To test out his theory, Simon took out his new hearing aids and sure enough, their conversation diminished to a quiet murmur, which he could scarcely distinguish from the dozens of other muffled noises around him.

"Wow!" Simon thought. "These things are amazing!" He put them back in his ears, sat behind the steering wheel of his car and started the engine. Immediately his car stereo began blasting some incredibly loud music. His hand instinctively flew to the volume knob and turned it down to an acceptable level. Simon realized once again just how bad his hearing must have deteriorated. "I can't believe that's how loud I had to play my music," He thought.

Simon pulled out into the street and headed for home. He recalled how his wife had asked him to stop by the local pharmacy on his way to pick up a few essentials for the medicine cabinet. After entering the drug store and finding all of the items he needed, Simon approached the cashier, placing his purchases on the counter.

The young woman behind the counter was a very attractive girl wearing a revealing low-cut top, which left little to the imagination. And although old enough to be the girl's father, Simon couldn't help but look. He was a man after all. He hoped he wasn't being obvious in his gawking and tried self-consciously to look elsewhere.

"Those are a couple of sweet melons just waiting to be picked my friend. Why don't you just reach out and grab one of them," Simon heard a voice he didn't recognize say. The voice startled him and Simon quickly looked around to see who had spoken, but he didn't see anyone around him and in fact couldn't see anyone else anywhere in the store. Yet strangely, it had sounded as if the speaker had been standing right behind him.

"Are you alright sir?" he heard the cashier say and he turned back to see her looking at him oddly.

"Um... yeah... yes I'm fine." Simon explained, "Just a bit distracted." His eyes settled right back on the woman's chest for a few seconds before he was once again able to pull his gaze away. When he caught her eye he saw her smiling at him, which caused him to blush with embarrassment.

"Look at that," The strange voice said. "She's beggin' for it. Why don't you make your move now? The store's empty. No one will know."

As the girl was ringing up the rest of his items Simon found himself walking closer to the counter and had to use all of his willpower not to reach over the counter and grab the woman. It was all so strange and so surrealistic. Simon was a law-abiding citizen, a husband and a father. He would never even think about committing such a heinous act yet now here he was scarcely able control himself. What the hell was wrong with him?

"Sir? Sir?" The girl said once again waking him from the strange dreamlike state and bringing him back to reality.

Simon looked up at the young woman and said, "I'm so sorry what was that you asked?"

She hesitated for a moment, starting to become obviously concerned about the peculiar way the man was acting then replied. "I said that will be twenty-seven dollars and sixteen cents. Sir."

Clumsily, Simon pulled out his wallet to retrieve his debit card as the woman began placing his items into a plastic bag. Her abundant breasts swayed gracefully to and fro as if in slow motion, all the while giving Simon a million-dollar view via the low cut top. Again he tried to look away.

"You know you want her man," The strange voice said. "Just take her. Just do it man."

"What?" Simon said aloud once again looking around him.

Now the cashier was starting to become very concerned and was looking at him with confusion. "Excuse me? Did you say something, Sir?" she asked.

Simon stammered, "Um... no... no... nothing... here... here's my debit card."

The girl slid a card reader across the counter uncertainly as her other hand reached underneath the cash register in order to be close to the panic button which was located there. She might be alone in the store but the night manager was in the office not far away and she knew if she pressed the button he would be out in a second. However, she soon found she wouldn't need to call for help, as the strange customer who she had caught staring at her breasts was now busy entering his pin number and no longer seemed to notice her at all.

"Th... thank you," the man said nervously. His forehead was glistening with sweat as he quickly snatched his bag from the counter and hurried out of the store.

"Sir! Your receipt!" The girl shouted after him but he was already out the door.

In the parking lot Simon stood slightly bent over, breathing heavily, feeling as though he might vomit. He was trying desperately to regain his composure. Not only was he upset by the strange voice he had just heard and the disgusting things it had told him to do, but also by something else. He realized he had actually wanted to do all the terrible things the voice had been suggestion. It had taken all of his willpower to resist its commands. What the hell was going on with him? Was he having some sort of mental breakdown or something?

Simon was not normally a bad person, yet back in the store he had wanted nothing better than to race behind the counter and throw the woman to the floor, strip off her clothing and rape her. He couldn't believe such a thought would have ever entered his mind, let alone almost actually have happened. Now, thank goodness, standing in the fresh air the evil sensation was rapidly fading, being replaced by a feeling of complete embarrassment.

Simon climbed back into his car and headed down the road. Along the way he was stopped for a traffic light when a man wearing dark sunglasses and carrying a white cane began slowly walking out into the crosswalk. As the blind man got close to Simon's car the light turned green but Simon still was required to sit and wait for the man to get safely past him.

"What are you waiting for chump?" A voice said inside Simon's head. "Run him down for Christ's sake. He's just a damned cripple, nothing but a drain on society. Run the gimp down and save us all a lot of grief."

Simon couldn't believe what he was hearing. It was that same voice; the one he had heard earlier. He could also feel himself losing control once again. His hands were gripping tightly on the steering wheel and his right foot was trying to press down hard on the accelerator. He managed to put his left foot on the brake pedal as his right was pressing the accelerator to the floor. The engine was roaring, but the car blessedly remained stationary.

The blind man must have heard the engine revving because he increased his pace and luckily just made it past the car's left bumper when Simon could no longer hold the vehicle back. His left foot slipped from the break as the tires burned rubber and the car shot like a bullet across the intersection. Had this occurred two seconds earlier the blind pedestrian would have been crushed under the weight of his car.

Then the car swerved to the far left, almost slamming into an oncoming vehicle before Simon was able to regain control. The strange voice was screaming in Simon's head now, "How dare you disobey me!" Simon began to feel incredible pain in the center of his skull. He pulled over to the side of the road and waited for a few minutes as the pain in his skull began to subside and began to feel a bit more like himself again.

Sitting in the car, sweating and breathing heavily, Simon realized that all of his problems had started when he put in the hearing aids. Simon slowly began to lift his hands to take out his hearing aids when the searing pain returned to the center of his skull and the voice commanded, "I know what you're thinking about. Stop it immediately or I'll make it much worse." The pain started to increase and Simon dutifully dropped his hands back to the steering wheel. As he did so the pain lessened to a dull ache.

He decided he was going to go back and confront Skip about what had been happening to him. He managed to negotiate a rough U-turn and drove as quickly as possible back to the place where his troubles seem to have started. He couldn't understand why, but for whatever reason the voice didn't return or try to stop him but instead allowed him to continue on his way.

Simon stumbled through the front door of the audiologist's office, staggered over to the reception window and began banging frantically on the customer service bell he found there. A few minutes later Skip stormed angrily through the door shouting, "Alright already. Keep your shirt on!" When he saw Simon standing there looking like a madman, his words caught in his throat.

He stood motionless for a second then spoke, "Simon? My God man what's the matter? Why are you back so soon? You only left here like a half hour ago and your checkup isn't for another week. What in the world could possibly be wrong?"

"Voices!" Simon said wide-eyed. "I... I'm... I'm hearing voices in my head... voices I've never heard before!"

Skip looked curiously at Simon and then breathed a sigh of relief and said with a note of sarcasm, "Of course you're hearing voices Simon. You're supposed to be. That's the whole idea of having hearing aids: to hear those things you couldn't hear before." Then he gave Simon a condescending smile. "It's absolutely nothing to worry about Simon, I assure you. But why don't you come on back in my office and we'll check them out for you anyway."

"No! No! No!" Simon insisted as he followed Skip back to his inner office. "You don't understand! Someone... someone bad is speaking to me through these hearing aids and he telling me to do the most incredibly awful things."

"Look Simon," Skip said. "That doesn't make any sense to me. Maybe these units are set too sensitively. You're probably just picking up someone's conversations around you or maybe getting interference from a television, radio or cell phone. I'm sure a minor adjustment will take care of it."

Simon said, "But there's more. Don't you understand? When I hear the voice telling me to do the bad things I feel like I have to, like I can hardly stop myself from doing them."

Now Skip was seated behind his desk and was starting to wonder if maybe this Simon character was a bit off his rocker, and maybe he should consider reaching into his desk drawer where he kept his hand-gun. It was getting late, the sun had set and he was alone in the office now with a potential madman. He preferred dealing with the octogenarians who were his regular customers; even unarmed he could probably overpower any of them that might choose to go bonkers. But Simon was still young and strong enough to be a problem. He decided to try and calm Simon down. The last thing he wanted to do was to have to shoot someone in his office. He especially didn't want to get blood all over his new recently installed carpeting.

"Look Simon. Even if you were hearing someone else's conversations, why in the world would you think it meant that you had to do what the voices said? After all, no mere voice can control you Simon. You're a grown man for God's sake. You're in control of your own actions."

Simon said with confusion, "But... but you don't understand... when the voice speaks to me... it's almost impossible to resist. I almost killed a blind man on the way over here and came very close to raping and murdering a young woman."

Now Skip began to realize just how crazy Simon was and he now wanted nothing more than to get this wacko out of his office, "I'll tell you what Simon, why don't you just leave the hearing aids here with me and I'll check them out and call you in a few days."

"If you try to take them out Simon," the voice inside Simon's head said, "I'll make your life a living Hell."

Simon started to reach up to take out the hearing aids and the incredible pain which had plagued him earlier returned with a vengeance. He felt his knees start to buckle as if he could hardly remain standing. When he let his hands drop to the desktop to support himself, Simon felt the pain immediately cease.

"Kill him Simon." The voice insisted. "Grab that letter opener and stab him with it!" For a brief moment time seemed to stand still as Simon envisioned himself bending over, grabbing the letter opener from the desk and thrusting it into Skips right eye socket and deep into his brain, then pulling it out with a jolt. He could hear Skip's dying screams of pain and terror as his blood and brains dribbled out through the open eye hole before he collapsed face forward on the top of his desk as a pool of glistening crimson formed below him.

"Simon? Simon? Are you alright?" Skip said from across his desk as the murderous image faded from Simon's mind.

"W... w... what?" Simon replied in confusion. He saw Skip sitting looking as confused as Simon now felt.

Then without even taking moment to think Simon quickly reached up and yanked both hearing aids from his ears and threw them at Skip. One landed on the top of the desk while the other skidded across the desk and hit Skip square in the chest. He had done it. He had acted quickly enough to beat the voice and had safely gotten the accursed things out of his ears.

"Fine! Fine!" Skip shouted at him. "I told you this was a no-risk proposition. You don't have to go off acting like a lunatic for Christ's sake." He was about to order Simon to leave his office but before he could he saw the man had already turned and fled, probably not even hearing Skip's rant as Simon slammed the inner office door behind him. Then he ran out the front of the office leaving the main door standing open to the cold night air.

Still traumatized by the evening's events, Simon stumble-stepped to his car, yanked open the door then collapsed into the front seat. He let out a sigh of relief as the sweat trickled down his face. He closed his eyes and sat basking in the glorious near-silence, which was his once again. He may have missed a lot of sounds before he had the hearing aids, but he didn't have the peace and tranquility that the quiet now brought him. This was better, he realized, much better.

"You didn't really think you could get rid of me that easily, did you my new friend Simon?" It was that voice once again. But how could that be? He had gotten rid of the hearing aids. Then with gut-wrenching terror Simon realized that somehow the voice must have found its way into his mind and was still in him.

"We have so much to do, Simon, so, so much to do." Then he heard the sound of ear-piercing maniacal laughter, but had no idea it was actually coming from his own mouth. He clenched his hands into claws and began tearing his ears to bloody shreds.

***

Skip closed the front door, turned and started back toward his inner office, but he momentarily stopped thinking he heard someone screaming somewhere in the distance. He shook his head and said, "I must be hearing things." This brought about a small chuckle as he realized the irony in what he had just said. Once back in his inner office Skip picked up the discarded hearing aids and placed them back into the appropriate compartment in his "reconditioned" drawer. The compartment read, "Sabatino, Vincent."

The story he had told Simon about the hearing aids being reconditioned units was, of course, a total lie: a scam that Skip often pulled on his unsuspecting new customers. There was no lab where the units were sent to be sanitized and reconditioned. In fact he could have given the hearing aids to Simon at his first visit, but Skip often found that by allowing a few days for "reconditioning" it seemed to make the lie more believable. He had many years of experience running this particular scam.

However, the first part of the story he had told Simon was at least partially true. He often did have surviving relatives of recently departed patients bring their loved-ones hearing aids back. Also, most of the time the units were practically like new and had been seldom worn by their owners. And it was also true that Skip really did pay them pennies on the dollar for the used hearing aids. But that was where the truth ended.

After buying them back, Skip simply tossed them into a compartment in a drawer with the names of the former owners written on a tag mounted on the front of the compartment. Some of the tags had multiple names, those being the original owner and subsequent owners. Skip hadn't had time yet to add Simon's name to the tag reading "Sabatino, Vincent" and realized he probably wouldn't bother since Simon only had them for a half hour or so. Skip knew very little about most of his dearly-departed former patients, including the one whose name he was currently examining.

"Vincent Sabitino?" Skip said aloud. "If I remember correctly, I believe he may have been one of my younger patients, but I'm not certain. I don't remember much about him. Anyway, I suppose that doesn't really matter." He closed the drawer and went back to his paperwork.

Had he actually taken the time to learn more about his former client, Skip would have discovered Vincent was a very troubled young man whose wealthy parents had tried to buy their son's love for years. No matter how much trouble he got into they would always come to his rescue and as a result had inadvertently created a monster in the process. When Vincent had begun experiencing hearing loss as a young adult his parents insisted on buying him the very best hearing aids, despite the fact that his hearing loss was a direct result of his recreational abuse of oxycodone.

Skip would have also been surprised to learn that Vincent had eventually taken his criminal activities to an extreme and after a four-state crime spree of rape and murder he had eventually been cornered by the FBI and killed in a shootout. His hearing aids were still present in his ears at the time of his death. Eventually, those same hearing aids found their way back into Skip's reconditioned drawer and eventually into the ears of Simon Baxter, his latest disgruntled patient.

***

Outside, a car engine started up as a driver with an insane look in his eyes and bloody shredded remnants of what were once his ears now dangling like limp crimson coated noodles from the sides of his head, pulled his car out of the parking lot and headed down the highway for the second time that evening. He was on a mission. There were people to kill—so, so many people to kill.

BIG FRANKIE

Young Timmy realized he might have made a very bad mistake. The model was far more frightening than he had anticipated. It hadn't seemed so terrifying when he initially asked his parents to buy it for him. Now that he thought about it however, hadn't he noticed something odd about the thing while he and his father were assembling and painting it?

In the darkness of his bedroom, this uneasy feeling had become stronger than ever as the wretched thing stood like a demonic sentinel out there in the shadows. Timmy was certain it was watching him, just waiting for him to fall asleep so it could... what exactly could it do?

A rational part of Timmy understood the object was nothing more than plastic, painted and glued together. Yes, it had movable arms, but they were just precisely fitted swiveling parts whose action was the result of a thick rubber band stretched between them. No matter how it bothered him, it was still just a model from the Aurora Company, an almost two-foot high replica of Frankenstein's Monster known as "Big Frankie".

It had been in early March of 1965 when ten-year-old Timmy Middleton saw the model kit advertised in his copy of "Movie Monsters" magazine. The thing had looked incredible. Timmy had been a major fan of all things horror related his entire young life. He watched horror movies and collected horror books, comics, magazines, posters, models —anything he could get his hands on.

His model collection consisted of almost every one of the Universal Studios monster models including Wolfman, Dracula, Frankenstein, Mummy and many others. He even had a special model customizing kit, which came with an assortment of miniature skulls, rats and other such items. This kit allowed the collector to modify his particular model so it became unique to his own specific tastes.

He had all of his models prominently displayed on his dresser, but they were only about seven inches tall. This new Big Frankie model was almost twenty-four inches tall and when carefully painted it looked very much like the Boris Karloff interpretation of the monster in the Universal Studios movie. To Timmy it was the equivalent of the holy grail of monster models.

Then to his surprise, it appeared in a local hobby store and he had wanted it more than anything he could imagine. Timmy tried his best to save his money he earned from his paper route but hadn't even managed to save even a third of the model's $4.95 price tag. He just knew he had to find some way to get it. Eventually he ended up pleading with his parents to get it for him for his birthday in July, and miraculously when he unwrapped his present, there it was. He and his father spent the weekend sanding, assembling, gluing and painstakingly painting the model so it looked as realistic as possible.

Now he was wondering what in the world he had been thinking. The model had oversized swiveling arms and wore the trademark black suit jacket with tattered sleeves, which were too short and exposed the creature's wrist and massive hands. A thick plastic replica of a heavy metal chain was attached at its shoulder, near its neck. The chain traveled down along its body where it attached to a huge chunk of simulated granite. The granite was possibly meant to represent a broken off piece of his grave marker and was engraved with the partial word "Fr."

In the light of day, the model was by far the coolest thing Timmy had ever seen but now, in the darkness of his bedroom, lit only by his night-light, the thing looked incredibly frightening.

Timmy's relationship with his chosen hobby, horror, was strangely of the love/hate variety. He was fascinated by the genre yet simultaneously terrified. He suspected things might be this way for all horror fans or at least for kids who liked horror. His bedroom looked more like a chamber of horrors than a place for a young boy to sleep, and he loved having it that way.

Yet at night, he slept with the covers pulled over his head and still used a nightlight. Every night as he attempted to fall to sleep, he would poke his head out from under the covers and look around at his collection making sure nothing was out of place. It was as if he needed to make sure there was nothing out there trying to get him. This all seemed futile, since his thin blanket wouldn't be any sort of defense against such imagined demonic monsters.

Now as he lay under the supposed protection of his covers Timmy could imagine that he was hearing the rattling sounds of Big Frankie's chains and the scraping of the large chunk of granite as grated across his floorboards. He envisioned the monster getting close to his bed then swinging the chain and boulder, using it to bash in his tender young skull. He fantasized his parents finding him in the morning, stone-cold dead in his bed with his head crushed while his blood and brain matter soaked into his pillow.

Timmy knew he was being ridiculous. Yet the way the horrible thing seemed to stare at him was extremely troublesome. As he lay there terrified, he was certain he could recall a Twilight Zone episode where a ventriloquist dummy came to life. Big Frankie was very much like such a thing. What if it was also somehow able become alive?

What if some ghost, or maybe a demon had crawled deep inside the plastic shell and had taken over its functions? Its legs didn't move but maybe it could just float above the floor. Timmy knew nothing like what he was imagining was even remotely possible, yet at night in the darkness of his room, it seemed as if anything could happen.

He ventured a quick peek out from under his covers certain to discover the horrid model just inches from his face, but it wasn't there. Gathering a bit more courage, Timmy pulled down the covers and looked over to the corner where he had placed Big Frankie and to his relief saw the model still standing just as he had left it.

With a self-deprecating chuckle, Timmy realized just how foolish he was allowing his over-active imagination to get the better of him. It was just plain silly. Even if the thing were alive, what could it possibly do to him? Even at only ten years old, Timmy was more than twice the size of the little model and was fairly certain one good kick would send it flying across the room and crashing into a wall where it would likely break into pieces.

Timmy realized it was time for him to put all of his wild imaginings behind him. He was ten, almost a teenager. There was no longer any reason for him to waste his time worrying about imaginary monsters. He tucked the covers up under his chin and closed his eyes preparing for a good night's sleep.

That was when he felt the icy cold touch of plastic on his ankle.

DINNER WITH ANDY AND MEG

The young woman's heart pounded like a jackhammer in the center of her chest. Her blood thumped with a deafening roar inside her skull, sounding like ocean waves crashing against the shore as she fled frantically down the dark alley on the hot and humid August night. Perspiration flowed from every pore as her clothing clung tightly to her sweat soaked body. Her feet felt like lead weights, her footfalls resounding like claps of thunder inside her panic stricken mind. The steamy air surrounding her reeked with the stench of decay. She was using up virtually every last ounce of energy she could muster trying desperately to escape. She was unaware that as she fled she was screaming at the top of her lungs.

She fought back the tears that seemed to be pressing on the backs of her eyes, which bulged wide with fear. But she knew if she gave in to such an urge and allowed the tears of terror to flow freely, she might very well lose her concentration, might falter and then it would certainly be all over. Behind her an ever-increasing mob of vile rotting living-dead creatures lumbered clumsily along with arms outstretched, growling, moaning that horrible sound they all seemed to make, clawing at the air with long yellowed gnarled fingernails.

She had outrun such creatures countless times before with little difficulty as they were all so slow and awkward, stumbling about in what might be considered an almost a comic fashion, had they not been so disgusting and so incredibly deadly. But tonight, something had gone very wrong; tonight she had inadvertently found her way into an unfamiliar section of a city with numerous connecting side streets and alleys, each of which appeared to be vomiting dozens of the deadly zombies.

The creatures' tattered clothing hung on decaying skeleton-exposed bodies as rags and remnants of what they had once been, mimicking the same hideous manner in which their own flesh tended to hang and slough off of their bones as they gradually rotted away. She supposed some day, if she only could stay alive long enough to see it, they would all simply decay and disappear. As she ran for her life, she started to wonder if staying alive was going to be possible for her for very much longer.

Bonnie well knew and understood the rules for surviving in this post-apocalyptic world, and the number one rule was to never let them out-number you, corner you or trap you. Even a small child might be able to outrun two or three of the mindless beasts, but when they overpowered you with sheer force of numbers the chances of survival quickly dwindled away to nothing. And that was exactly where Bonnie now found herself—surrounded by an ever-growing number of the walking dead creatures, too many to allow for any sort of successful getaway.

She looked around for a possible avenue of escape, but found none. She could smell the stench of decay getting ever nearer as the creatures began surrounding her. She could hear their mechanical guttural growling getting ever closer behind her. Just when she thought she would have to accept her fate and would surely be eaten alive, she heard the honking of a car horn and saw the silhouette of what appeared to be a dark van or panel truck speeding down the alley in her direction knocking down zombies, literally smashing them to pieces as body parts flew in all directions.

When the van was about ten feet in front of her, the driver slammed on its breaks, skidded sideways and brought the van to a stop with the side door facing Bonnie. A moment later the door slid open and Bonnie saw an arm wave frantically, beckoning for her to come inside, as she heard a man's voce shouting, "Hurry! Jump in quickly, before it's too late!"

Without hesitation, she pushed aside two disgusting female zombies who had momentarily turned away from her and had begun focusing their attention on the newly arrived van. She quickly sprinted toward the open door and literally threw herself inside. A moment later the door slammed shut and she was plunged into darkness. She seemed to land on a dank musty smelling rug of some sort and thought she could smell an oily, industrial odor inside the van. She heard several zombies thumping against the outside of the door. The man who had just saved her life, seen only in silhouette was working his way back into the driver's seat.

"Come on!" The shadowy man said, "Hurry! Up front! Get in the passenger's seat! It's the only chance we have of getting out of here alive!"

Bonnie did as the mysterious man instructed, quickly climbing into the passenger's seat and securing herself with her safety belt with shoulder harness. She looked over at the man in the driver's seat and was surprised to find he was a young, handsome man, just a few years older than she was. He had longish dark hair, was well built and seemed surprisingly clean considering the deplorable condition of the world they lived in.

He was busy flipping switches like a pilot about to take off in an airplane. It was then Bonnie noticed the strange array of dials and knobs crudely retrofitted to a box mounted to the van's dashboard.

Outside, the zombies had begun to crowd all around the van, scraping, clawing and banging on the outside, trying to find a way to get in, to get to the two delicious morsels, just waiting to be devoured. Bonnie surprised herself by strangely thinking of the phrase, "meals on wheels" then experienced an uncontrollable shiver at the thought.

"Look down by your feet!" the man shouted, "See that black rubber square on the floor? Put your feet solidly on that square and put your hands in you lap."

"But... but..." Bonnie attempted to say.

"Do you want to live or die?" the man scolded. "Now do what I told you! Put your feet on that square and put your hands in your lap! Do not... I repeat... do not touch any of the doors or any metal in here! Do you understand?"

Bonnie quickly nodded her understanding and immediately did as she was told, assuming the position the man described with her feet planted firmly on the soft thick rubber mat. To her right, at the passenger's side window, a particularly hideous creature had its rotting face pressed tightly against the glass, its eyes roaming about wildly; its wretched tongue licking the surface of the window like some sort of mentally deficient animal, which in essence, it was. Bonnie cringed and held back an almost uncontrollable urge to vomit at the horrible sight.

Then most of the other creatures had begun pounding wildly against the outside of the van as the young man fiddled with knobs and dials on whatever the contraption was that was mounted to the dashboard. "Here we go," he said, as if Bonnie was supposed to know what he was about to do, which of course, she did not.

Suddenly, the air around her seemed to hum and she began to feel the hairs on her arms and the back of her neck stand on end. Then the humming became louder and she noticed that the hideous creature, which had attached itself to her window, was suddenly beginning to twitch and spasm. All around the van every one of the undead beasts was thrashing and convulsing uncontrollably. Then Bonnie finally realized what was happening and why the man had asked her to keep her feet on the rubber mat and not touch any metal. He was somehow sending a high-voltage electric current of some sort throughout the outside of the van and was electrocuting any of the decomposing creatures that had come in contact with the metal exterior, as well as any of the things which were in turn touching the ones hanging on to the van.

The particular creature, which had attached itself to her window, convulsed worse than ever, his body twitched spasmodically, his gray-filmed eyes rolled back in their sockets as he began to uncontrollably spew a greenish-yellow liquid all over the window. The wretched creature's hair began to first smoke then smolder, and then was finally set ablaze as the mindless thing stared helplessly in through the window at Bonnie.

For the briefest of moments she almost began to feel pity for the beast as smoke began pouring from the corners of its undead eyes, its flaring nostrils and then finally from its slack-jawed mouth. The entire process seemed to go on for hours but in reality took but a few seconds. Then all of the zombies surrounding the van began to drop one by one onto the street, now reduced to smoldering heaps of burning shuddering flesh. The air was filled with the foul odor of rotten burning human hair and flesh.

Without a moment's hesitation, the man flipped a few more switches then put the van into gear and raced down the alley, driving bumpily over top of the twitching, burning corpses. When they were a safe distance from the alley the man turned to Bonnie and said, "You can relax and take your feet of the rubber pad if you like. I turned off the juice."

"Who... what... how... who are you?" Bonnie stammered.

The man offered his right hand in a friendly handshake gesture and said pleasantly, "My name is Andrew but you can call me Andy."

At first, Bonnie was reluctant to shake his hand after what she had just witnessed, as if somehow his hand held another electrical charge, which would fry her the way it had fried the creatures in the alley. Eventually she took his hand, "My... my name is Bonnie... say... what was that you just did back there?"

"Oh that. Well, that was nothing. I just gave those dead heads a taste of good old-fashioned e-lec-tricity—courtesy of a series of industrial strength batteries I have rigged up in the back of the van."

Bonnie asked, "But how did you... I mean... how do you know how to do all that?"

Andy replied, "Well, back in the good old days, before the world went down the crapper, I was an electrical engineer. I know all kinds of stuff like that. Most of it is useless in the stone-knives-and-bear-skins world we now live in, but some of it comes in handy from time to time... like tonight for example."

"Well I certainly appreciate it," Bonnie replied. "I usually have no trouble outrunning those things, but tonight something went wrong and I got turned around somehow and they managed to ambush me."

She sat quietly for a few minutes then self-consciously began to notice her own fetid odor: the stink of sweat, fear, caked on filth and an unwashed body. She reached over and rolled down the passenger window about half way.

"I'm sorry about my smell," Bonnie said. "I know I must really stink. Needless to say it's been a long time since I've been able to wash."

Andy replied, "Not a problem. Baths are few and far between theses days, and compared to that crowd we just left, you smell just fine. Besides, you can take care of getting a bath and a clean set of clothing when we get where we are going." Bonnie was suddenly thrilled at the prospect of being able to wash once again.

The van navigated from street to street driving around the city. She believed Andy was taking a circuitous route, which would keep him as far away from zombies as possible, but she had absolutely no idea where they were going. After a while she realized they were leaving the city and heading out into the suburbs.

"Where are we going?" Bonnie asked with a bit more uncertainty in her voice than she had wanted. She understood there were many dangers to fear in this new world and not all of them were zombie in nature. Bonnie often found she had as much to fear from her fellow man as she did from the walking dead. She unconsciously reached into her right pants pocket to make sure she still had her switchblade handy.

"Well," Andy said. "I figured the best thing to do under the circumstances was to get as far away from danger as possible. We have a place out in the country that is safe and where we hardly ever see any of those ungodly creatures."

"We?" Bonnie asked curiously. She had heard of pockets of survivors who formed small communities. She had been searching for such a group and hoped she had finally found one.

"Oh yes. Sorry." Andy explained, "I have a place out in the country where I live with my wife Meg. I only come into the city when I absolutely have to—to get those things I can't seem to find at home. I was returning home when I heard you screaming."

Bonnie sat surprised for a second. Had she screamed? She could not recall, but supposed in her terror she most likely had done so. Now that she had given it some thought it was probably a good thing she had screamed, or else Andy might not have ever found her.

"Do you and Meg have and kids?" Bonnie asked off handedly then suddenly thought better of it. Many couples had lost children to the insatiable appetites of the hell-born creatures. What if that had happened to Andy and Meg? Now that the words had left her lips she wished she hadn't said them.

"No. Meg and I never got around to having any kids," Andy explained. "I suppose that was fortunate, considering how everything turned out." Bonnie let out an inaudible sigh of relief. Then Andy asked her, "Do you live in the city somewhere or are you just passing through?"

Bonnie hesitated for a moment then said, "No. Not really. I suppose I was just sort of passing though, looking for food, maybe hoping to find some survivors, whatever. I don't really have any firm plans these days."

"Yeah. I know what you mean. Well, it looks like tonight was your lucky night," Andy said. "You have found a survivor and we have plenty of food. When we get to my place I promise I will fix you up a good late night meal. How long has it been since you've eaten real food? You look a bit on the scrawny side, if you don't mind my saying so."

Bonnie looked down at her pathetically thin condition and said, "I suppose you are right. I really can't remember when I ate last. It's hard to keep track—days, maybe. I think I may have had a bag of pretzels a few days ago, but I can't recall... that might have been a week ago. The days all seem to run together."

Andy reached down into a brown sack next to his seat, took out a large bright red apple and handed it to her. He said, "Here, try this. It should hold you over until we get home."

Bonnie took the fruit and began to hungrily gnaw on it, allowing the juices to run shamelessly down her chin.

"I think you'll be quite happy with the dinner you'll have at our place," he said, "and I can't wait to introduce you to my wife Meg. I'm sure you'll both get along great."

Very little else was said for the remainder of the trip. After they had traveled for about a half hour or so along an dark and quiet country road, Andy slowed the van and made a sharp right turn onto what appeared to be a gravel driveway which ended at a set of large metal gates. Bonnie soon learned Andy's house was located at the end of the roadway. To gain access, Andy had to leave the van and unlock a padlock securing the gates, which were equipped with razor wire across the top. When he returned to the van he explained the fence was just one of the many precautions he had to take to keep the creatures from getting onto his property. "Every so often one or two of them find their way to the fence," Andy said. "When they do, I simply wheel down a few of the batteries, hook up the cables, turn on the electricity and fry 'em."

Bonnie was a bit leery about being locked inside the property, which was more like some sort of compound, trapped behind an eight foot razor-wire fence that could be quickly charged with enough electricity to kill an elephant. But she believed she would be much safer on the inside of the fence than she would be on the outside. Plus she had survived this long and was certain she could still take care of herself if the need arose. And she did not believe she would have any problems since her new companion, Andy seemed OK; especially considering the risk he had taken to save her life. Once they had passed through the gates, Andy locked them again, before returning to the van and driving slowly and cautiously up the dirt driveway to the house at the end.

When the pair approached the house, Bonnie could see candlelight reflecting in some of the windows. She must have looked a bit taken aback because Andy quickly explained, "Yep, candles. Keep in mind, just because I'm an electrical engineer doesn't mean I can produce juice from thin air. The local electrical grid has been down for months. I have a few gas-powered generators for real emergencies and some rechargeable batteries like the ones in the van, but for the most part we have to get by with candles, just like everyone else."

Bonnie nodded her head in understanding without speaking. It was weird how Andy had been able to read her thoughts as if they were not strangers but actually a couple. She wondered if her face was such an open book or if he was simply able to read and intuit all people well. Then with a degree of jealousy she thought, "Too bad this one's married. We might make a good team." She immediately derailed that train of thought, worrying if he might be able to once again know what she was thinking. She suddenly was hit with a feeling of melancholy, realizing just how lonely and in need of human companionship she had become.

Andy opened the front door of the large farmhouse with a key and the pair passed into a downstairs foyer. It was a grand place with a high ceiling from which hung a huge and unusable crystal chandelier.

Bonnie looked around, awestruck, then said, "This place is amazing! Did you live here before... you know... before... everything... or did you find the place afterward?" With no government, no laws, no police, all formalities of a civilized society had long since broken down. People roamed aimlessly from place to place barely clinging to survival, living wherever they could. If someone found a house they liked, which appeared to be safe from the living dead, they simply would move in. She knew some lower and less civilized types would not be above killing the current residents to gain ownership. It truly had become a survival of the fittest type of world.

"We could have never afforded a place like this in the old days," Andy said. "We stumbled upon it, abandoned, shortly after everything went south and have been living here ever since. Everything was pretty much as you see it now including the wire fence. The original owners must have either been survivalists or simply paranoid. But I figured whatever... it suited our needs perfectly. Whoever the owners may have been then never returned, alive or otherwise."

Bonnie suddenly remember Andy's wife, Meg and asked, "Where do you suppose your wife is?" For a moment her uncertainty returned. No matter how appealing this man seemed and no matter what he had done to help her, he was still an unknown commodity.

For all she knew the stranger might not even have a wife. This whole thing could be a ruse to get her into this farmhouse where he and perhaps some of his friends might subdue her, rape, torture and kill her. But so far, her mysterious host had made no hostile moves against her and for all intent and purpose he appeared to be acting in a manner that was just the opposite, paying little attention to her as they walked through the dimly lit living room toward what she believed was the kitchen. Once again she reached into her pants pocket to feel the security of her concealed switchblade.

"She is probably still resting," Andy replied. "We try to sleep whenever we can, because when we are awake it seems we are always working or foraging for food and supplies. I used to think my engineering job was a pain in the butt, but this whole survival thing is a much, much worse."

The pair made their way out to the large country kitchen and as he lit a few more candles, Andy said, "Don't worry. I'm certain when Meg smells the food we make she will be up here shortly."

"Up here?" Bonnie asked. "You mean she's down in the basement?"

"Yeah. We moved our bedroom downstairs when the weather got hot," Andy explained. "There's obviously no more air conditioning and we have to stay cool any way we can."

Bonnie thought how nice it must be for Meg to have a man like Andy, who seemed so preoccupied with tending to their needs that he thought little of the fact he had been alone with another woman. Granted, she might be a bit gaunt, as well as sweaty and unclean, but she was still an attractive worm that had what it took to seduce a man.

If Andy had been a different sort of man, he could have easily tried to attack her when they left the city. He could have raped and killed her and left her body by the side of the road and no one would have had any idea what had happened to her. She would have just been another dead body rotting along the side of the road in a world full of rotting dead bodies. She was alone in the world and had no one to care about her, so she was extremely vulnerable.

He reached into a plastic thermal cooler and extracted what appeared to be several eggs and some bacon. Bonnie stared at the sight, scarcely able to keep herself from drooling.

"Are... are... those... real eggs? And... and is that... real bacon?" she asked unbelievingly.

"Yes they most certainly are," Andy said. "You probably couldn't tell when we drove up, because it was so dark, but this property is actually a small farm. I have a barn around back with several chickens, two cows and a few small pigs. We are fairly self sufficient around here. It keeps me from having to go into the city very often except when I need only the most essential supplies—the things I can't get here."

Bonnie looked at him with surprise, "But how do you keep things cold and fresh without electricity or refrigeration?"

Andy explained, "Below the barn is a cold storage root cellar. It doesn't keep things frozen like a freezer, but it does a pretty good job of keeping food fresh for a while. I also dry some fruits from our trees and salt and dry meats. That reminds me, I should warn you that the woods out behind the farm are full of a variety of traps. I catch small animals like squirrels, rabbits and such, not to mention the occasional zombie that might somehow get past the perimeter fence. I also have a large vegetable garden out back as well. Like I said... we are pretty self-sufficient. Most of what we need we can get right here."

He reached into a cabinet and brought out a large cast-iron frying pan, placing it on the top of a stove. He looked again at Bonnie and said, "No gas, no electricity, no microwave or convection ovens anymore, but this old wood stove does a good job of cooking whatever we need to cook." He placed the strips of bacon into the frying pan and after a few minutes cracked and added the eggs, allowing them to cook in the bacon grease. The smells, which permeated the kitchen, were so luscious; Bonnie thought she would lose her mind from simply soaking in the pleasurable aromas.

Andy turned and said, "This will be ready in a minute. Why don't you go to that cooler over there and grab yourself a soda or fruit drink. Or if you like I can rustle up a glass of fresh milk."

Bonnie thought she had died and gone to heaven. She said with genuine appreciation, "Th... thanks... soda will be fine." She walked over to the cooler and grabbed a can of cola. She could not believe she was about to eat a real meal —the first in only God knew how long. She popped the cap on the soda and listened to the glorious sound of the escaping carbonation.

By the time she returned to the table, a large plate of bacon and eggs was waiting and looked to Bonnie like the most incredible meal she had ever seen. She sat down and without even taking time to pick up a fork or knife she began to devour the food using her fingers. After a few moments when the initial hunger frenzy was satisfied, she became slightly embarrassed by her actions, wiped her greasy hands on her filthy shorts then picked up the fork and slowed her pace, trying to eat in a more civilized fashion.

Andy who was watching her the entire time, smiled and said, "Don't worry about it, Bonnie. I was the same way when Meg and I found this place and were able to eat real food once again. It's OK. Once the initial hunger passes, your body will naturally allow you to slow down and you'll be able to better enjoy what you are eating. Speaking of which, how do you like the food?"

"It's incredible!" Bonnie said with grease dripping down her chin, "It is beyond incredible! I honestly didn't think I would ever eat another hot, cooked meal again. It is beyond my wildest dreams."

While Bonnie continued with her feast they both heard a thumping noise coming from the basement. Andy glanced over toward the basement door, with a momentary look of apprehension present on his face. Then he quickly recovered and once again his expression took on that of the congenial host. Bonnie did not miss the momentary change in demeanor and although she was suddenly alert and concerned, she did her best to conceal her uneasy feelings.

"It sounds like Meg is awake," Andy said indicating everything was fine. "I'd better go down and tell her we have a guest for dinner. I'm sure she will be very happy."

Andy opened the basement door and ducked through it quickly closing it behind him. Bonnie could hear him running rapidly down the stairs, his footsteps echoing loudly on the old wooden treads. For a moment she thought she smelled a foul odor wafting up from the basement through the briefly opened door, but it had closed so quickly she could not be certain, especially since the kitchen was filled with the pleasant smells of food cooking. She looked down at her plate, no longer starving and suddenly unsure if she was even still hungry. She started to feel a growing sense of uneasiness in the pit of her now full stomach. She began to feel that something strange might be going on behind the scenes in this otherwise unthreatening household. She could tell something was definitely wrong.

She heard Andy calling from the basement below, "Bonnie? ...Hey Bonnie? ...Come on down. Meg can't wait to meet you."

Bonnie stood uncertainly and walked very slowly toward the basement door. It felt as if she were moving in a dream, as if in slow motion. The door stood ominously with its off-white, slightly yellowed and flaking paint and its old-fashioned crystal glass doorknob. She placed her left hand cautiously on the knob, once again feeling through her jeans for her switchblade and gaining comfort knowing it was there. She turned the knob slowly, then opened the door and could see the old wooden cellar steps illuminated in a wash of candlelight from below. A stone wall occupied the right side of the stairs and the left side appeared opened to the basement behind a rickety hand railing. As she descended the squeaking stairs, she again smelled the foul stench of decay growing stronger, and the hairs on the back of her neck stood on end as a cold chill ran down her spine.

Part of her, the natural fight or flight instinct, was screaming for her to turn and run, but another part, the more logical part of her mind was trying to convince her to go on. It was telling her she had been allowing her uncertainty to get the better of her. So she ignored the urge to flee and continued walking down the stairs.

When she reached the concrete floor at the bottom, she looked to the left and saw Andy standing in the flickering candlelight in front of what appeared to be a tall canopy bed surrounded by a thick velvet curtain. He wore a strange, almost detached smile on his face. She walked slowly toward him.

"Meg is so happy you have come by to visit. We don't get many visitors out this way," Andy explained. "She sometimes gets upset when I have to leave her behind to go to the city to get those things she needs but we simply can't find out here."

Bonnie was feeling worse about the entire situation by the minute, and was about to give in to her impulse, turn and run back up the stairs, when Andy quickly reached out and firmly grasped her by her left wrist. "Don't worry," He said. "Everything is going to be fine. I just want you to meet my beautiful wife."

With his other hand, Andy quickly pulled back the heavy black bed curtain and revealed a sight for which Bonnie had not been prepared, a sight she could not have imagined in her worst nightmares.

Seated on the bed was a female zombie, secured to the bed by a heavy iron chain attached on one end to an anchor cemented into the wall and on the other end to a sturdy leather collar encircling her neck. The creature's face was a mass of festering sores and rotting, pealing chunks of flesh. Her one eye was covered with a gray film of death while the other was completely gone, leaving a dark black gaping hole from which a long worm hung precariously, attempting to burrow into an open wound on her cheek. Suppressing the urge to vomit, Bonnie could not think of the thing looming before her as a woman but as some sort of sexless hell-born creature, despite its still feminine anatomy. It wore a sheer teddy-style nightgown, which revealed shriveled, sagging breasts, likewise covered with gray, decomposing flesh.

Andy spoke, "You see, when we escaped from the city and found this place, Meg had taken ill. I had tried everything I could to make her better, but we just didn't have the right medicine to help her and eventually she... well... she just... died. At least I thought she had died, but then, miraculously she came back to me and we had another chance to rebuild our life together."

"But... but... she's one of them now," Bonnie said stuttering. "She's a freaking zombie! Can't you see that?"

Andy said angrily, "How dare you speak of Meg in that way. She is not like one of those horrible creatures; she is different; she is special. She is still my wife, my Meg, and I still love her. And as such it is my job to do whatever I can do to make her happy. So sometimes I have to go into the city and get her those things she needs; those things we just don't have out here." Then he gripped more tightly on Bonnie's wrist and said, "Such as fresh living human flesh —like yours."

Andy tugged hard on Bonnie's arm, temporarily putting her off balance, trying to pull her toward the bed where the creature strained out to the furthest extent of its chain, arms outstretched, struggling to reach out and catch hold of Bonnie. Bonnie screamed in pain as a small lock of her hair was pulled from her head when the creature's reaching fingers must have managed to grasp and pull out a small clump.

While Bonnie fought desperately to keep her distance from the savage thing, Andy tried to force her closer to allow his living-dead wife to get a solid grip on her. Then Meg suddenly remembered the switchblade. She reached her right hand down into her pocket and quickly withdrew the knife. In one swift and continuous motion, she snapped open the blade, brought her arm around in an arc and slashed wildly at Andy.

Although she did not produce a mortal blow, she had managed to create a gaping gash, which ran across the bridge of his nose, and his right cheek, just under his eye. As is common with many facial wounds, the cut immediately began to bleed profusely. The attack caught Andy by surprise and he lost his grip of Bonnie's wrist, as he also lost his own balance, teetering backward, landing in a sitting position at the bottom of the mattress, his hands pressed tightly against his face, blood flowing freely between his fingers. He screamed a string of obscenities brought on by a mix of anger and pain.

Smelling the scent of fresh blood the Meg-creature reached out and grabbed tightly onto Andy's shoulders, pulling him down backward as she sunk her teeth deep into the left side of his neck, tearing out a large chunk of flesh and severing his carotid artery. A fountain of blood shot freely from the wound pumping in cadence with his now failing heartbeat.

Bonnie understood Andy's fate was sealed and took the opportunity to escape, turning and sprinting for the stairs. She reached the kitchen and saw the keys to the van sitting on the center of the kitchen table where Andy must have left them. Amid the cacophony of Andy's death screams and Meg's savage growls streaming up through the open cellar door, Bonnie hurried across the kitchen, out the door toward the waiting van and freedom. She did not know where she would go or what dangers she might face in the next town but she understood she had to keep moving, keep trying and keep surviving.

COLD, COLD WOMEN

She had been the love of his life, the reason for his very existence. In fact, Dylan had considered her the warmest and most affectionate woman he had ever met. In his past, so many cold, cold women had hurt him so many times before taking all the love he had to give and then tossing him aside like so much garbage.

After years of dealing with this rejection Dylan had become wise to such deceitful women. He had experienced enough pain. He found he was never able give fully of himself in any relationship. He knew to watch for the signs. When he saw a woman turning cold, he would end it before he could be hurt again. After a while, he had begun to wonder if he would never find a truly caring woman.

Then he met Celia. She was everything he wanted in a woman and more. She was warm, compassionate and loving. She was the one woman who could break down the protective walls Dylan had built around himself. She taught him to give fully of himself once again without fear or concern and she had made his life complete—at least for a time.

But then he sensed that she too was beginning to grow distant and cold, just like the rest of them. These damned cold, cold women. She didn't think he noticed, but he did. He knew the signs. After a time he realized she was no different than the others and soon she too would leave him. He was furious that he had allowed her to get so close to him, to break through his defenses, to get him to open up to her. Why had he been such a fool?

Now she lay quietly next to him in bed, her cold dead corpse growing stiff with rigor mortis. Her neck bore the blackened bruises from strangulation—her eyes bloodshot with petechial hemorrhaging. He was certain he could smell the stench of decay already forming about her and only after a few hours.

Life had made Dylan wise. He had ended it before she could hurt him any more than she already had. Why had she grown so cold? He didn't know, but it really didn't matter. Now she too would be buried in his back yard along with the many others who had tried to hurt Dylan. She had once been special but now she would become just another of the dozens of the cold, cold women now resting in the cold, cold ground.

IF THINE EYE OFFEND THEE

And if thine eye offend thee, pluck it out: it is better for thee to enter into the kingdom of God with one eye, than having two eyes to be cast into hell fire.
– Mark 9:47

And if thy right eye offend thee, pluck it out, and cast it from thee: for it is profitable for thee that one of thy members should perish, and not that thy whole body should be cast into hell. – Matthew 5:29

The cold October evening drizzle fell relentlessly upon the lone figure sitting cross-legged on the wet pavement in front of the liquor store. The proprietor of the establishment was a kindly man, conscientious of the troubles of others and as a result, had not been able to bring himself to ask the vagrant to leave. Nor would he call the police to do the unpleasant job for him.

The storeowner assumed the disheveled man was such a sad and pathetically harmless creature, sitting and begging for the unwanted change of those more fortunate than he that the most considerate thing he could do for the man was to just leave him be.

The squatter was dressed in faded, torn jeans, a well-worn old black leather coat, under which he wore a soiled gray hooded sweatshirt, which drooped downward under the weight of its sodden condition, hiding his face in shadows. Despite the time of night, he also wore dark black wrap-around sunglasses further shielding his appearance from any curious onlookers—not that anyone paid attention to what seemed to be nothing more than a burned-out homeless beggar.

On the ground in front of his folded legs was a tin cup with a few dollars in change inside. It had been a slow night and by the obvious absence of the sounds of metal against metal, he suspected not too many people had been willing to part with their change that evening. That was, of course, unless they had dropped a few dollar bills into his cup, which he knew was highly unlikely.

John sat in the shadows, mumbling incoherently to himself, which he seemed to do more and more of lately, while pedestrians hurried by, anxious to get to their destinations. Whatever it was he was babbling was indistinguishable to anyone but himself. And most of the passersby either didn't see him or simply ignored him. Still others might glance at him with angry looks of disgust before hurrying past, many forming a deliberate arc of avoidance around him. Occasionally, someone would drop a coin or two into his cup and John would mumble "Thank you" or "Bless you" or some other phrase of appreciation. He kept his replies to a minimum, not wanting to engage anyone in actual conversation.

His hands were tucked deep in the pockets of his coat, their purpose two fold. First, the worn cloth liner of his pockets managed to still provide some warmth for his ungloved fingers; and second, the deep pockets offered a hiding place for the switchblade he held tightly in his right hand. He knew he could never be too careful when living on the streets. There were plenty of evil souls out there in the world, and no one understood that fact better than John Martin, himself.

***

He hadn't always been the babbling street beggar he appeared to be, sitting in the shadowed darkness, avoiding contact with his fellow man. John had once excelled at everything he did, no matter how difficult and with ease. Yet he was also naturally lazy, unambitious and as such had no desire for higher education.

What he longed for more than anything else was simply to have the time necessary to sit quietly and let his mind contemplate the one subject that was of the most importance to him—that being the existence of the human soul. He didn't consider himself a theologian or philosopher by any stretch of the imagination, but he had always believed that buried somewhere deep inside of him, he had the natural ability to not only someday prove the soul's existence, but to actually see it—if he were just able to figure out how.

Once, as a young boy, while suffering with a flu and extremely high fever, John noticed something strange about his elderly grandfather who had been visiting for the day. It was a fleeting thing, only the briefest of glances, but he was certain he had seen it. A glow had momentarily surrounded the man and John wished he had been able to see it more clearly. It had appeared then disappeared so quickly, he had not been certain of what he had seen, especially in his feverish and weakened condition. But he was sure he had seen something. Then a week or so later, his grandfather died suddenly of a massive heart attack. John believed that had he been with his grandfather at the time of his passing, and in the same feverish state as he had been in the previous week, he might have actually seen the man's soul leave his body.

Many years later one of his friends talked him into trying a hit of LSD. Although he had found the incident quite unpleasant and one he wouldn't want to repeat, John had to admit he actually did learn something from the experience. The hallucinogenic effects of the drug seemed to temporarily open his eyes, giving him the ability to see things he had never imagined before. From that day on, John believed if he could find the right combinations of drugs, he would someday be able to open a door inside of his mind, which would lead to his developing a sight beyond sight, and likely the ability to actually see the human soul.

John worked a series of low-skill, minimum wage jobs; each of which he made sure he was guaranteed to eventually end up losing, finding himself collecting unemployment compensation. This bouncing on and off of the unemployment rolls suited John just fine. Whenever the long-awaited day arrived when John would find himself back collecting government checks he would do his best to ride it out for as long as he could and only work when he absolutely had to. During times of severe economic recession he was able to enjoy numerous government-sanctioned extensions of unemployment benefits and had more free time than he could have ever hoped for.

Prior to his last layoff John had worked as a stockroom helper for a local pharmacy. Being a small, privately owned business, it didn't have the stringent inventory controls of the larger chain stores. Since the high school LSD incident John had been experimenting with a variety of drugs, as he was certain the answer to his quest for the soul lie in the proper combination of pharmaceuticals. While working in the stockroom John had managed to accumulate a number of pills, which he labeled and properly recorded. He broke up the pills and combined them into various concoctions for his experimentation. He kept a detailed log of his research, documenting the exact weights and measurements of his mixtures, as well as his successes and failures.

Sometimes the drugs just made him sleep. Sometimes they caused him to hallucinate. And sometime the results of his drug experiments were nearly catastrophic. But despite the risks, he was sure he would eventually find the precise combination to give him the outcome he was looking for. He didn't have to wait long, as after a short time he was not only successful, but more successful than he ever would have imagined in his wildest dreams or most terrifying nightmares.

One day, about a half hour or so after taking his latest mixture of various over-the-counter sleep aids combined with alcohol, John was sitting on the stoop outside of his apartment, observing people walking by, hoping for some positive results. A pretty young woman, who lived in the apartment across the way, named Nancy, came out of her front door and waved a greeting to John as she had done many times before. He always found her attractive and could tell by the way she acted around him she was interested in him as well. John had thought about asking her out, but felt he truly didn't have the time or energy for a girlfriend at this point in his life, so he had always tried to keep things somewhat distant between them.

He cordially returned the wave with as much enthusiasm as his latest drug-induced stupor would allow. That was when he noticed it. At first he saw a glowing aura form around Nancy's body and he knew he might have finally found what he had been hoping for.

Then suddenly, without warning, he felt a tremendous pain inside his skull and for a moment he worried that his brain was about to explode. His first fleeting thought was of a possible stroke or aneurism, but then just as quickly the excruciating pain subsided and he was elated to discover he was still both alive and hopefully still healthy.

"Are you alright John?" He heard Nancy say from a distance. She must have noticed his reaction to the crippling headache. Not looking up he signaled with a wave and replied, "Yeah... yeah... I'm fine... just had a headache or some... " But before he could finish his sentence he had looked over at Nancy and was suddenly stunned speechless. Nancy was gone. That is, the Nancy he knew was gone and in her place stood some sort of horribly disfigured animal-like creature.

It was one of the most hideous sights John had ever witnessed. The thing stood about as tall as Nancy but appeared to be hunched slightly. Its hair, though the same color as Nancy's, was wild and frizzled, shooting outward in every direction in long greasy strands. Its flesh was gray and mottled and even appeared encrusted with scars and scabs in places. It and was completely naked from head to toe and had lots of long body hair. The creature's drooping breasts hung long and pointed downward like two horrible pendulums swaying to and fro.

John chose not to look at the rest of the creature's body, fearing what he might find lurking down below the waist. Instead, he made what might have been a greater mistake and looked at the beast's face. Its cheeks were sunken in appearance and its giant eyes bulged from its dark and hallow-out sockets. The thing's nose that of an ape. Its mouth was an oversized cavern filled with large yellowed fangs. Drool spilled down over the creature's huge lips as the mouth began to form a strange smile.

John had no idea what it was he was seeing. How could someone as lovely as Nancy be suddenly turned into such a revolting slobbering thing before his very eyes?

"John? Are you alright?" The hideous creature asked discordantly in Nancy's sweet voice. "You look like you just saw something terrible."

For a moment, John just sat and stared at the hideous sight before him. He could not comprehend what was happening. He could hear Nancy's voice, but it was coming from the horrid thing that scarcely resembled the woman he knew—or at least the woman he believed he knew.

"I... I..." John stammered. "I gotta go!" And with that he jumped to his feet and staggered on wobbly legs down the street, hurrying around the corner and away from the wretched thing. He kept his eyes cast downward deep in thought, trying to make sense of what he had just seen, while still fighting the mind-blowing effects of the drugs he had taken. After a moment he was startled by the angry honking of a car horn and realized he had inadvertently stepped off a curb and into traffic.

"Hey! Watch where you're going, you stupid asshole!" He heard a driver shout at him. John looked up to see who had shouted at him and was horrified by what he saw seated behind the steering wheel of a taxicab. Like Nancy, the creature behind the wheel was a horrifying twisted version of a human so dreadful as to no longer be considered a man. The thing was even uglier than the Nancy creature had been with a huge, hairy muscular, vein-riddled ape-like arm hanging out the driver's side window. That same arm was now extending its fat middle finger in John's direction and might have actually seemed comical had it not been for its incredibly ugly face. Large, pulsating veins similar to those in its arms traveled up the creature's thick neck and continued up the sides of its mottled face, disappearing into its hairline. Its grinning mouth seemed impossibly large with what appeared to be hundreds of razor sharp pointed teeth. Its eyes were huge and filled with an anger and hatred the likes of which John had never seen before. The creature looked like it epitomized the essence of evil.

"Get off the street you drunken bum." The horrible man-beast said in the driver's gruff human voice. In terror, John stumbled backward much too quickly and tripped over a curb, landing down hard on his backside on the pavement behind him.

"You OK?" Someone asked from behind John. He heard the sound of young children chuckling, as they sometime do in such situations. The voice he had heard sounded like a young woman, likely the mother of the laughing children. He looked up cautiously, fearful of what he might encounter and was relieved to not find some heinous creature, but was eye to eye with a normal pretty-looking little girl: a toddler, perhaps almost two years old.

But upon closer examination, John noticed she was not quite as normal as he originally thought. Her eyes had something of a strange look to them as if they were in the midst of a gradual transition from human being to something else. Likewise the luster of her young skin was not a pink as it should have been, looking slightly gray in color.

John began to crab walk backward away from the strange child when he noticed what must have been her two older siblings perhaps six and eight years old. He was shocked to notice as the ages of the children increased so did the hideousness of their appearances. It was as if they were gradually changing and evolving into something horrendous. That was when he observed the children's mother and the crowd gathering behind her.

"Can I help you?" The woman said with a large fang-filled mouth that looked as though it might be capable of devouring John's head in a single bite. As he looked with stunned immobility at the massive maw he saw long thick streams of some type of reddish goo-like drool dripping down from the fangs. The creature's tongue rolled out over its teeth and John could see some sort of vile insectile creatures attached like barnacles to the organ. These tiny bugs seemed to be eating the flesh of the tongue and burrowing under its skin.

As he quickly pulled his gaze away and unwillingly scanned the rest of the crowd John observed that every one of the gawking spectators was more repugnant than the last. He had no idea what in hell was going on with the world around him, he only knew he had to get home to his apartment so he could hide out from these despicable beasts and try to figure out what was happening.

John staggered to his feet and keeping his eyes cast downward while groping the sides of the buildings he made his way as quickly as possible back to his apartment, tears streaming down his face and babbling like a crazy man. He thanked the heavens that he didn't meet up with any other of the horrid creatures and was pleased to find that Nancy or the horrifying thing she had become was no longer outside waiting for him.

He pushed his way through the front door and into his apartment, being sure to secure every one of his locks and deadbolts. John suddenly recalled the insects devouring the flesh of that woman's tongue and felt his stomach heave. Fortunately, he made it into his bathroom just in time and fell to his knees at the toilet, vomiting and heaving like he had never done before. Sometime later when his gut was thoroughly emptied and after the retching and dry heaving subsided, John slowly tried to stand hanging onto the sink for support. He needed to brush his teeth and run a cold washcloth over his sweating face.

John stood at the sink, his weak arms barely supporting him as he leaned on them, hovering over the washbasin as his eyes stared down into the bowl. What had happened out there to everyone? Why had they all changed and look so hideous? Then the realization hit him like a baseball bat to the face.

He had done it! He had actually seen the human soul. That would explain everything! But if he had in fact seen what he thought he saw, why had the souls looked so incredibly horrifying and evil? Then he came to an unpleasant realization. The toddler, barely two years old had a soul that had not yet been corrupted by the world around her. That was why she still looked relatively human. John could tell that she was just starting to change however, likely from being negatively influenced by her environment. And the older kids the six and eight-year olds looked progressively worse. He deduced that must be because their souls were becoming degraded more and more each day. Then the kids' mother, and the taxi driver and the rest of the crowd—their souls had all obviously become corrupted to the point of no return.

And then there was Nancy. The lovely neighbor he thought so fondly of. She seemed like such a sweet and wonderful person on the outside, how could her soul be so horribly vile and revolting? Then he thought, "Perhaps the world we live in tarnishes all of our souls, and we in turn contribute to ruining the pure souls of others, including our own innocent little ones."

John realized that perhaps the human soul, even the soul existing inside the best of humans was likely a horrifying slobbering beast struggling to get out and wreak havoc. Perhaps it was some genetically evolved force that formed back in the time of our origins before we became what we now think of as civilized human beings. This thing, this soul, which was responsible for giving us the intellect and cunning to survive and rise to the top of the food chain, still lives inside each of us. But we all unconsciously do what we must to keep the beast at bay—force it to be locked down deep inside of us with the hopes it might never get out. He then knew this soul, this beast within was never meant to be seen by any man.

Then another thought struck him. There was a mirror on the vanity above the sink. John slowly raised his eyes upward to look at his own soul; he simply had to know. The last thing John could clearly recall was hearing his own bellowing screams of anguish.

***

The patron hurried out of the liquor store, trying to avoid getting too wet in the steady downpour. He didn't see John squatting on the sidewalk as he ran by and accidentally bumped into him, knocking his wrap-around sunglasses to the ground.

"Oh man. I'm terribly sorry," the man said as he saw the beggar on the ground groping haphazardly for his fallen sunglasses. "I was in a hurry and wasn't paying attention. Here, pal, let me get those for you." The patron reached down and picked up the sunglasses then handed them back to John who turned his face up toward the man.

"Oh my God!" the man shouted, shocked by what he saw looking out from beneath the shade of the hood. The man on the ground stared up at him from two hollowed out sockets where his eyes should have been. At the tops and bottoms of the gaping holes were deep-scarred furrows and the man instantly realized why. "Dear Jesus man... did you... Oh my God you did... you clawed out your own eyes!"

John put on his glasses, lowered his head and returned to incoherent mumbling as the shocked man stumbled away into the night. No one would have been able to make out what John was repeating but it they could understand him they might recall the phrase as part of a bible verse—perhaps one they had heard in church as a child. What John mumbled was, "If thine eye offend thee, pluck it out."

HOMECOMING

"Home is a place you grow up wanting to leave, and grow old wanting to get back to" – John Ed Pearce

"When you finally go back to your old hometown, you find it wasn't the old home you missed but your childhood" – Sam Ewing

"Nothing but the dead and dying, back in my little town" – Paul Simon and Art Garfunkel

"You can't go home again." – Thomas Wolfe

Mason always believed someday he would return. There was something about his hometown and the many memories of his happy childhood there, which seemed to beckon to him. Ashton, Pennsylvania was somewhere in his mind and close to his heart throughout his entire life. It was odd how no matter how long he was away or where he happened to live Ashton was the only place he truly considered home. There were times when he believed he could actually feel it pulling him, almost calling to him in a sad and mournful voice like the heartbroken cries of a jilted lover. "Come home... come home... come home."

However, life had to be lived and there were things Mason Fredericks wanted to accomplish in his life, which he just couldn't find in his simple little town. As a result, after graduation he had said goodbye to his hometown to attend college in another state and had never returned: not for any reason. He had missed all of his high school class reunions and all of his cousins' weddings. In fact, he didn't even return to attend family funerals, including those of his parents and his older brother.

During quiet moments at night or when he was traveling alone on long business trips, Mason often had pleasant memories of his youth in Ashton. He often thought about the parks, the local stores and of his childhood friends. He had been a paperboy and had known just about everyone in town.

At different times in his life, he had considered stopping back to see what had become of his precious Ashton, but he never did. He knew about the adage, "You can never go home again," which was a take on an original quote by Thomas Wolfe, and he believed he understood what that meant. He knew if he were to go home, all that would await him there would be change and disappointment. He loved his hometown but knew he would have trouble dealing with the changes.

The playgrounds, the schools, the stores, the houses, the people all would be different now. The world is constantly moving forward and as it did, it left the happy memories of young boys like Mason in its wake, replacing them with whatever was to follow. He often imagined the Ashton of his youth as a series of plastic railroad models laid out on a card table. Then while enjoying his fantasy, he imagined life coming along in the form of a rowdy child, who with a beefy arm would simply sweep his memories onto the floor where they would shatter into pieces.

Now, after more than forty years he had done it. He had finally returned home. Mason stood on the sidewalk, staring in amazement at what he saw. He had prepared himself to see many changes. So many that he assumed he would barely recognize his hometown. But that hadn't been the case at all. To his shock, the town looked exactly as it had looked when he was a boy. Over there was Leon's Barber Shop and there was Marco's Shoe Repair. He turned and saw Woodman's Restaurant and Gerhard's Dress Shop. It was incredible! The town looked exactly as he had remembered it from his childhood... exactly.

Then he realized something was wrong. What he was seeing wasn't possible. He recalled when he had left for college at age eighteen Woodman's Restaurant had no longer been in business. The owner Stan Woodman had passed away and his children had no interest in the business. As a result, his widow had chosen to shut the place down. And hadn't Marco the shoemaker retired, closed down the shoe repair shop and moved to Florida back when Mason was still in high school? Yet here they all seemed to be. None of this made any sense.

"Hey Perry Mason!" A voice called from the distance. He hadn't heard the voice or that name in almost fifty years, but he recognized both immediately. It was Jimmy "Duke" Wellington, a well-known local troublemaker who had been two years older than Mason. Duke had always call Mason "Perry Mason" because of the popular TV Show from his childhood.

Then an icy chill crept down the back of Mason's neck when he realized it couldn't possibly be Jimmy Wellington because he knew Jimmy died in an automobile accident on his way home from high school graduation over forty years earlier. Mason looked in the direction of the voice and sure enough it was a twelve-year-old version of Duke Wellington and he was approaching a skinny young boy of about ten with a newspaper sack over his shoulder.

Mason felt his breath catch in his throat. He knew that boy. Somehow, impossibly that boy was him: a young version of Mason Fredericks. Mason suddenly felt weak, his legs became wobbly, his hands trembled and a buzzing noise began to rise inside his head. Then everything around him went black.

***

Mason awoke confused. The last thing he remembered was standing down town. Then something... something happened. In his confusion, Mason had the strange detached feeling he often experienced after waking from a dream. Maybe that was what had happened. Perhaps he had been dreaming about something. He wished he could recall what it had been.

He looked around and discovered he was in the middle of a cemetery. He had no idea how he had gotten there. He recognized it as Brockman's Cemetery, which he recalled was located near the western end of Ashton—an area locals referred to as the top of town. He remembered that his parents, as well as his older brother, were buried in this graveyard.

Mason looked down at the tombstones laid out in front of him and discovered he was standing at the exact location of his family's burial plots. He suddenly felt a pang of guilt for having not attended their funerals. There had been no good reason for his absence, no justifiable excuse. Although at the time, his justifications did seem legitimate enough, at least to him. When his parents passed, he had been working in China as a representative for his company seeking new business opportunities. When his brother called with the news that his parents had both been killed in an automobile accident, Mason explained that he simply couldn't get back to the states for the funerals. The deal he had been brokering was too big and far too critical for him to leave at this jointure.

Mason's brother had been furious with him but Mason insisted there was nothing he could do about the situation. Then after a heated argument, just before his brother disconnected he told Mason he never wanted to speak to him again and that he should never bother to return home. Mason knew he was wrong and his older brother had every right to feel the way he did.

Now standing in this place of the dead, Mason was suddenly filled with sadness at the realization of how he had disrespected his parents and had let down his brother. They were all dead now and it was much too late to do anything about it. The melancholy inside him seemed to grow more intense as it finally sunk in that they were gone for good and he would never see them again.

Of course, he had known this reality for many years, but there seemed to be something so final about seeing their headstones carved with their birth and death dates that made it all so real to him, perhaps for the first time. Mason supposed this was what people meant when they spoke of closure. For the first time in his life, he realized he was all alone in the world. This realization troubled him more than he could have imagined.

In the distance, Mason saw a long black hearse followed by a similarly dark sedan coming along the gravel lane toward him. They stopped close to where he stood separated from each other by about ten feet. Two tall bleak looking men in dark suits exited the hearse and walked to the rear where one of them opened the rear tailgate. Mason instantly recognized the one opening the gate. It was Jim Kulp, a member of his graduating class and son of the funeral company's original founder, Bradford Kulp. Jim had apparently taken over the family business, as Mason and most townspeople assumed he would.

Mason wondered who the poor soul in the back of the hearse might be. Then the doors to the black sedan opened and four strangers in similar dark suits got out and joined the other two behind the hearse. Looking like sentinels, they lined up in formation, three on each side and slowly began sliding the casket from the hearse as its handles passed along the line.

Then Mason saw a weeping woman exiting the back of the sedan wearing a dark dress and black scarf over her head. To his shock, he realized it was his cousin Marylyn. Even though he hadn't seen her in close to forty years she looked every bit as pretty as he had remembered her— much older but nonetheless beautiful. His heart went out to his cousin. He recalled she had married her high school sweetheart Bernie Walters, and they had been together all these years. Surely, it must be devastating for her to lose him after so long. Then Mason wondered why their kids weren't here, not to mention Bernie's many friends and relatives. Mason assumed having lived in the area all of his life Bernie should have had a great precession of cars not just these two pathetic funeral vehicles. He suddenly felt great compassion for his poor cousin.

Mason decided he would approach her and offer his condolences for her loss. He realized he would likely have to introduce himself, as she hadn't seen him in so long and she would likely not recognize him. He walked up and stood beside her as the pallbearers slowly walked the casket over toward the graveyard.

He said, "Marylyn? It's me... I'm sorry... about Bernie... I guess... Geeze... I just don't know what to say." He raised his hand to place it consolingly on her shoulder but stopped short when he heard her speak his name.

"Oh Mason," Marylyn said with a sigh.

Mason was surprised. "Why... um... Marylyn... I'm surprised that you recognized me... you know... after all these years."

Marylyn sniffled and dabbed her eyes, "Mason, why did you stay away so long? I remember how we were so close when we were children. You were like a brother to me and I really missed you so much over the years. And now to have to see you... like this." She began to cry again.

"I... I understand Marylyn," Mason said sounding contrite. "I missed you as well. I... I often thought about coming home... but I never seemed to get around to it. I'm so terribly sorry."

She blubbered, "I had so hoped you would have been able to meet my daughter, Sarah. I often told her stories about you. We followed your career and cut out articles whenever one appeared in the business section of the newspaper. Sarah's all grown up now and has a daughter of her own. I'm a grandmother. Can you believe it... me a grandmother?"

"That's... that is very hard to believe Marylyn," Mason replied. "I, myself... I never married or had any children. I guess I could never find the time. But I'm home now Marylyn, maybe I can find some way to make up for lost time. "

"So... well... I guess this is our final goodbye Mason," she said with tears now running down her cheeks.

Mason was confused and replied, "No Marylyn. You don't understand. I'm home now. And I retired last year so if I want, I can be home for good."

Just then, Jim Kulp walked up to Marylyn and said, "Are you going to be alright now Mrs. Walters? Is there anything I can get for you before we proceed?"

"Hey Jim," Mason said. "It's me Mason Fredericks. You probably didn't recognize me. I haven't seen you since graduation."

Marylyn said, "No. But thank you Jim. I'll be all right. You can proceed with what you have to do."

Mason was even more perplexed than previously. "Jim. It's me, Mason. From high school? There's no need for you to be so antisocial."

"I feel sort of strange not having a ceremony or minister for you today Marylyn," Jim said blatantly ignoring Mason. "Are you sure that is what he would have wanted?"

"To be honest, Jim. I have no idea what he would have wanted," Marylyn explained. "He had no living relatives and left no will. I just want to get this over with and head home."

Mason said, "What do you mean Marylyn? Bernie had tons of relatives in the area and probably just as many friends. Where are they all?"

Jim said to Marylyn, "OK. This won't take but a few minutes. You can wait in the car if you'd like."

Marylyn turned and went into the sedan, closing the door behind her. Mason watched the team of dark-suited men standing next to the casket, which now sat next to a recently dug grave he hadn't noticed before. It was located right next to his older brother's plot.

"Well Mason," Jim said looking down into the hole as the casket was lowered, "You did your best to stay away all these years and now you're back for good. Who said you can never come home again?"

PASSAGEWAYS TO PERNICIOUSNESS

Todd stood confused in the blackness. He discovered he was alone in a long dark alley in some unfamiliar city. Both sides of the street appeared to be bordered by tall buildings, which he recognized as probably being abandoned. Not a single light in any window was lit, nor were there any other signs of life whatsoever. It was all so unsettling.

He realized by the chill he suddenly felt racing throughout his body, that he was shirtless, clad only in a pair of thin cotton pajama bottoms; sleep pants was how they referred to them nowadays; and he discovered he was barefoot as well.

"How in the world did I get here?" Todd asked himself, having no answer to his own question. He looked further up the alley and noticed a blue light in the distance, seeming to originate somehow from the ground in the middle of the blacktopped street. He approached the site cautiously, his unclad feet sensing the rough texture of the paving beneath them and the unearthly chill it radiated. The eerie blue light ahead only served to make Todd feel even colder.

When he got within a few feet of the strange illumination he saw it was originating from a hole, which had apparently erupted in the middle of the street. This was becoming stranger by the minute, taking on a surreal, almost dreamlike quality. Putting his confusion aside, Todd walked to the edge of the cobalt blue glowing fissure, now curious about what its purpose might be. Although he was somewhat apprehensive, he didn't seem to be afraid.

The opening appeared to be about two feet in diameter, not perfectly round but having irregular edges where it met the street's surface. Todd inched cautiously closer to the edge of the hole, wanting to look down into the brilliant blue glow, to learn its mysterious secret. But as he leaned forward to peer inside, he felt the pain of incredibly icy cold against his bare lower legs. He looked down and saw two long, thin, bluish-gray hands holding tightly onto his ankles. The hands were attached to thin arms with bulging ropey muscles rising up from the hole.

A pale blue mist like steam or fog arose out of the strange fissure. As he stared down at the opening, Todd saw an icy frost begin to form over his feet and lower legs where the hands held him in place. Todd could not comprehend why he did not resist or attempt to break free, but instead remained standing, transfixed.

As an unimaginably freezing cold began to spread rapidly upward Todd finally recognized that he was in grave danger. The sensation spread quickly through his legs and up into his abdomen, then to his torso and down both of his arms. A thin mist of vapor seeped from his mouth as he exhaled. Oddly, it brought back a momentary childhood memory of playing outside in the winter while eating candy cigarettes. He and his friends would pretend they were smoking by blowing steam from their mouths on cold winter days. But that pleasant memory was short-lived.

He felt his neck grow frigid and stiff as his next breath seemed to freeze in his throat. Todd knew then that he was surely going to die. The last rational thought he had before his brain completely shut down, was the sensation of being pulled downward into the mysterious glowing blue gateway as all around him he heard maniacal laughter.

Todd sat up in bed with a jolt. A cold sweat ran down his back as he panted, gasping for breath and feeling as if he might actually be suffocating. "Oh my sweet Lord in Heaven!" he said to the empty darkness of his bedroom, struggling to regain his composure. He then realized he must have had some sort of nightmare; even though the vision was already starting to fade, Todd instinctively reached to his left and turned on the table lamp next to his bed.

He threw his legs over the side and sat with his elbows resting on his trembling knees. He was trying to get his bearings as the last remnants of the nightmare dissipated to nothingness. But even with the details gone, an unpleasant feeling of dread still remained. Once Todd was somewhat awake he became aware he needed use the bathroom. He assumed it must have been that need to pee which woke him up. Shaking his head to disperse the remaining cobwebs of slumber, Todd stood and sleepily shuffled into the bathroom.

Still not quite feeling alert he chose to sit to do his business, assuming it would be better to be safe now than sorry tomorrow when he awoke to discover his aim had not been as true as he had originally thought.

As he sat in the darkness of the bathroom relieving himself Todd tried to recall anything about his dream but he couldn't. Then he oddly began to hear a distant humming noise coming from somewhere in front of him and he could suddenly smell a faint odor, which reminded him of freshly cut grass. He also smelled something else— something dank and earthy, like that of recently turned soil. This made no sense, as he was inside his home on the second floor sitting on the toilet. He wondered if perhaps one of his cats had knocked over a plant or something during the night. He decided it could wait until morning.

Then he noticed something happening in the darkness directly in front of him on what should have been the bathroom wall. A large circle of pale green light at least two feet in diameter began to form as if out of nowhere. As Todd stared at the strange spectacle, the green glow began to illuminate brighter and the outdoor smells grew stronger. But unlike the scent of a meadow or forest on a beautiful spring day, there was something foul and ominous about this smell—as if something rotten and decaying lurked just below the initially pleasant aroma. The stink was like that of dead leaves in the fall or perhaps fertilizer spread upon a field or maybe like something worse—perhaps like a dead, bloated animal baking along the roadside on a hot summer day.

Todd realized what he was experiencing was impossible. How could such a thing ever be possible? He felt trapped, helpless with his pajama bottoms down around his ankles, sitting slack-jawed on the toilet, staring at the mysterious phenomenon unfolding before him. Even if he had the presence of mind to try to flee he had insufficient time to react, as suddenly long weed-like tendrils shot out from the green glowing portal and began to wrap themselves tightly around his exposed legs and arms.

He felt a searing pain wherever the vines came in contact with his skin—not so much a burning, as it was the feeling you get when you touch a plant with tiny needle-like irritating barbs, the types that sink their tines deep into your flesh like splinters. The pain he felt was similar to that but was magnified to an unimaginable level.

He opened his mouth to scream but his cry was cut short when several of the snaking vines shot forward into his mouth, over his tongue and down into his throat. The pain of their thousands of prickly barbs on the tender meat of his tongue, inner mouth and esophagus was unbearable. He felt his breath being cut off by the invasive tendrils and he could sense movement as he realized he was being pulled helplessly off of the toilet and into whatever strange, horrifying netherworld existed beyond the glowing gateway. Then just before his world went black he heard strange and for some reason familiar maniacal laughter.

Todd opened his eyes once again with a start and sat upright in his recliner. He was sitting in the living room of his apartment. "Man what the hell was that?" he wondered. He felt as if he had just awoken from a very bad dream and was surprised to discover he was trembling. "Wow! That must have been some doozie of a nightmare!" he said to the empty room.

He could no longer recall the apparently terrifying dream and wondered what it might have been about. Todd stood on quivering legs and walked out to the kitchenette to fix himself something to drink. He filled a cup with water and put it into the microwave for three minutes in preparation for making himself a nice, hot cup of tea—

which always seemed to relax him. The microwave oven was mounted over the kitchen range. As he was reaching into the cupboard to get some teabags he heard a strange noise coming from inside the stove below. What made it seem even more unusual was the fact that Todd never used his oven, for any reason. He stepped back and stared down at the glass front of the oven not sure what he was expecting to see. He noticed that the glass appeared to be changing shape, from its normal rectangle to a circle, like that found on the front of a washing machine, but it had grown to over two feet in diameter.

Then the glass began to glow bright red and disappear, leaving in its wake a luminescent cavernous ruby opening where the front of the stove had once been. Todd could feel heat coming out from the opening and could smell something burning; something hot and sulfurous— something quite unpleasant. He was too stunned to move but knew he had to do something, either call the fire department or find his fire extinguisher—something. But instead he stood dumbfounded, staring at the fiery opening.

That was when several rope-like coils of some semi-solid flaming lava-like substance shot out entwining his legs and wrists, searing the flesh from his body while simultaneously fusing to his now exposed bones. The pain was beyond unbearable. Todd howled with agony as the lassos of fire began to pull him screaming into the oven orifice. The last thing he heard was the ding from the microwave signaling that his hot water was ready for the tea, which he would never drink, and what sounded like the wild laughter of a madman.

"Oh!" Todd said with a stifled cry as he awoke to find himself seated on a bus of some sort heading rapidly down a highway. It appeared to be early in the morning on what looked like a very pleasant day. He was dazed and not quite sure where he was as an apparent dream began to fade from his memory.

"Are you alright young man?" a voice said from next to him. Todd looked to his left and saw an elderly woman looking at him with some concern.

"Ah... um... yes," he replied. "Yes. It was nothing... I suppose... I must have dozed off... and had some sort of dream or nightmare or something." Things were starting to come back into focus. He remembered why his was on the bus and where he was going. He looked out the window and could see the industrial waterfront of New Jersey and understood his trip was almost over.

He was on a bus taking him to the Port Authority of New York City. Todd was an author of horror fiction and was known for his wild imagination and descriptive scenes. This imagination was very beneficial when writing stories but it often showed its negative side by invading his sleep and contaminating his dreams with horrifying images.

Todd recalled how he had been invited by his publisher to attend the Book Expo America Convention New York City, where he was scheduled to spend some time at their booth speaking with people and signing books. He had been up very late the previous night working on his latest novel and had to get up at 4:30a.m. to catch the 6:30a.m. bus out of Kutztown, Pennsylvania. It was no wonder he had fallen back to sleep and had missed the entire trip.

He couldn't recall any of the elements of his dreams but suspected they had not been pleasant, as he seemed to have a chill running down his spine from a cold sweat, the effects of which were currently being exacerbated by the bus's air conditioning, which he felt was set far too low. Todd realized that he had to use the bathroom. So he excused himself as he stood and squeezed passed the elderly woman in the aisle seat. Due to the bouncing and jostling of the bus, when he entered the restroom he chose to sit to do his business rather than stand and as he did, he had a strange sensation of déjà vu that he couldn't explain; but for some reason, he sensed something just felt very wrong.

He finished without incident and started to return to his seat. As he walked carefully down the aisle swaying to and fro from the bus's movement, Todd noticed the dark black rubber floor runner and for some reason was oddly reminded of a blacktopped street. Suddenly that unusual sensation of having had a similar experience returned and he was once again filled with an ominous feeling of dread.

He couldn't imagine what might be making him feel this way, and he did his best to shake off the sensation as he got closer to his seat.

Looking out the front window he observed something. The bus was sitting in traffic in a long line of similar busses all waiting to enter the Lincoln Tunnel just outside of New York City. It had been years since Todd had been in the city and so he took a moment to look out the window at the tunnel entrances before taking his seat. He was unprepared for what happened to him next.

He saw the long line of busses several lanes wide each curving to the right working their way into one of the tunnel entrances. Todd had no idea why the site of these three large openings in the side of the mountain bothered him so much, but he suddenly believed with all of his being that if the bus entered the tunnel, he and everyone on the bus would die. He passed the elderly woman at his row and approached the female bus driver.

"You can't go in the tunnel!" Todd said with a panicky voice. "You have to turn around or back up or something... you just can't go in there."

"Sir, I don't know what you are talking about but will you please just calm down and return to your seat?" the driver said.

Todd insisted, "But you don't understand we can't go in there. If we do, all of us, everyone on this bus will die."

"Sir, I must insist that you return to your seat immediately!" the driver tried again, "And I must point out that it is illegal to make terroristic threats on any form of public transportation! Now either return immediately to your seat or I will be forced to report you to the authorities."

"Why can't you understand me?" Todd pleaded. "I'm not making threats... I'm telling you the truth. We just can't go into that tunnel!"

The rest of the passengers on the bus were becoming agitated by Todd's behavior. Some of them looked at the scene with disapproval while a few of the older passengers were becoming visibly distressed by the commotion. A large muscular man stood up and approached Todd. The bus crept ahead at a painfully slow pace as the line of traffic was bumper to bumper.

The man tapped Todd on the shoulder and said, "Look buddy, the lady said to return to your seat. I suggest you be a gentleman and do as the nice lady asks." His tone was polite, but the look in his eyes and his body language was very serious and potentially threatening.

Todd ignored the man and once again addressed the driver with anger. "OK. Look. If you won't back up then please just let me out here. I'm telling you I won't go into that tunnel."

Before the driver had a chance to reply, the big man put his hand on Todd's shoulder saying, "Come on pal. Why don't you just go back to your seat and sit down and relax, nice and peaceful like."

Todd reacted without thinking as he turned and swung a fist at the man, striking him in the jaw with a right hook. Todd may have been a good writer, but he was of a slight build and was no fighter. As a result the blow went barely noticed by the larger man; that is to say it did nothing to seriously injure him, but it most certainly did get his attention. Reacting in kind the man's fist shot out like lightning and struck Todd in the chin, knocking him back against the overhead storage bin and dropping him to the floor in an unconscious heap.

***

Todd opened his eyes and was once again unsure about where he was. There were lots of bright lights around him. He could hear the beeping sounds of machinery and several people talking. He tried to move but realized he was strapped securely to a table of some sort. Even his head had been immobilized so he was completely unable to move anything but his eyes.

He tried to speak but his voice caught in his throat, which apparently was dry and parched, allowing for barely a whisper to escape. He heard snippets of conversations around him, which sounded to be medical in nature: terms like "scan", "films" "head injury" and "potentially severe" and such. What was happening to him? Then he felt the table move forward with him strapped to it. His first thought was that he was being transported somewhere but then he was able to see a bit in front of him and knew he was being shuttled into some sort of machine.

Although he had never had an MRI or a CT scan, Todd had seen pictures while doing research on the Internet for one of his stories. He had never given much thought to them before but now he could see the large round opening of the machine up ahead and understood he was going to be slid inside the device.

He recalled panicking on the bus and lashing out at some big guy who was telling him to sit down. Then he noticed a pain in his jaw and head and realized the guy must have cold cocked him. Maybe he had struck his head and had been knocked out. Perhaps that was why he was going into the machine. But he suddenly knew he didn't want to be put into the machine.

Once again the same unexplainable feeling of foreboding he had sensed on the bus was returning with a vengeance. He couldn't believe what he was feeling. He had never been claustrophobic in his life so why was he now so worried about the confined space? But maybe it wasn't the space, maybe it was something else; perhaps it was the circular shape of the opening. It seemed to remind him of something he had seen somewhere. Then suddenly as if a dam of lost memories burst wide open inside his mind, Todd began to recall every detail of his nightmares and the horrifying images of the terrible passages he had experienced.

He began to struggle desperately but couldn't move in his restraints. He looked forward and could see the terrifying circular opening of the machine getting closer as his lower body began to slide inside. Then he saw the surface of the machine begin to change from effervescent blue to green and finally to bright red. This was insane. How could it possibly be happening? Then he heard wild maniacal laughter and realized it was coming from his own mouth.

STORAGE

"What an ungodly time of the evening to visit a storage locker!" Ryan thought, reprimanding himself for the poor timing, yet knowing he had little choice because of his hectic schedule. He had to stop whenever he could and unfortunately that usually meant doing so in the evening after a long and tiring day at the office. Fortunately, or perhaps unfortunately, the storage facility was located along the road he traveled as part of his daily commute.

He realized it was ridiculous for him to feel so uneasy about the simple task of stopping by for ten minutes to retrieve whatever his wife might ask him to pick up. Yet every time he had to do so, he felt like something about the place was wrong. And tonight things felt exceptionally wrong. He couldn't help but notice how it seemed to be getting prematurely dark and how he was the only person in the facility. Ryan sat in his car for a few minutes with the engine running, looking out through the windshield, taking in the seemingly endless shadowed rows of storage units stretching out before him. The sight reminded him of a time back when he was in junior high school art class and they were studying the concept of perspective. He and his classmates had been required to draw railroad tracks starting wide at the closest point and tapering forward until they joined at the horizon line. This was how the rows of storage units in the *Store More Storage Facility* now looked to him. They appeared to go on forever.

Even in the daylight, Ryan hated the place and detested the very idea and so-called need for such a facility. Ryan was only using his storage shed on a temporary basis because he had no choice, as he and his wife, Julie, were between homes. They had recently sold their small two-bedroom rancher and were waiting to move into a much larger four-bedroom split-level, which they were having custom built. Unfortunately, the contractor had run into a few snags and the build was taking longer than he had originally promised. As a result they were forced to put their possessions in storage and temporarily move into a furnished apartment while their new home was being completed. Because he was responsible for their inconvenience, the builder had agreed to pay the cost of the apartment and the storage unit as well as their moving expenses. All things considered, Ryan felt it was about the best solution for a bad situation.

But that did little to make up for the inconvenience he and Julie were facing. What bugged him most about the storage facility was he suspected that many if not most of the hundreds of units in the place were not just temporary in nature like his, but were in reality used by people who simply had too many possessions and couldn't bear to part with them. So the people voluntarily forked out the one hundred or more dollars every month for the sole purpose of storing tons of what Ryan thought of as garbage—most of which should be decomposing in landfill somewhere or should have been chopped up at a recycling facility. He couldn't understand why people insisted on hanging on to such worthless junk, let alone why they would want to pay a premium to store it.

He had watched a few episodes of the A & E Channel reality show *Storage Wars*, where people competed to get the best deals hidden in unclaimed storage lockers. He couldn't comprehend earning a living bidding on stuff no one really wanted anyway. But he supposed the old adage "one man's trash is another man's treasure" must be correct. He also on occasion stumbled onto A & E's show *Hoarders,* which he preferred not to watch, as it really bothered him.

Yet if he accidently channel-surfed onto the program, he couldn't help but watch. It was like a train wreck. Every time he had an occasion to see an episode, he was at first mesmerized, then revolted, then he was usually motivated to immediately choose one of his closets, clean it out and trash everything he felt they didn't need. Both he and his wife detested the idea of having too many material possessions.

So it went against his grain to be forced by circumstances beyond his control into this Mecca of human refuse, especially at night. Ryan stared out through the windshield of his car feeling like there was something particularly wrong with this place that went beyond his simple dislike for it. Tonight he had stopped by to pick up a few kitchen items that Julie hadn't originally thought she would need for a while, but now discovered she did. Luckily, he had planned ahead, had packed the shed in a logical fashion and knew the boxes with the kitchen supplies were close to the front of the locker and could be easily accessed. And that was just the way he wanted it. The sooner he got out of this extremely uncomfortable place, the better.

Ryan stepped out of his sedan with his flashlight at the ready and left the motor running as he always did whenever he arrived at the shed at night. He left his driver's door open just in case he needed to get back inside quickly. Ryan wasn't typically prone to such feelings of apprehension or irrational fear but there was just something about the place tonight, which seemed even stranger than normal. The moon, although full and bright, had suddenly become hidden by a thick layer of clouds. "Funny," Ryan thought. He hadn't heard any forecast of inclement weather. And the lone security light, mounted on a rickety pole more than fifty feet from his shed, was flickering weakly doing little to provide necessary illumination.

He walked slowly toward the roll-up door of his unit feeling strangely as if someone was watching him from the shadows. He looked around while squinting his eyes in a feeble attempt to see through the growing gloom. Maybe he was imagining the sensation, or perhaps the security camera was working after all. It stood high on the same pole as the failing light; its single eye tilted downward, moving back and forth in a semicircle like a robotic sentry. Despite its appearance, Ryan still didn't believe the thing was functional.

He recalled the day he and the moving van arrived with
his furniture and he had stopped at the front office to meet
with the owner. The man sat behind the front desk like an
emperor ruling over all he surveyed. Ryan later learned the
owner was actually his builder's brother-in-law. The man
was one of those disheveled people who Ryan just naturally
took an instant dislike to. He was an overweight, greasy,
sweating hog of a man in a pair of oversized plaid shorts
and a stained, yellowed wife-beater. His head was bald
save for a white fringe that was too long and hung over his
ears—which were sprouting long thatches of gnarly white
hair, making it difficult to determine where his head hair
ended and his ear hair began. Likewise the man's
shoulders were covered with cotton candy like
tumbleweeds of white hair, which matched his thick white
furry arms, as well as the tufts that protruded from his
armpits and chest like silky white ornamental grass.

Ryan also felt certain that hygiene was as foreign a
concept to the man as reading a magazine that might not
contain pictures of naked women. This thought was
substantiated by the massive, collapsing piles of such
pornography, which covered his filthy desk.

Yes, Ryan was quite certain the camera was a fake and
the place had no real security—save for the chain link
fence surrounding it, the card access at the entrance gate
and the keys to the padlock for his shed. Ryan realized
suddenly that if some maniac ever broke into the place and
decided to attack him, his chances of getting any help from
that security camera were nil. He grabbed the handle of his
flashlight tighter, holding its meager plastic body,
pointlessly, as if it were a weapon of some real substance.

As Ryan bent to insert his key into the lock securing
the roll-up garage door, he heard a sound that seemed to
come from one of the lockers several units to the right of
his. He stopped what he was doing and stood upright,
waiting to determine if he could hear the noise again. It
had been a strange sound, sort of like a whimper or a faint
sigh or maybe even a moan. Although he had been certain
he had heard something, all seemed to be silent now. The
strange sound did nothing to help his already active

imagination or his discomfort, and it only made him want to get his stuff and leave even more quickly than before.

He returned to his task and just as he removed the padlock from its hasp he heard the whimpering again, followed by a faint thumping sound. He immediately imagined the sound to be like that someone would make if they had weakly bumped against one of the metal walls surrounding the storage unit.

"Hello?" Ryan asked into the darkness, which seemed to be getting more intense by the minute. He also noticed that a light mist had begun to creep slowly along the ground, working its way through the cross ways between the banks of storage units like a translucent gray serpent. He listened for another minute then hearing no other sounds started to turn back toward his shed. The place was really starting to get under his skin now, despite the knowledge that his discomfort was irrational. Ryan realized he had to get himself together. So he stood silently and took a deep cleansing breath, which really did make him feel much better. Then he heard the thump again.

Against his better judgment, Ryan slowly began to walk down along the rows of locked storage sheds toward the location of the sound, which regrettably took him further away from the security pole and deeper into the gloom. He trained his flashlight on the doors of the sheds, stopping at each one and listening for the sounds again. Each time he stopped he would look back longingly toward his car which was still sitting idling with the driver's door open. Ryan cursed himself for not turning on his headlights and was about to go back and do so when he heard the sound again. It appeared to be coming from the next unit down.

He focused his flashlight on the door handle and noticed to his surprise there was no padlock in the hasp. He looked around, hoping to possibly see the headlights from some other tenant coming by, but he found he was still alone. For a moment Ryan considered calling 911, but realized how foolish he would seem trying to explain to the police how he heard a strange noise coming from a locker that wasn't his. They would likely become suspicious and possibly accuse him of trying to break into someone else's shed. He looked back at the spot where the security camera should be and realized even if it were working; the light was so dim where he now stood no one would be able to see him anyway. Then he heard a whimper and a light thump once again. It was definitely coming from the locker where he now stood.

Mustering all of his courage, Ryan bent down grabbing the door handle and attempted to open the garage door. It was surprisingly heavier than the door that was on his own unit so he had to set down his flashlight in order to lift it. He slowly raised the door, opening the shed fully. Unfortunately, with the amount of darkness and mist surrounding him, Ryan was unable to see clearly inside the unit but from what he could tell it looked like any other cluttered storage unit—just a ten-by-ten metal building filled with an assortment of furniture and boxes piled inside. Then once again he heard a slight moaning sound, which seemed to be coming from deep inside the shed.

Ryan reached down and picked up his flashlight. As he stood he thought he saw something moving out of the corner of his eye, off to his right. He pointed his flashlight in that direction but saw nothing but the strange mist, which had now seemed to take on the appearance of a thick fog. He looked back to his left to check on his car and could barely make it out in the thickening atmosphere; he could see the faint glow of his dome light, but the car and the open door were no longer visible.

This was all getting too strange for Ryan to deal with. He had just made up his mind to turn and head back to his car when he heard the light thumping sound again. He whirled and focused his light on the inside of the open shed door.

"What the!" Ryan exclaimed, when to his amazement he realized that what he originally thought was a storage unit full of someone's various belongings was nothing more than some sort of curtain: a painting or tapestry designed to replicate the inside of a storage shed. Ryan gently pressed against the surface of the tapestry and felt it move inward until it bumped against something solid behind it. At the same time he heard the faint moan once again. Then he heard a whispering raspy voice pleading, "Help me... please... help me."

Ryan grabbed the right side of the curtain-like tapestry and quickly pulled it back while training his flashlight inside the shed. What he saw caused his stomach to clench with disgust and made him freeze in uncontrollable terror. He took in the entire ungodly spectacle of what was inside the storage unit in one unbearable glance.

Behind the curtain wall was what could only be described as some poor soul's Hell on earth. There was a structure in the center of the room; a rack of sorts made from thick heavy pipe welded together to form a giant rectangular framework. Hanging from the rack was the body of a young man, not much older than Ryan. His hands, neck and feet were manacled with heavy rusted metal and chain, secured with padlocks and welded to the heavy framework.

There was a complex network of plastic tubing encircling him with dozens if not hundreds of tubes and needles intravenously connected to the man. Some of the tubes were clear and seemed to be feeding him from a bag filled with a transparent clear fluid, which was positioned high on a stainless steel pole. Ryan suspected this device might be supplying what was likely the minimal amount of nutrients necessary to sustain life. There were also thicker tubes coming in and out of the man's abdomen, which gave Ryan the impression they might too be some sort of feeding mechanism. At the same time plastic tubes red with fluid were leading from the man's body to a bag on a hook near the man's feet.

"Blood," Ryan said in a soft voice. Then he thought, "This man is being force-fed and kept barely alive with some type of IV drip and feeding tubes while at the same time his blood is being slowly drained from his body." Then a single word of understanding popped into Ryan's mind, "Harvested." And he realized he was probably correct. This young man's blood was being produced and harvested for some reason. "But why?" He wondered. "For what purpose?"

Ryan knew the need for certain types of blood was often critical, but he could not imagine the value of any blood type being sufficiently high enough to warrant someone doing something so rash. Then he wondered if perhaps the man were being kept alive so someone could eventually harvest his organs, one at a time. That certainly would bring in a lot more money than selling blood. Yet that too didn't seem quite correct.

The chained young man weakly attempted to raise his head, his hooded red-rimmed eyes scarcely able to focus. "Hel... help me," he managed to squeak out through dried, cracked and bloody lips.

Ryan suddenly snapped out of the strange trance which had overtaken him and stammered, "Wa... what happened to you? Who... who did this?"

"Help... please," the man said weakly. "Get... help... now... please." Ryan took out his cell phone and looked reassuringly at the wretched man. "Look... see... I have a cell phone... I can call for help."

The man's eyes opened wide in terror, staring past Ryan at something he was seeing behind him. His split lips seemed to be forming some silent word. The man appeared to be mouthing the word, "NO."

Upon the realization of what was happening, Ryan felt a cold chill creep like a centipede down the center of his spine as the hairs on the back of his neck tingled with some primal warning of imminent danger.

Sill holding his cell phone tightly in his hands, Ryan turned slowly to confront whoever waited behind him. At first he saw nothing but the darkness and the ever-thickening fog then a silhouette began to emerge from the mist coming ever closer and finally taking shape.

Once again Ryan was frozen in terror, unsure if what he was seeing was real or some strange trick of the light. He was not even sure he could possibly be seeing what he thought he was seeing. There was someone or more accurately, something standing in the gloom, partially illuminated by the glow of his flashlight, which was pointing down toward the ground. He was unsure if what he was seeing was a man, an animal or some horrible twisted mutation between human and beast.

It stood about seven feet tall, was shoeless and shirtless but wore pants that appeared to be faded jeans, which were ripped and tattered. The thing's chest was massive, hairy, muscular, and was covered with crosshatches of thick ropy scar tissue as if the result of poorly healed lacerations. Looking down the muscular arms to the creature's hands, Ryan could see long gnarled fingers with claw-like yellowed fingernails.

But the real horror came when Ryan lifted his flashlight and stared at the creature's hideous face. It was humanoid, but far from human, with an oversized mouth filled with long needle like teeth all of which appeared to be stained crimson with blood. Its nose was more of a snout than a nose—pig-like in appearance with dark flaring nostrils from which deep plumes of air now pushed through the fog in cadence with its heavy breathing. The smell of the thing was incredibly horrid, as foul as that of a barnyard animal but with more woodsy, savage and feral stink combined with a deeper stench of rotten meat.

Then Ryan looked into the creature's inhuman eyes, which were blacker than black and in which Ryan not only saw a surprising intelligence, but something much worse: a type of hunger the likes of which he could never hope to fully comprehend. From behind the creature an enormous set of leathery wings opened and blocked any remaining moonlight, casting Ryan into total darkness.

Ryan's trembling fingers reached for the 9-1-1 buttons on his cell phone although he knew the gesture would likely be futile. Even he were luckily enough to hit the correct buttons and an army of policemen miraculously showed up, Ryan suspected they would be of little use against such a hellish beast. The word "hellish" sounded right to him because truly no such abomination of unimaginable horror could possibly have come from anywhere but Hell. The cell phone was knocked from Ryan's hand as he felt sharp claws scrape deep furrows across his forearm.

The agony that exploded in his arm was instantaneous and when he opened his mouth to scream he realized he was unable to move. He understood immediately his paralysis was not just from terror but that the creature's claws must have sent some fast-acting paralytic toxin into his blood stream, because he could no longer feel the pain in his hand.

A massive clawed hand wrapped around Ryan's throat, cutting off his air supply. The creature's hideous face was now just a few foul smelling inches from Ryan's own; its stench was overwhelming. The thing's eyes grew wide with excitement and seemed to glow with anticipation, as Ryan's own vision blurred then finally went black.

***

"Hell if I know what happened," the overweight sleazy owner of the storage facility said to the investigating police officer. "The guy who you said owns this car is one of my renters, all right. That's his locker right there. But I have no idea where he might be."

The officer looked up at the security camera in the distance and asked, "Does that thing work?"

"Well... no not really," the man said sheepishly. "In fact, it's not even a real camera. It's one of those decoy things that move back and forth but really don't film anything. According to local code I'm not required to have real cameras inside the complex, but I figured the decoy might do a good job of helping to keep honest people honest."

"You do advertise security camera monitoring. Isn't that right?" the officer inquired.

The man hesitated for a moment then said, "Sort of, but not really. I do have a camera that does work out at the main gate. It monitors everyone coming in and going out. You can check the footage out front. But I already did. After this guy arrived last night no one came in or out of here until I arrived early this morning. I drove around and did my normal morning rounds and then I found the car. I called you folks. The car was sitting with the door open and the motor still running just like it is now."

As if on cue, the car sputtered, then the engine died. "Must have run out of gas," the man suggested, looking at the cop who silently nodded his agreement.

"Well," the policeman said. "We had a call this morning from this guy's wife saying he never came home last night. She said she called his cell phone repeatedly, but he never answered. She said that was unlike him, so she became worried and called us."

The greasy man replied, "Yes, it's all so strange. Stuff like this never happened in my storage facility before."

The officer would check to make sure what the owner was saying was true, and although he thought the man to be less than completely honest in his business dealings, he appeared to be telling the truth regarding this particular situation.

"I'm going to look around a bit more then call a tow truck to haul this car to the impound lot. I assume you will be here to let them in when they arrive?"

"Not a problem officer," the owner said. "Whatever you need."

The policeman walked slowly up and down the aisle looking for any signs that might shine some light on this mysterious disappearance. At one point he thought he heard a faint and distant sound like a moan, but when he saw a cluster of leaves blowing down the aisle, he realized it must have been the wind.

***

Ryan slowly opened his eyes to complete darkness. He felt pain throughout his body—in his legs, arms and even his neck. He tried to move and realized he was unable to do so. He didn't know if he was still paralyzed or simply too weak to use his body. Even trying to think seemed to exhaust him. He felt something hard, like metal around his neck, wrists and ankles and realized with horror he was manacled. He wanted to rattle the chains and to cry out for help, but he could not. It was like he was trying to move someone else's body with his own mind.

He suddenly recalled the image of the chained man in the storage shed and the horrifying winged creature. He knew now for certain where he was and just how terrible and hopeless his own situation had become. Exhaustion and a type of futile acceptance overtook him as he once again faded into the blessed blackness of unconsciousness.

CUTANEOUS HORNS

Doctor James Watts sat quietly at the café counter enjoying his breakfast of scrambled eggs and toast when the odd man walked through the front door. He heard the frightened murmur of the obviously troubled restaurant patrons as the tall reddish-faced man wearing a long black trench coat walked up the aisle then took a seat at the counter next to him. The man had two curved horns jutting from either side of his forehead.

James looked at the man, studied the bizarre appendages for a moment then between bites of his toast calmly said, "Cutaneous Horns."

"Excuse me," the odd-looking man said. James noticed the man's hands were as red as his face.

James nonchalantly replied, "I said I see you have Cutaneous Horns."

The man said nothing, but just stared, confused, at the doctor.

"You see," James continued. "I'm a dermatologist. And I've read about your condition. Cutaneous Horns are hard conical projections coming from the skin. They are made of compacted keratin. They are often referred to as horns because of their resemblance to animal horns. They usually arise from benign, premalignant or malignant skin lesions."

"Hum..." the stranger replied, as if contemplating. "But at first weren't you afraid I might be some sort demon? And that maybe I came here to take you to Hell."

James scoffed, "Nonsense. There are no demons and those are nothing but Cutaneous Horns. And I'd be willing to wager your red skin is the result of a dermatological condition, possibly an advanced form of Rosacea."

"So then I'm not a demon?" the man asked.

"No, of course not," James replied. "Don't be ridiculous."

The man sat quietly for a moment, listening to the increasing rumblings of the customers behind him. After a time he said, "Well then. How might you explain that?" He pointed to the floor behind where James was sitting.

James looked down and was shocked to see his own lifeless body sprawled out in the aisle—his color ashen. The customers were all gathered around him mumbling. They were in an obvious panic and not sure what to do. He turned and looked back at the stranger who was now grinning at him with a mouth full of long, pointed brown and yellow fangs. James noticed something crawling around between the creature's sharp teeth and realized to his horror they were some sort of worm-like maggoty insects.

"Not... Cutaneous... Horns?" James managed to squeak out in a rasp.

"Nope." The hideous being replied, taking James by the arm and leading him down the aisle and out of the café.

ICEHOUSE

The decrepit old stone structure bore the typical look of a building left to the mercy of the elements—its facade covered with mold, moss and creeping vines where nature had taken over during the years. Vines covered blackened, rotting, decades-old plywood, which now shielded rusted metal frames where once blown-glass windowpanes had hung. Similar sheets of weathered wood covered gaping openings in the tattered kudzu-encased roof as well. Upon close examination however, the camouflage painted front door would look to be surprisingly new, strong, and constructed of heavy gage steel. In reality, it was actually quite secure.

The building was located in a densely wooded area, far from view of the main highway and close to an easy flowing stream. It butted against the base of a steeply rising mountain. Surrounding it were massive shade trees, whose branches intertwined, forming a giant canopy overtop and keeping the structure completely shaded. The undergrowth crawling about the building was so dense, unless you knew the structure was there it was likely you could pass within ten feet of it and never see it.

The building had once been an icehouse during the early part of the twentieth century. It was now under the ownership of one Jansen Whitmore, a young man who had inherited it from his father's estate several years earlier. The building and surrounding property had been in the family for generations but had remained unused since the mid-1920s. Prior to his inheriting the property, Jansen had never even known of its existence and was quite surprised to learn of it. He had no idea why his father had kept the place a secret, nor did he care. Jansen had his own ideas for how he would use the property, so just like his father; he made sure no one else knew of it.

Early on Jansen had done some research and learned the reason the icehouse was located next to a stream was so during the winter months the former workers would haul snow and ice from the river to the icehouse where the workers packed the building with insulation, often made up of straw or sawdust. This would allow the ice to remain frozen for many months, often until the following winter, and then they could use it even during summer months. The back of the icehouse had two large wooden doors with cast iron hardware, which opened into a cavern under the mountain. His great-grandfather had taken advantage of the coolness of the cave and added a concrete floor as well as inner walls and ceiling of stone and more straw and mud, further insulating the already cool caverns making them ideal for storing ice year round. It also made the place perfect for storing perishable items.

"Perishable items," Jansen thought with a smile as he drove his old panel van up the winding dirt and weed-choked road, leading to the icehouse. He pulled up to the front door and stepping out of the van looked around and listened to make sure he was alone—satisfied to hear only the mildly flowing stream and chilling wind blowing through the leaves of the trees above him. The late afternoon was unseasonable cool for July, but that suited Jansen just fine.

He unlocked and opened the front door of the icehouse then switched on the portable generator to provide light, as the place had no direct hookup to any public utilities. Looking around once again to assure his solitude, Jansen walked to the back of the van, opened the doors and unloaded the large canvass bundle tied with a heavy rope from its interior and hoisted it over his shoulder. It was surprisingly heavy.

"Dead weight," Jansen thought, smiling at his own ironic sense of humor.

Inside the icehouse, he placed the bundle on a mobile cart he kept there. Then after moving his van to a more secluded section of the property deeper in the woods, he returned, locking and bolting the front door behind him. Jansen walked to the two large doors, which led back into the cave—into the large cavernous room he loved so much and pulled them open.

The back area was just as he had left it, not awash with bright hot lights, but dark with strategically placed cool blue spotlights. The place looked more like a museum than the inside of a cave. That was because a sort of museum was exactly what it had become. It was his own very special museum.

Jansen looked over to his right and saw a man in a suit and tie sitting silently behind a large desk with his back straight and his arms resting on the top of the desk. There were a variety of legal-looking documents spread out before him. Behind him was a backdrop of bookshelves adorned with hundreds of legal volumes. Atop the walnut desk was green glass shaded lamp; a banker's lamp it was called. "Should be called a lawyer's lamp," Jansen said aloud, chuckling once again at his joke.

To his right and saw the platform displaying a man dressed in a plumber's coveralls hunkered down appearing to work on a set of pipes leading up to a large white porcelain claw-foot tub. He appeared to be deeply involved in his work. Inside the bathtub was a naked woman who appeared to be in the act of scrubbing herself in a sea of simulated resin bubbles.

Jansen smiled with pleasure, knowing these works of art were products of his own creation and each had their individual, personal meaning for him. For example, the lawyer had been his father's estate lawyer. Jansen hated to have to kill him and bring him here, but he was the only other living creature who knew of the icehouse's existence and Jansen couldn't risk having him blab about it to anyone. The place had to remain secret.

The plumber had been a man he had hired to repair some pipes at his house, but to Jansen's surprise, the man had agreed to do some work on his wife's plumbing instead. For their joint sins, they would be here on display for Jansen's viewing pleasure. When the police detective had questioned Jansen, he told them he suspected the cheating lovers must have run off together. Now they could spend eternity together as far as Jansen was concerned. Perhaps a thousand years from now some futuristic archeologist might find his way into the cave. Jansen wondered what he might think of his displays.

There were also many other displays scattered about the museum, perhaps a dozen or more, each of which contained someone who Jansen had felt had wronged him in one way or another. Funny, the more people he killed and displayed in his museum, the easier it became for him to find others who he was certain had done him an injustice.

Nearby there was another display in the process of being completed, depicting a scene from the inside of a police department, complete with an exact replica of the workspace of the detective who had so rudely questioned him. Jansen knew the detective was certain he was responsible for all of the disappearances, but he had no proof as far as Jansen was aware. But Jansen also knew if someone didn't do something to stop the man, he would most likely eventually find the evidence he needed. The only thing missing from the tableau was the police detective himself.

Once again, Jansen smiled his wicked little smile, knowing that as soon as he wheeled the cart in from the other room he would be able to start work on completing this scene as well.

SINGLE PANEL

The young man stood by his high school locker with his hand gently resting in a consoling gesture on the trembling shoulder of a girl who appeared to be weeping uncontrollably. Outside the cold late autumn wind howled and the icy rain pelted the school's windows as if to accentuate or perhaps even mock the dreadful news the two had only received upon arriving at school.

"I just can't believe it!" Aubrey Jenkins sobbed. "I can't believe he's dead. I mean I didn't really know Jeremy all that well, but still it just seems so incredibly unfair."

Sam Delany was having a great deal of difficulty offering the much needed solace to the girl, as he was doing everything within his power to hold back his own fragile emotions. The last thing he wanted was for his classmates to see him crying.

"I'm so sorry Sam," Aubrey said tearfully. "I really have no business blubbering on like this to you. Especially since Jeremy was your close friend. You knew him much better than me or I suppose, better than anyone in the school. I should be the one comforting you."

"That's OK, Aub," Sam said struggling to maintain his composure. "I'm doing OK. It's just a really tough thing to deal with you know?" In addition to suppressing the extent of his sadness, Sam was also hiding his true feelings toward Aubrey. The two had been close friends since childhood. However, it seemed lately Sam was starting to look at Aubrey quite differently than he had in the past, less as a friend and more as a young woman.

However, what Aubrey said was true. Sam had been Jeremy's good friend and now the boy was dead—struck down, while standing right in front of his house waiting for the school bus, by a distracted driver who hadn't anticipated the extent of the hazardous weather conditions.

Jeremy Spencer had been the "new kid" at their school. His family had only recently moved to the area just the previous summer. It had been tough for Jeremy, starting in a completely new high school as a senior with absolutely no friends.

Sam was an easy-going congenial sort of person and one who tended to get along with just about everyone he met. He empathized with Jeremy's plight and felt sorry for him. He couldn't imagine what it must be like for Jeremy leaving all of his friends behind in his senior year of high school and starting all over in a new unknown place. As a result, Sam went out of his way to talk to Jeremy and they soon became great friends.

Sam learned they shared a mutual hobby as well, that being sketching and cartooning. Sam was amazed at how advanced Jeremy's skills were and did everything he could to learn whatever techniques he could from Jeremy. He often tried to replicate Jeremy's style and although he often came close, he never managed to create more than a second-rate copy. There was something so unique and special about Jeremy's art that it was impossible to duplicate all of its nuances.

After becoming friends, Sam learned that Jeremy and his family had moved from Southern California to Ashton, Pennsylvania because his father had accepted a promotion at his company, Technofacture International, which had a facility at the eastern end of the town just beyond the borough limits. It had been a tough call for his parents to make, but in the end, they decided his father should accept the promotion. Then Jeremy had to leave behind the warm beaches of Southern California for the cold hills of Schuylkill County, Pennsylvania. The move gave new meaning to the word culture shock, as the two locations were polar opposites in virtually every way.

As Sam and Aubrey stood by the locker discussing Jeremy, they heard raucous laughter coming from a group of three large boys, growing louder as they got closer. Sam looked up over Aubrey's shoulder and could see the cluster consisted of Big Billy Coogan and his two flunkies, Johnny Domaski and Geno Deangelo.

Coogan was the sixth generation descendant of an Irish immigrant who arrived in America in the 19th century. Local rumor had it that the senior Coogan had used ruthless and illegal means to build a fortune in the coal mining industry on the backs of his underpaid laborers. This was at a time before the labor union movement. Years later, his son and eventually grandson had switched the business from coal to oil and natural gas and as a result, their wealth had grown exponentially.

Billy Coogan was a bulky young man with flaming red hair and a pallid complexion stippled with freckles. More importantly, he was a sadistic bully who, along with his two cohorts, gained great pleasure from making the lives of other students a living hell. Sam did his best to avoid Coogan whenever possible because Billy was one of the few people who truly hated Sam. The sad truth was, if Coogan didn't like someone he took every opportunity to target them, as did his toadies Damoski and Deangelo who both did whatever Coogan told them to do.

As the group got within earshot of the couple Coogan said loudly and deliberately, "Dudes. Did you hear what happened to that new kid, you know, that fag from California? What the hell was his name again?"

"Jeremy," Deangelo said.

"Yeah that's right," Coogan agreed, doing his best to pretend that Jeremy was so inconsequential the simple act of remembering the boy's name was beneath him. The truth was Coogan knew his name very well and detested Jeremy as much as he did Sam. This was primarily because the two friends were the only kids in the entire school who weren't afraid to stand up to Coogan and his cadre even though they were smaller and many pounds lighter.

Only a few weeks earlier, Jeremy had drawn a hilarious black and white single-panel cartoon caricature of Coogan portrayed as an idiotic-looking buffoon with hooded eyelids over crossed eyes and his finger stuck deep up into his nose with a trickle of snot drizzling down the penetrating finger. To add insult to injury, Jeremy had shown Coogan's nose, which in reality was quite large, in an even more oversized caricature. Then to make matters worse, the caricature's oversized mouth hung wide-open in a moronic slack-jawed manor with a stream of drool leaking from the corner.

Jeremy had been so bold as to tape the picture to the front of Coogan's locker early on a Monday morning and most of the class had seen it before the habitually-late Coogan ever got to school. Coogan had threatened to beat Jeremy to a pulp. However, when he eventually cornered the boy and saw the stern look in his eye Coogan knew Jeremy wasn't going to back down. So he chose instead to "spare" the boy a beating for this one-time offense since, "he's just a stupid new kid who don't know no better."

Now standing across the hall from Sam and Aubrey Coogan said disdainfully to Sam while sneering at him, "I heard that dumbass queer-bait butt-buddy of yours got hisself squished this morning right in front of his own house, out along the highway. What a stupid douchebag."

Hearing this Sam began to tense: his sorrow quickly replaced by an ever-growing rage. He needed an outlet for his grief and it looked as if Billy Coogan was about to provide one for him. Aubrey sensed the change in Sam's demeanor and said softly, "Ignore them Sam. They're just trying to get to you. Don't fall for it Sam. There are three of them. Just stay cool. OK? Please?"

Coogan and his friends were laughing loudly as Billy said, "Yeah. Did you guys hear what happened to him? I heard he got splattered big time. They said it was so bad that the ambulance dudes were puking their guts out. I heard they had to go around picking up pieces of his frigging body parts and then had to stuff them in like giant garbage bags or something. It just all seems so fittin' to me. He was nothin' but trash when he was alive and now he's trash for good, all in pieces and in garbage bags. Ha ha."

Sam's face reddened and Aubrey decided she had better say something before things got out of hand. "Shame on you Billy Coogan! Didn't your mother ever teach you to respect the dead? You should be ashamed of yourself."

Coogan looked at her as if noticing her for the first time, as if she were nothing more than an insect. He snickered and said, "Well if it ain't little Princess Aubrey. Maybe you should be glad that little artsey-fartsy faggot got hisself squashed. Now maybe you can have Sammy boy all to yourself; that is, if you can convince him to switch teams." Then Coogan and his friends burst out in uncontrollable laughter.

Sam made a lunge toward Coogan, but once again, Aubrey blocked him and said, "Just forget it Sam. They're not worth it. Nothing he says matters anyway. He'll get his. Believe me. Someday he'll get his."

"I'd like to give him some of what he deserves right now," Sam growled; his eyes burning holes in Bill Coogan, who although doing his best to appear unconcerned, knew he had probably gone and pushed Sam too far. He knew Sam wouldn't hesitate to take him and his goons on all at once. He also knew if that conflict did happen, although they would likely beat Sam unmercifully, it wouldn't be without their taking some injuries themselves. Not to mention they likely would all end up expelled for fighting in school.

Coogan waved his hand dismissively at the pair and said to his cronies, "Let's get out of here and leave those two love birds alone to bawl like babies over their dead pansy boy. We got lots more important things to do."

Still fuming from the encounter Sam and Aubrey walked purposefully in the opposite direction heading for their first class of the day. As they turned a corner, Sam's eyes began to tear up from a combination of anger, sorrow and overwhelming frustration. He turned away so Aubrey didn't see him. She actually had seen him although she would never let on that she had.

Aubrey said, "I wish Jeremy was still alive. If he was here I'm sure the two of you would come up with really cool some way to get back at stupid Billy Coogan."

Sam knew she was right. Jeremy might not have confronted the three head on, but he certainly would come up with some creative scheme to get back at them. Jeremy was not just a talented artist but was creative in many other ways. He also had a knack for figuring out what made people tick: their likes and dislikes, their hopes and even their deepest fears. As such, Sam knew Jeremy would have definitely come up with some incredibly nasty way to get even with Coogan. He wished he had half of his late friend's creative gifts, but he simply did not.

***

Bill Coogan approached his locker still laughing with his friends about their earlier clash with Sam and Aubrey. "Did you believe the nerve of that fairy Sam kid? I think the dope would have actually tried to take us on if his little beard girlfriend hadn't been there."

"Yeah," Johnny Domaski agreed. "Beard is right. Who's he trying to kid?"

Coogan opened the door to his locker and started to speak, "You know it. We woulda bashed his..." but the words caught in Coogan's throat. He stared into the locker for a minute then his already pale face became ashen.

"You... you OK, Bill?" Deangelo stammered. "You kinda look like you seen a ghost or something."

"Um... ah... yeah. I'm fine. It's nothing." Coogan said after a moment's hesitation. Then he quickly closed the door to his locker, his hands involuntarily trembling. He turned and walked quickly down the hall trying to get as far from the locker, as quickly as possible. His two friends hurried behind him and could tell something was very wrong, but they didn't dare question him again.

Coogan's stomach was cramping with tension from what he had just seen. How could that even have been possible? Inside his locker was an almost identical copy of the same insulting single panel cartoon—the one Jeremy had drawn weeks earlier. It was the same one Coogan had personally torn to pieces. However, instead of it hanging on the outside of the locker for everyone to see, it was inside where only he would find it. He was certain he was the only one who knew the combination to that locker. So how in the Hell could that picture have possibly gotten in there?

Coogan suddenly stopped in his tracks and told his friends, "Look. I got something I gotta do alone. You two head to study hall and tell that douchebag Flemdick I'll be along as soon as I can." He was referring disrespectfully as he always did, to one of his teachers and first period study hall monitor, Bryce Fenwick. Coogan's cronies had no idea where the ridiculous nickname came from but because Coogan came up with it, they always laughed as if it was the funniest thing they ever heard.

"What should we tell him?" Johnny asked. "We don't want him bustin' on us just 'cause he's pissed at you."

"I don't give a rat's rosy red ass what you tell him," Coogan shouted as he turned to head down the hall. He waved his beefy arm dismissively and said, "Just tell him I'll be there as soon as I can." Coogan wasn't worried in the slightest about being late nor did he care what that moron Flemdick thought about it. He knew the teacher was in the middle of a divorce, was having money issues and owed Coogan's old man a boatload of cash. As far as Billy Coogan was concerned, he could do whatever he damn well pleased and Flemdick would have nothing to say about it.

He headed back to his locker, determined to figure out what was going on and who was screwing with him. One thing he knew, whoever it was, they were going to pay big time. Coogan stood outside of his locker knowing what he needed to do but more than a little unsettled about doing so. Mustering his courage, he opened his locker and stared at the single panel cartoon. It looked exactly like the one Jeremy had drawn... but not quite. It was slightly different, and the eyes looked wrong. Instead of having a dull hooded and stupid look like the previous caricature, they seemed to be wide open and staring angrily, directly at Coogan.

Reluctantly, Coogan reached inside the locker and grabbed the drawing to study it closer, certain it had to be some sort of copy but when he rubbed his thumb across a small corner of the sketch he saw the ink smear and knew that it was freshly drawn. "Stinkin queer!" Coogan said, realizing that Jeremy must have found some way to get into this locker the previous day to play this prank on him. Coogan felt a bit of satisfaction knowing this prank was the last one the little fairy would ever pull.

"Serves him right. Glad his stupid ass is dead. Good riddance to bad rubbish," Coogan said to no one in particular. He took the drawing crumpled it up into a ball and tucked it into his pants pocket. He decided he would have to get a new combination lock for his locker as soon as possible.

He didn't know how Jeremy had gotten the combination but chances were good if he had it, he had likely shared it with his little pussy boyfriend Sammy. In fact, now that he thought about it, Jeremy might not have even been the one who had put the drawing in his locker. It could just as easily have been Sam who had actually done the drawing and not Jeremy.

Coogan knew they were both artsy-fartsy types and both liked drawing cartoons. The more he considered it the more he began to believe that it was not only possible but also probable that Sam had been the one who had copied Jeremy's original cartoon and put it in his locker. That might explain the slight differences between the two drawings. The fact that he had found it on the same day Jeremy died was probably just a stupid coincidence. However, this realization did little to relieve the uneasy feeling he was experiencing.

He turned and went to what was left of his first period study hall. After the end of period bell rang, Coogan and his cronies headed down the hall toward their next class. All the while Coogan had his eyes open for Sam, because he had a very special message to give him as well as a present.

Coogan was fuming. The more he thought about Sam the angrier he got. He had made up his mind. He was going to pull out the crumpled cartoon and force the little queer to swallow it. Then he saw the boy with Aubrey walking down the opposite side of the hall.

Coogan and his crew surrounded the couple and without a moment's hesitation, he grabbed Sam and slammed him up against a set of lockers. Sam felt the steel handle of one of the lockers dig into the small of his back sending pain coursing through him and knocking the wind temporarily from his body.

Damoski and Deangelo pushed Aubrey roughly out of the way and held Sam tightly against the wall of lockers, as Billy Coogan's face was just inches from his. Sam could smell the bully's foul breath while at the same time the spittle from Coogan's shouting stippled his face.

"You stupid little faggot!" Coogan shouted. "You honestly thought I wouldn't figure out what you did—your little practical joke. Well, I did and you screwed up big time! Now you're gonna pay queer-bait... you're gonna pay like you never paid before."

Coogan reached into his pocket, pulled out the wadded clump of paper and raised it up to Sam's lips. "Here you go you gobbling faggot. You like putting things in your mouth don't you? Well eat this you little queer." He began trying to stuff the wad of paper into Sam's tightly closed lips.

"Coogan!" A deep voice shouted from behind him. It was the high school principal, Mr. Wolf, also known as "Lightning" by most of the students. He was someone even the toughest of students feared. He got his nickname from the speed at which he swung his paddle, which he often used to enforce his authority through corporal punishment. Rumor said that "Lightning" had brought even the biggest and meanest kids to tears with the speed and force of his paddle.

Coogan froze as Mr. Wolf pulled him away from Sam. His two cronies immediately let the boy go and did their best to slink out of sight. Wolf saw them, knew them well and decided he would deal with them later.

"What's this all about?" The principal said.

Sam looked at him in shock and said, "I don't know, Sir. Aubrey and I were just walking to our next class and Coogan and his boys attacked me."

He then looked at Coogan who said, "Mr. Wolf. Look I'm... I'm really sorry. It's just that I lost my temper. Sam here put something very insulting in my locker. I don't know how he got my combination, but I didn't like what he put in there."

Wolf looked at both boys for a moment. Sam was looking scared and apparently unaware of what Coogan was talking about while at the same time, the larger boy seemed certain of the accusations he had just made.

"Billy. Do you have any proof about what you're saying?" Wolf asked.

"You bet I do," Coogan replied as he simultaneously began to un-crumple and smooth out the drawing now slightly wet from Sam's lips. "Here you go. Sam put this in my locker. See for yourself."

Wolf looked at the wrinkled paper, confused by what he saw. He turned the paper around and handed it back to Coogan saying, "I don't know what you're talking about Billy. There's nothing insulting on this paper. In fact there's nothing on the paper at all."

Coogan couldn't believe his ears. He grabbed the paper away from his principal with perhaps a bit more force than was appropriate by the angry look Mr. Wolf was giving him. He stared at the paper; it was completely blank.

"How the hell did you do that?" Coogan shouted at Sam. "Did you use some kind of disappearing ink you little queer!" Once again, he made a lunge toward Sam. But this time he was stopped by Wolf's tight grip on the back of his neck.

"I think you'd better come with me Billy," Mr. Wolf said. "Maybe you can calm down a bit while we wait for your mother to come and take you home."

"But... but... but..." Coogan tried to reply, but his protests were useless.

***

As he sat on a chair in the waiting area outside of the principal's office Billy Coogan stirred restlessly, waiting for his Mother to arrive. He fiddled with his various notebooks opening one he knew to be virtually empty. As the first page flipped open, he saw to his horror a single panel cartoon—the same one that had been in his locker, but again it was different. In fact, it seemed to change even as he stared at it.

The cartoon was no longer simply a rough black and white caricature sketch, but was detailed and realistic. It looked just like Billy Coogan. In fact, in some color now graced the image as well. The eyes were bloodshot, riddled with crimson veins and opened wide with wild fury. They began to change and now looked less like Coogan's eyes and more like… yes he was certain, they looked more like Jeremy's eyes.

Coogan felt as if the horrible eyes were boring a hole through him. That was when he noticed the change in the finger lodged far up the cartoon's bulbous nose. The snot was now such a vivid red it appeared to be wet. The longer Coogan stared at it the more it seemed to consist of real blood. He was even certain he saw it move and slowly trickle further down from the nose.

But the most disturbing thing was the slack-jawed open mouth. Its former stream of drool had now become a sickening dark greenish-red mixture. And inside that open mouth dozens of slime-covered white maggot-like insects squirmed and crawled lazily over-top of each other, bathing in the slimy mouth sludge.

Coogan held back a scream, grabbed the page, tore it out and threw it on the floor breathing a sigh of relief. Then to his shock and horror when he looked down at the formerly blank notebook page, there was another identical single-panel sketch. In a flurry of wild manic movements, Coogan continued to rip out page after page, each one revealing the same horrifying cartoon time after time. Soon sheets from his notebook covered the floor around his as he continued to rip out one after another.

"Billy Coogan! What do you think you're doing?" A voice called out from across the room. It was the principal's secretary, Mrs. Glassman. She was standing with her hands on her ample hips and her face was red with anger.

Just then, Billy's mother walked in to see her son still manically tearing pages from his notebook. The floor was barely visible beneath the sea of pages, all of which were completely blank.

Billy was mumbling incoherently while simultaneously weeping as tears coursed down his reddened face. No matter how many pages he tore from the book, the cartoon reappeared and he understood there was nothing he could do to stop it from haunting him.

It simply wouldn't stop appearing: not that day, not the next and not the next. In fact, for as long as he lived no matter what the doctors at the sanitarium tried to explain to him and no matter what drugs they gave him, Bill Coogan still saw the single-panel drawing.

And what could anyone do for him anyway? It was obvious the late Jeremy Spencer was not about to let the cruel remarks Coogan made on the day of his death go unpunished, not now and not ever again.

THE BRANDS

The silent man sat cross-legged on the dusty wood-
planked attic floor. The air around him was both stiflingly
hot and was redolent with the musty scent of decades old
cardboard boxes stuffed full with discarded memories of
ages gone by. The man however was completely oblivious
to his surroundings. He sat upright with his side leaning
against a wall and his chin resting against his chest as a
thin stream of drool trickled down soaking his already
sweat-stained tee shirt. The owner of both the foul smelling
shirt, as well as the stream of drool, was sound asleep.

A bottle of Seagram's Seven lay on its side next to him,
empty. Near the mouth of the bottle was a dark spot where,
at some point during the past several hours, some of the
remaining liquid must have spilled and soaked into the
aged floor. The musty air now also held the faint scent of
whiskey.

Tobias Matthews gave out a slight chuffing sound as he
began to awake from his latest drunken stupor. How he
had managed to keep from teetering in the wrong direction
and falling over was a mystery. He squinted, looking about
the room with bleary eyes unsure if it was day or night and
not really caring either way. Instinctively, he reached down
for the whiskey bottle, only to find it empty. With an angry
shout he threw the bottle across the expanse of the attic
where it struck a wood-framed side wall and shattered.
Tobias put his head down into his hands, lay on his side
and began sobbing uncontrollably.

He couldn't comprehend how drastically his life had
changed during the past year; and that change was not at
all for the better. A year or so earlier he had been a

successful hard-working member of the American middle class with a house, family and responsibilities. Now he was just an out of control drunk. Tobias supposed everyone had a breaking point and he apparently had reached his.

Up until that point Tobias had lived his life exactly as he had always been taught since childhood. He always did as he was told and followed all the rules. He studied and did well in school, graduated from a prestigious college, secured a good paying job, married his high school sweetheart, advanced within his company, bought a house, had two kids—managing to do all of this in what he had always been told was the right order. But all of the planning hadn't prepared him for the massive kick in the crotch life had in store for him.

The small, private company where he had dedicated the past fifteen years of his life was unexpectedly bought out by a much larger corporation. Then the economy started to go south. Decisions were made—the kinds of decisions people were not to take personally because they were "strictly business decisions." Or this was at least what Tobias had been told the day he was called into his boss's office and informed that his services were no longer needed, "nothing personal," just one of those "business decisions." So the job he had expected would carry him for his entire career and eventually into a comfortable retirement with a nice pension, had ceased to exist with the simple stroke of a pen. And the secure life he once had taken for granted was no more.

Tobias was unable to find another job in his field no matter how many applications he filled out, how many recruiters he spoke with or how many doors he had slammed in his face. Unemployment compensation, severance pay and his meager savings were able to carry him for only a few months. He and his wife Angie had never lived frugally and in reality tended to live far beyond their means. The result was they had accrued a significant amount of high interest rate credit card debt. They both simply assumed his job would always be there and his income would continue to grow. The housing market had likewise crashed, and the couple soon discovered that the new home they had moved into a year earlier was worth about seventy-five thousand dollars less than the mortgage they still owed on it. And that mortgage was one they no longer could afford to pay.

Angie had managed to secure a minimum wage job to help out as much as possible, but Tobias had refused to do likewise. He felt he needed to keep his time free to go on interviews for the next high-paying job, which he was certain awaited him just around the next corner, or maybe the next, or perhaps the next.

But six months after losing his job, they in turn lost their home to foreclosure and were forced to sell all of their furniture and treasured belongings to pay off at least some of their massive debt. Despite this too-little-too-late effort they still were forced to declare bankruptcy when they couldn't pay what remained. The now desperate family had no other choice but to move into the basement of Tobias' parents' house. It was either they accept that demeaning fate or else find themselves homeless.

Then three months later after weeks of constant fighting and endless frustration, Angie announced she was leaving Tobias and moving back home to her mother. She took the two kids with her and immediately filed for divorce.

He later learned she had been having an affair with her boss at work and she was in fact, leaving Tobias to marry him. The only satisfaction Tobias could garner from the discovery was that despite his title and position, Angie's new lover still earned less than Tobias had earned at his old position. This was a strange, twisted satisfaction indeed, since for the moment Tobias brought home no paycheck while and at least Angie's future husband had a job.

Then just two weeks earlier, Tobias' parents were both tragically killed in a car accident when his father apparently had a heart attack at the wheel, lost control of the vehicle, went over the side of a bridge and fell seventy-five feet into a rain-swollen river. This had been the last straw for Tobias and had sent him into a drinking binge after the funeral that had continued practically non-stop to the present.

Tobias knew he was named as the sole beneficiary in his parents will and as such would not only inherit the house but would also receive his parents' savings and life insurance. But as his current string of rotten luck would have it, he discovered several unpleasant facts. His parents only had enough life insurance to cover their burial expenses and had used most of their savings to purchase and refurbish the old home where Tobias now lived.

Since they had only moved into the home four years earlier the couple still had a substantial mortgage they were paying. "Like father, like son," Tobias thought. Because this meant their mortgage debt now would become Tobias' responsibility. So what originally looked like a windfall of good fortune was just another albatross of debt to be hung around his neck. He understood he was simply waiting to lose yet another home within the next few months; then he would be homeless once again.

Tobias always knew life could often be unfair, but he never imagined it could be so brutally unfair—especially to someone who had spent his life doing what society deemed was right and living by the rules.

While he lay on his side, sobs hitching in his chest as he struggled to regain his composure, Tobias saw something that caught his attention, something that appeared to be very old and was barely visible between two stacks of musty-smelling cardboard boxes. It looked like some sort of wooden box or container. Tobias had no idea why the item had suddenly caught his attention. After all, he had spent the past day or so combing through his parents' storage boxes with the hopes of finding something of value, but had struck out completely and had never even noticed the box before. But he was not surprised he had missed finding the potential treasure since all the while he had been searching he was for the most part drunk.

Maybe, just maybe, the old wooded box might hold some jewelry or ancient coins or something else that would free him of his financial woes. Now standing awkwardly, Tobias began to move box after box working his way back to find the mysterious wooden container. Sweat seemed to stream from every pore in his body, not just from the extreme heat in the attic but likely from the effects of his alcohol consumption.

After a few strenuous moments, Tobias reached the unusual box and pulled it out from the shadows into the meager light filtering down from the single naked overhead bulb. There was a small window in the attic as well, but it had been painted shut years earlier and apparently this area had been ignored during his parents' remodeling project. With just a cursory look, Tobias could tell the box was very old indeed and must have at least some value to an antique dealer or collector.

The box appeared to be a well-crafted, ancient item, hand-made of finely polished wood. He suspected that even empty the thing might be worth a good deal of money to the right person. But perhaps he would get lucky; maybe it would be filled with something even more valuable than the box itself. That was exactly what he needed.

Tobias was surprised to find there was no lock or hasp securing the lid closed. His heart sank realizing that if it had once held valuables there would have been some means by which it could have been locked. But there was nothing of any sort. He slowly lifted the lid and his disappointment was realized by what he found inside: tools, just tools.

The box held a small assortment of very old hand tools. He found a small square-headed wooden mallet, a wooden clamp of some sort, a few flat metal nails, a metal chisel with a wooden handle and two odd tools he could not identify.

"Oh man!" Tobias said aloud with disappointment in the empty room. "Just my lousy luck. No jewelry, no cash, just a bunch of worthless tools." Although he assumed an antique dealer might be interested in buying the tools, he instinctively knew their value would not be sufficient to get him out of his present financial conundrum.

He looked at the raised lid and saw an inscription, which appeared to be hand-carved into the underside. It read, "Property of Ezra T. Mathews, Williamsburg, Virginia". Tobias thought for a moment "Ezra T. Mathews? I spell Matthews with two T's but this is spelled with one. Could be a relative I suppose. I don't recall my parents ever mentioning anyone named Ezra." Then he remembered his father telling him once that his ancestors had been early settlers in the 1600s and had lived in Virginia for a time before eventually migrating north to work in the coal mines of Pennsylvania. Tobias' grandfather and great-grandfather had been miners, but both his father and he had never worked in that industry, as they had both been sufficiently educated and held white-collar positions. "This guy Ezra could have been one of my ancestors from way back," Tobias said, wondering just how old the box and tools might be.

He looked again at the two unusual tools, which he still couldn't identify. For some unknown reason they seemed to suddenly fascinate him. The tools were made with teardrop shaped wooden handles, appearing to have been hand carved and which were about four inches long. There were dark metal objects protruding out from the wooden handles adding another several inches to their overall length. Tobias reached into the box and picked them up for a closer inspection.

As soon as his fingers came into contact with the tools, a strange tingling sensation shot through his entire being, affecting virtually every nerve ending in his body. It was not as though the tingling feeling was unpleasant, just strange. In fact, it felt quite soothing, perhaps even calming. Then just as quickly as the sensation had started it stopped; his body began to return to normal, making Tobias actually feel a bit disappointed the unusual feeling had ended.

What was even stranger than the sensation had been was that he now noticed he actually felt much better than he could have expected; the negative effects of the alcohol now seemed to have been completely erased. He no longer felt hung over, and his senses seemed more alert than they had been in weeks. This resulted in his suddenly noticing the foul stench from his own accumulated perspiration and far too many days without bathing.

"Man I stink!" Tobias said aloud with a self-deprecating chuckle. "Woo baby! I am in dire need of a shower!" He immediately made up his mind to head downstairs to his late parent's bathroom—his bathroom now he supposed—and remedy the repulsively odorous situation. He left the toolbox open on the floor but unconsciously took the two strange wooden-handled tools with him.

Tobias walked into the bathroom and set the tools down on top of the vanity, paying little attention to them. He turned on the shower and began peeling off his sweat-stained clothing, which clung to him as if they had been applied with some sort of vile-smelling adhesive. As he slowly turned to enter the shower, he noticed something about the tools he had not previously seen. The darkened metal ends extending from the wooden handles were shaped like two distinct letters; the one on the left was a capital letter "M," and the one on the right was a "T."

"Letters?" Tobias pondered to himself. "Humm... I wonder what sort of tools they might be."

As he got into the shower and washed under the cleansing hot water, he tried to clear his mind of all of his troubles and was surprised to find how easy the task was. Perhaps it was because of the pleasant feel of the hot shower, which he always enjoyed, or perhaps it was something else. Whatever the reason, for the first time in a long time, Tobias was beginning to feel like himself, his old self, once again.

He began to think about the two strange tools once again with their mysterious letters. In fact, suddenly that seemed to be all he could think about. Something about them had grabbed hold of all of his attention.

"M and T..." he thought. "M and T... T and M... Hey wait a minute, T and M. My initials are T M."

He pulled aside the shower curtain to look at the tools only to discover that instead of sitting in the order M then T with M to the left and T to the right; they had become reversed with the T to the left and the M to the right; the same order as Tobias's own initials.

"What the hell!" Tobias thought as he quickly closed the shower curtain, as if to suggest the thin fabric could protect him from whatever weirdness was taking place a few feet away. He was certain he had set the tools down in the reverse order of how he now found them. But how could that be? How could they now be reversed to match his initials? Perhaps he was mistaken; maybe he had set them down in their current order unconsciously and had simply not noticed. Yes. He decided that had to be the case, since nothing else made any rational sense.

He continued with his shower, once again contemplating what the purpose of the tools might have been. He was sure they were very old and had to have been hand-made. But he wondered just how old they might have been and where they had come from. He recalled the name scratched on the inner lid of the box and the location of Williamsburg Virginia.

Tobias knew about the colonial Williamsburg tourist attraction where people could walk around original buildings from colonial times. He wondered since his family had come to the US as colonists, if the man Ezra Mathews with one T might have been his great, great—God only knew how many greats—grandfather. But why would Ezra Mathews have tools with the initials T and M? Wouldn't he have had E and M?

"And what could they possibly have been used for?" he said as the steaming water fell around him. "Maybe they were some type of stamp or marker, or perhaps used to initial sealing wax on envelopes. Maybe they were used to stamp an impression into leather."

Stepping out of the shower and drying off, Tobias looked closer at the strange tools. He checked out the back of the wooden handles and saw they appeared to be intact and not damaged or mushroomed in any way as they might have been had they been struck repeatedly with a mallet or hammer as in the case of a stamping tool.

Then he looked again at the blackened metal tips of the tools and a thought suddenly appeared in his mind. "Brand," was the word he thought. "These tools could be some sort of branding tools." Tobias recalled the charred ends of his fireplace tools after years of usage and saw the resemblance the two lettered tools bore to those tools—the blackened metal the result of being subjected to excessive heat over long periods of time. He was suddenly certain the tools must have been used as some sort of branding tools.

He decided he would have to do some research to see if he could locate more information about the strange tools. He figured with his knowledge of computers and search engines he had enough rough information to at least get started.

He dressed and picked up the two brands—yes, he was now certain the tools were used for branding and he could now only think of them as brands—and headed down to his late father's study. He powered up his father's computer, now thankful he had bought it for them several years earlier and had also provided them with a high-speed internet connection. He suspected his folks had hardly ever used it and Tobias had likely used it more since moving into the house with his family than his parents ever would have.

Tobias decided to search based on a variety of combinations of the letters "M", "T" and the words "brand" and "Virginia." He first tried "M and T brand" but got no results that looked in any way promising. Then likewise he tried the string, "brand M and T VA," thinking perhaps the abbreviation of Virginia might bring alternative results. But still he had no luck. Then finally he tried "brand M and T Williamsburg VA," hoping that by using the actual town of Williamsburg it might allow the search engine to find something but all he got was similar unsatisfactory results. Tobias had mixed emotions and felt a bit confused because he didn't understand how he could be so positive the results he was receiving were not the ones he needed when he had absolutely no idea what he was actually looking for.

Then suddenly as if out of nowhere, a single word popped into his head, "Punishment". He had no clue where the word came from, but it simply felt right to him. Tobias then typed the string "Williamsburg Virginia Punishment Branding M and T" in the Google search bar and with certainty, he saw a heading for a URL that he instantly knew was exactly what he needed.

A link appeared for a website which read, "Colonial Crimes and Punishments: The Colonial Williamsburg..." Tobias noticed a brief description of the website listed below the link reading, "'T' for thief was branded on the light-fingered criminal's hand..." and he shouted, "Yes!" knowing he had to visit the website.

As soon as he clicked the link, Tobias was surprised to see a picture, albeit an obvious Photo-shopped recreation of a horrifying scene from Williamsburg, Virginia history. In an article by a man named James A. Cox, he saw a photo created by someone name Dave Doody of a man's hand, being securely held in place about the wrist by another man. Burned into the flesh of the seized open palm was the letter "T"; and not just any "T" but the exact same shaped "T" that was present on one of the very tools that now lay on the desk next to the computer. It was identical to the hand-carved tool in every way, down to the smallest detail. Tobias stared down at the tools with his mouth agape.

He then spent the next several hours researching various articles and learned that the courthouse in Colonial Williamsburg Virginia had a very small jail, which was not suitable for long-term incarceration. There was, however a gallows constructed in the yard behind the courthouse. As a result, there was only one of two ways an accused criminal could leave the courthouse: either by being set free or by hanging.

If a criminal were convicted of stealing, before being set free the letter "T" for "Thievery" would be branded into the flesh of his hand. If someone had killed someone, perhaps in a bar fight and it was determined the crime was not premeditated murder but an accident then an "M" for "Manslaughter" would be branded into his hand before he was set free. Sometimes these criminals were also forced to spend time in the stocks at the center of town as well before being released.

These brands, being permanent and visible to everyone, not only marked the criminals for life, but also provided a very helpful perpetual record for the Williamsburg judicial system. Because of this, if someone convicted of thievery or manslaughter and was so branded, returned to the courthouse on a similar charge, it was likely that the next time they left the courthouse it would be by dangling from the end of a hangman's noose, kicking their feet until they suffocated.

Tobias was astonished by what he had discovered. He knew without a doubt that the two tools he had found were not just cheap replicas, but were actually two of the original branding tools used in the Williamsburg, Virginia settlement. He assumed the tools must have some great financial worth, but that was not however, what was foremost in his mind. He wondered how many human hands had been branded by the tools, how much pain and punishment they had provided and how many of those who had been branded eventually ended up being hung for repeat offenses.

As he had been gathering his research, Tobias was unconsciously formulating the crux of an idea in the back of his mind. The words "punishment", "branding", "guilty", "conviction" as well as others were bouncing around in his subconscious as if swirling in a mental alphabet soup of disassociated ideas, just waiting to somehow come together to form some sort of clear and understandable concept.

Then just like before when the words "brand" and "punishment" had miraculously popped into his mind, the jumble of snippets ping-ponging through his brain suddenly came together to form an idea—and not just an idea, but an understanding. Tobias suddenly knew exactly what he must do. He had a mission: one that he believed was placed into his mind by a higher power. He unexpectedly understood everything. All that had happened to him over the past year had not been his fault, not of his own doing. He had been blaming himself for everything and now he realized he was not responsible for any of it; and in fact, he was the victim. And as with any such unfortunate situation, where there is a victim, there must also be an aggressor: a responsible party. And Tobias now instantly knew very clearly, each and every one of the offenders who was responsible for his misfortunes.

His company, his boss and all those who made the company's decisions were the ones who were to blame for his losing his job. They were the ones who insisted on saying the firing was "nothing personal" and it was "just a business decision". Tobias knew better; it was personal. It is always personal when it affected his life. And now he suddenly realized just how personal it was going to become.

Then there was the bank, which held his mortgage and its loan officers with their fancy suits and ties and their manicured fingernails. They were the ones responsible for stealing his home from him. He had worked his butt off for over fifteen years to buy that house and now it was gone. If they hadn't taken his home none of his problems with his wife would have ever occurred.

Tobias also decided Angie's new lover had to answer for his role in destroying their family. He didn't really blame Angie; he probably should have, but in his confused mind he believed her to be as much of a victim as he was. Her boss had taken advantage of her at a time when she really needed a friend. Tobias believed if that man were out of the picture, Angie would come back to him and great him with open arms. She would beg Tobias to take her back and would be a true and faithful wife from that day on. He was certain of it.

And in the case of his parent's deaths, he was unable to find anyone to blame, as their deaths had simply been an unfortunate tragedy. He did recall however, how dissatisfied he had been with the way the funeral director had made their faces appear so false and waxy as they lie in their coffins. Although it was true their bodies had been badly damaged in the accident Tobias believed the man could have done more. Especially since the majority of his parents' insurance money went to pay for that funeral—the man shouldn't have cut corners. Tobias knew there was only one person, the funeral director who was definitely accountable for that debacle.

He had a clear picture now not only of who was to blame for each of his recent heartaches, but he also knew what he had to do about it. "Punishment," he thought. He looked down at the branding tools he held in his hands and smiled understandingly.

Over the course of the next several weeks Tobias systematically hunted down and savagely butchered each of the people he knew had been responsible for his hardships. And when he did capture them, Tobias made sure their deaths were long, drawn-out, painful, brutal, vicious and bloody.

Each of them was tortured repeatedly and brought to the brink of death, but not finally killed until he was certain he had finished enjoying their hours of suffering. And in every case, just before he issued the final killing blow, he would take his two very special branding tools, heat them with a portable gas torch until they were red hot and then he would burn "T" and "M" into the bubbling, steaming flesh of their foreheads as they screamed and pleaded for their own deaths to mercifully arrive.

During his rampage of slaughter, Tobias took absolutely no precautions to protect his identity; his mind was too far gone for him to worry about such trivial things. He believed he was on a mission ordained by a higher power to seek his vengeance and as such he had every right to do so. If the authorities could not bring themselves to understand his responsibility, then so be it. As a result, he left plenty of evidence for the police investigators to follow, which of course, eventually led them straight to him. The fact that his initials were burned into the foreheads of his victims was simply the icing on the cake as far as the detectives were concerned.

Before long, Tobias found himself arrested and locked in a prison cell awaiting his trial. He explained to his court appointed attorney that he was simply carrying out a punishment on his attackers and that God himself had justified his actions, by providing him with the tools necessary to do what had to be done. Tobias said he felt no remorse for his actions and had no fear for what fate the judicial system might have in store for him. He had done what he had to do and cared nothing for the consequences, whatever they might be. He felt good, very good, as he sat on the edge of his cot, alone in his jail cell staring down at the floor.

Then suddenly in the silence of his cell he thought he could hear the distant rumbling of voices—faint but slowly growing louder. It sounded as if he was walking toward a room full of people, but that was not quite correct. Since he was sitting on his bunk and not moving and the sound was still getting louder, it was as if the crowd of people was moving toward him. He couldn't make out what they were saying as their words all seemed to flow over top of each other resulting in a steady inaudible humming sound like that of thousands of insects.

He raised his head and looked across his tiny cell into the shadowed corner of the room from where the sound seemed to be originating. He suddenly could see something materializing on the far wall resembling a painting or a mural of some sort. He couldn't believe his eyes. In the image which was rapidly forming there were several men and women dressed in old style colonial clothing all sitting together in some sort of terraced gallery of wooden benches with a podium or lectern at the center. And the translucent image had depth, as if it had been somehow painted in three dimensions.

Then the incoherent buzzing sound grew louder until it became an earsplitting roar, forcing Tobias to cover ears with his hands, which did little good because he soon discovered the deafening sounds were not really in his ears but were actually occurring inside his mind. Just before Tobias was sure his brain would explode from the maddening din, the sounds instantly stopped and the room was once again silent.

He cautiously removed his hands from his ears and looked out at the mural on the wall. It was then that Tobias realized what he was seeing was no longer a painting because paintings didn't move. The group of people appeared to now be animatedly engaged in excited silent conversations with each other and some of them were periodically pointing toward Tobias as he sat astounded on his bunk.

Although he couldn't hear a word they spoke he knew they were discussing him. The lead figure at the center of the image sat behind the large wooded podium and wore a dark robe and long white braided wig. The others were dressed in dark colored hand-made clothing, which appeared to be fashioned from dyed wool. They were all silently shouting at the same time and attempting to get the attention of the man in the wig.

The man behind the podium slammed down a large gavel and the rest of the men and women in the image closed their mouths obediently. Tobias realized what he was seeing was a seventeenth century courtroom with some sort of drama being played out right before his eyes and the man in the wig was most likely a judge. But it was more than that, because now the judge was looking directly at Tobias. Impossible as it seemed the man's eyes were locked on his own and his lips were moving, uttering some sort of accusatory declaration, which Tobias couldn't hear or understand.

When the judge's lips stopped moving the man brought down his gavel silently against the podium and as if on cue two other men walked into the room each from separate darkened doorways on opposite sides of the image. They both wore black hoods with eyeholes cut into them and they were also clad in long black robes. One of the men carried a rope fashioned in the shape of a hangman's noose, while the other carried something in each of his hands. The objects glowed with a bright orange illumination and Tobias recognized them as the same branding tools he had found in his parents' attic and which had served him so well during the previous weeks of revenge.

Next, with a signal from the judge the two men— executioners, Tobias realized—turned and began to step from the image, their black leather boots landing with a dull smack on the floor of his jail cell. He was stricken with unimaginable terror and was unable to speak as the pair approached him and their shrouded figures surrounded him like a cloak of darkness.

***

"What do you supposed happened to him?" the first guard asked upon finding the chalky white corpse of Tobias Matthews curled in a semi-circle on the floor of his jail cell.

"I don't know," the second replied. "...maybe a seizure of some kind or maybe a heart attack. Whatever the cause, he just saved the taxpayers the expense of a trial."

Then the first guard said, "Yeah, you're right. But... but look at his face. The way his eyes are bugging out of their sockets like he saw the devil himself."

"Looks almost like something scared the life out of him," the second agreed. "And look at his hands... the way they're closed up tight like he's gripping something."

"That'll be one for the medical examiner to figure out. Cause this guy's as stiff as board right now."

The guard got on his walkie-talkie and relayed the message about Tobias to his superiors. Days later, the medical examiner determined the cause of death was asphyxiation apparently caused by Tobias swallowing his own tongue. But there were several things about the death that he could not explain. The first was the appearance of a bruise around Tobias' neck, which appeared to be caused by a rope; yet, no rope or anything resembling a rope was found anywhere in the room.

And the second, even stranger phenomenon was what the examiner found when he pried open Tobias' hands breaking his rigor. In the palm of the left hand was burned the letter "T" and in the right hand the letter "M".

BREATHE

The claustrophobic sensation of suffocation was more than Ron could stand. Someone had gagged him and although his nose was clear, he still couldn't seem to get enough air. Ron could see nothing; he was in a world of complete blackness. He was certain he was going to die the agonizingly slow death of oxygen deprivation. This had been his life-long fear. He didn't know who had done this to him or why, but one thing he did know was if he didn't find some way out of this situation he would likely go insane long before he finally did die. Although he technically might be able to get enough oxygen through his nose to keep himself alive, it would do nothing to satisfy his need for a deep cleansing lung full of air. He could do nothing to keep his ever-increasing panic attack at bay.

Ron needed to breathe. He had to find some way to get free so he could breathe; all he needed was to breathe. His hands and feet were bound so he tried wiggling his mouth to try to loosen the bandana holding the gag in place but to no avail. The more he struggled, the more air he seemed to need and the more he realized how little air he was actually getting. It was maddening. His panic was rising. He could no longer think rationally. He was drenched in an icy sweat and could smell the stench of his own rising fear. He knew in just a few more seconds if he didn't get free, he would go completely insane. He struggled uselessly as his air supply seemed to dwindle further.

Then he suddenly awoke to darkness. He felt the comfort of a pillow under his head and knew it had all been a horrible dream. He was at home in his bed and it must have all been a horrible nightmare. Ron really did have sinus issues as well as chronic lung issues and was a mouth-breather. He could never seem to get enough air, especially during allergy season, even when he used his Albuterol inhaler. As a result, he was also extremely claustrophobic and some of his worst nightmares revolved around his not being able to get enough air. Thank God, this one was finally over.

Unconsciously, Ron reached up to verify his mouth was clear of any obstructions even though he understood he had been dreaming. However, when he did, his knuckles scrapped along some sort of rough wooden surface just a few inches away from his face and then the horrifying reality came rushing back to him. It was strange how his mind tricked him. Maybe insanity was better. Because he now remembered, he was not resting comfortably in his bed. Someone had buried him alive.

TOOLS OF THE TRADE

The knife shimmered in the glow of the candlelight, its blade honed to a razor sharp edge. Its scrimshawed ivory handle was amazingly detailed with scenes from the original owner's homeland. Angelo Morelia had no idea where that particular homeland was, nor did he care. He had removed the blade from the cooling dead hand of one of his victims. A chinaman was how Angelo thought of the man although in reality he had no idea where the man had originated. He was obviously some sort of Asian. Angelo didn't consider himself either a racist or a bigot. He liked to think of himself as an equal opportunity businessman.

At that time the only thing he knew or cared about was that someone needed the man to be killed, and his doing so netted him a healthy bundle of cash and a nice unsuspected memento to boot. And this knife was no longer just a keepsake from a conquest. It had found its way into his personal arsenal of weapons: his tools of the trade.

And that trade was murder for hire. On the streets he would have been called a hit man, but Angelo preferred to think of himself as the ultimate problem solver. If someone had a nuisance that they needed to have eliminated they simply contacted Angelo through one of his many non-traceable avenues of communication and the negotiations would begin. Once the deal was set he received half of his payment up front and the remainder when the job was finished.

Angelo rewrapped the knife back in a fine cloth and placed it into its appropriate drawer in his special toolbox. It was a heavy-duty mechanics style metal box on wheels with multiple drawers as well as a few cabinets. It came with a combination lock so that only Angelo could access the contents inside. This wasn't to suggest that the combination couldn't be deciphered or that some determined person might not be able to force his way in. But that was not of immediate concern to Angelo since the purpose of the lock was simply to serve as a deterrent for people who had no business looking into his private business, people such as his wife or teenage daughter.

To the casual observer Angelo Morelia was just another suburbanite living his life day to day and struggling to give his family all the things they felt they needed in this overly materialistic world. His subdivision was a bedroom community where people usually only saw one another on occasions, perhaps giving a friendly wave on the way to work, maybe out doing yard work in the summer or shoveling snow in the winter. For the most part, everyone minded their own business and basically kept to themselves, which was perfect for Angelo's needs.

Most of his neighbors knew almost nothing about Angelo, other than he was some sort of independent consultant. He and his family didn't live above their means and by design he did all he could to appear to just be another neighbor doing what he could to support his family.

Angelo pulled open the bottom drawer and withdrew a long filament of wire with hand grippers on both ends. He gave a slight smile of pleasure remembering how well this tool had served him in the past. How many times had he used that little gem? Two times? Three? Funny, but he couldn't recall. But he could remember the sight of his victims' bulging eyes as the garrote did its job of snuffing out their lives.

Perhaps, he thought, if he were lucky he might get to use it again someday soon. But he knew it wouldn't be tonight. For this assignment he would be using something more basic and something that he felt was quite mundane. But the customer was paying good money for this job and as such was always right.

His latest project was to eliminate a certain head accountant for an unnamed import/export business. He knew the accountant's name, Bradford Glickman and that the unidentified owner of the undisclosed business wanted him dead. Apparently the owner had discovered Mr. Glickman had been skimming money from him for many years and had transferred the funds into an off-shore account.

Unbeknownst to the felonious Mr. Glickman, his employer had not only managed to locate the funds but had also cleaned out the accounts, transferring the money back to his own bank. And this not only included everything Bradford Glickman had stolen from him but everything in the accounts. After all, the soon to be deceased Mr. Glickman would very shortly no longer have any need for the money anyway.

The reason Angelo felt the assignment was to be somewhat unexciting was because the accountant's boss had requested that Mr. Glickman be shot once right between the eyes at close range: simple direct and to the point. Angelo had offered some other creative alternatives, but the customer insisted on short and sweet. Angelo assumed Glickman's boss was also a boring accountant and he had reluctantly agreed, understanding that sometimes a job was just a job. There would most certainly be plenty of other opportunities to express his murderous creativity at a later date. For twenty-five thousand dollars in cash, he could play it as straight as Glickman's boss wanted.

Angelo could have easily done a bit of digging and found out where Glickman had worked and maybe even discovered the name of the man who was hiring him, but that wasn't how Angelo worked. He earned his living through death and discretion. He found new clients by personal reference and word of mouth. He simply couldn't afford to be too curious. Just do the deed, collect the money and disappear was his motto.

Besides, his daughter Amy was in her junior year at a private high school and was starting to look at several Ivy League colleges. That all cost a lot of money, so just like every other nine to five working stiff, sometimes Angelo had to do what was required, rather than what he might want to do.

He opened one of the deep drawers and removed a Smith and Wesson Model 986 nine-millimeter revolver. It held seven shots, which would be six more than he would need for tonight's job, but he had been looking forward to trying it out. He also had a homemade silencer, which he could mount to the front to keep the noise down. It was too bad the gun would have to disappear when he was finished. He hated when he had to give up one of his tools. He tucked the gun into his jeans at the small of his back, pulled his jacket down over it, placed the silencer in his jacket pocket and headed out to his car.

When Angelo arrived at the quiet luxurious suburban colonial, which he was told was the home of Bradford Glickman the sun had set and darkness had fallen. Angelo had also been informed that Glickman's wife and two children were out of town for the weekend, so he would not have to deal with the potential problems associated with family members and collateral damage.

As was his method Angelo went around to the back of the property and found a basement window, which he expertly opened, dropping inside and landing quietly on the cement floor. He was dressed entirely in black and wore a fake beard and mustache, as well as a ball cap to disguise himself in the event of outside security cameras at either this or other homes. He had parked his car several blocks away and had made his way to the property on foot without being seen.

Carefully working through the cluttered cellar, Angelo tiptoed quietly up the wooden open staircase, being cautious to keep his feet over top of the stair joists to reduce the possibility of loud squeaks. With a skill honed by years of practice, Angelo made it stealthily to the top of the stairs and slowly opened the cellar door, which led to a darkened kitchen.

As soon as Angelo began to walk across the kitchen the hair on the back of his neck began to stand on end. Something, he didn't know what, was very wrong. There was a scent in the air, coppery, metallic. It was quite strong and for a moment Angelo thought he could actually taste it in the form of microscopic particles floating through the air. He recognized that smell; it was impossible not to be in his profession and not recognize the scent of blood, and lots of it.

From what Angelo could tell in the light streaming into the kitchen from the adjacent living room, the kitchen was free of any traces of blood. That meant whatever he now smelled had likely taken place in the living room. Angelo pulled out his nine, screwed on the sound suppressor and held the gripper comfortably in his hand with his finger near the trigger and at the ready. He turned and carefully looked into the lighted living room, not sure of what he would find or if he even wanted to know what awaited. His primal instincts were telling him to turn around and leave immediately, but he had made a deal for twenty-five large and he couldn't leave until he was certain what had happened.

What Angelo saw when he turned the corner was unlike anything he had ever witnessed in his entire life. And considering he had earned a profitable living murdering people, he had seen quite a bit. But nothing prepared him for the vision spread out before his unsuspecting eyes. The only phrase that came to mind to adequately describe the carnage in that living room was "charnel house." In the matter of a few seconds, Angelo took in the entire unbelievably gory sight.

It seemed no matter where Angelo looked in the blood splattered living room he found body parts: a hand here a leg there. Arms, fingers and strips of shredded flesh seemed to be draped over every solid surface in the room. Some dangled from the chandelier while others were draped over lampshades. The tan carpeted floor was saturated with gore and the ceiling, walls and drapes were splattered with crimson droplets.

And in the middle of the room in front of the sofa Angelo saw one of the most horrid tableaus he could have ever imagined. Lined up in a neat sickening row were four severed heads: a man, a woman and even worse, two young children—a boy and a girl. Glickman's and his entire family had been torn to pieces. But Angelo had been told his family wasn't even supposed to be here tonight. Angelo couldn't begin to imagine what had happened to them.

Most people would have felt sympathy for the murdered family, but that was not Angelo's way. After all, bringing death was how he earned his living. Then he suddenly remembered his own reason for being here. He was supposed to kill Glickman and it was to be neat and tidy. This house of horrors was anything but. Then suddenly Angelo became furious. He had just realized he was now out twenty-five grand. Whoever had done this had cost him a lot of money. And Angelo would use all of his resources to find out who had shafted him and they would pay. Oh yes, Angelo would use all of his murderous creativity on them when he found out who the perpetrators were.

Angelo decided it was time to get out of this horrific place, but as he started to back out of the living room he saw something move very quickly out of the corner of his eye off to the right. But when he turned to look with his gun raised and at the ready there was no one there. At the time he thought he saw the movement he had also heard a slight swishing sound like a quick breeze. The hairs on the back of his neck were now standing tall as an icy chill raced down his spine. He was back on full alert now. Then he thought he saw movement off to this left and once again heard the same swishing sound. What the hell was going on?

Angelo quickly turned his head to the left but once again saw nothing. Yet he had been certain he had seen movement just a millisecond earlier. He stood motionless, his eyes and ears searching for any sign of activity. But there was none. Once again he began to slowly back out of the room when he saw a slight motion coming from a shadowed corner across the room. Angelo raised his gun and pointed it directly at the corner shouting, "Whoever you are you had better come out here where I can see you or I'm gonna start shooting."

At first there was no response. Then after a few interminable seconds Angelo saw someone walking slowly into the light. He didn't know what he was expecting to find, but it was most certainly not what now made its way out of the darkness.

It was a woman—apparently a beautiful, mysterious looking woman wearing a semitransparent evening gown. Angelo assumed at one time the gown had been white but now the thing was old, worn and yellowed—at least in those places that were not splattered with gore. The woman had long, flowing black hair and even from his distance, he could see she had dark, yet glowing enchanting eyes.

She stood completely still, her arms hanging limply by her sides. Her lips were blood red, which seemed even more accentuated by her milky pale skin. She looked to Angelo like some sort of specter, something unearthly. Then he realized how such a thought, although appearing real enough was nothing more than his imagination obviously brought on by the scene of horror that was spread about the room between himself and the strange woman.

Then Angelo wondered if this woman might too be a victim, a survivor of this holocaust. Maybe she had somehow miraculously not been slaughtered in the carnage. Perhaps she had been a houseguest who had been sleeping at the time of the murders and awoke to find the massacre. He didn't know and if he were to be perfectly honest it really didn't matter.

Unfortunately for the young woman, she had seen Angelo and that alone meant he would have to silence her permanently. Like it or not she had become collateral damage. This thought troubled Angelo, not because he would have to kill the woman, but because he knew he might have to do so in the same fashion as whoever had slaughtered Glickman and his family. He would have to make it look like she was just another victim of the same maniac. And he had no idea how he might pull that off.

Despite his profession Angelo had never committed such a brutally heinous act in his entire life. In addition he didn't have the tools with him necessary to duplicate the crime. In fact, he wasn't even certain his toolbox arsenal contained any tools capable of creating such mayhem. He decided to delay the inevitable for a few moments with the hope of possibly coming up with a more palatable alternative.

"Who are you?" Angelo asked the young woman. "What happened here? Who did this?" He waved his arm gesturing at the carnage before him. "Who killed these people? And why did they let you live?"

The woman just stood staring at Angelo not saying a word. He began to wonder if perhaps she was in shock.

Then Angelo had an idea. He decided in her present condition the woman might be willing to go with him. She seemed almost catatonic enough to simply be led wherever he chose to take her. The two of them could slip out the back door and walk down the street in the darkness to his car.

Once there he could drive her to a remote location, maybe a place near a lake where he would strip her naked and put a bullet in her head. He smiled when he realized he might have to rape her first to make it look like she was the victim of a sexual assault gone wrong. Angelo liked that idea, especially seeing that flimsy see-through outfit.

"Look," Angelo said. "I need you to come with me. We have to get out of here. I want to take you... to get help. I'll drive you to the police station. This place... well... we just can't stay here." Angelo hoped his sympathetic voice would be convincing enough to get her to go with him with as little resistance as possible.

Again she didn't respond nor did her expression change in any way. She simply stood silently across the gruesome expanse of blood and dismemberment, staring at him. For a brief moment of frustration, Angelo considered putting a bullet in her from where he stood and not worrying about whether or not her death was obviously different from that of the Glickman family. He knew both his bullets and gun were untraceable. The cops would rack their brains trying to figure out what had happened, but that wasn't his problem. In fact, now that he had given the idea some thought he found it quite amusing. He could imagine the local keystone cops stumbling about foolishly. The idea was starting to grow on him. "Why not?" Angelo thought to himself.

He raised his gun and pointed it directly at the silent woman. Then without another word or thought he pulled the trigger. He heard the almost inaudible sound of the silencer as the bullet flew across the room. He heard it strike the wall but impossibly the woman was suddenly gone. How could that be? Angelo had been looking right at the strange woman a second earlier and now she had somehow mysteriously vanished.

Angelo looked around the room but couldn't find a trace of her anywhere. He took a cautious step backward then stopped as he heard something behind him. It sounded like deep heavy breathing accompanied by a slight trace of a moan or perhaps even a growl. He quickly spun around to find himself staring into the black glowing eyes of the woman who was now standing just a foot or so in front of him.

How was such a thing even possible? He had just shot at her a few seconds earlier from a distance of about twenty-five feet. How could she have not only dodged his bullet but gotten across the room and behind him so quickly? It wasn't humanly possible. "Not humanly possible," he thought again.

His gun was still in his hand and was now pointed directly at the woman. All he had to do was squeeze the trigger. But he realized he couldn't pull the trigger. In fact, Angelo realized he couldn't move at all. The woman's bizarre hypnotic stare had somehow paralyzed him. He tried to break his eyes free from her gaze but he was helpless to do so.

Then he noticed something. For the first time the woman's expression began to change. She acquired a look of satisfaction or perhaps even joy. He realized she was aware she had him right where she wanted him. And he also noticed the woman was not nearly as beautiful as she had appeared to be from across the room. Her eerie black eyes were rimmed in red and the flesh hung around them with brown sagging circles. Her breasts now clearly visible through the translucent gown hung limply downward and the pallor of her skin was more of a dusky gray than the milky white he had originally assumed.

Then all at once everything seemed to make a senseless sort of sense. Angelo suddenly knew this woman-like creature had not been a surviving victim at all, but somehow she had been the one responsible for the bloody massacre. She had slaughtered Glickman and his family. But how could she have done it? She had no weapons, no tools.

Angelo tried to move his right index finger. All he needed was enough motion to generate a slight pressure on the trigger and he would splatter this crazy broad's guts all over the kitchen table behind her. But no matter how hard he willed his finger to move it wouldn't budge.

The woman, never taking her eyes from his lifted her right hand high enough for Angelo to see it peripherally. The hand was thin, gray and wrinkled with exceptionally long fingers, longer than he had ever seen before. As Angelo looked on helplessly, the fingernails on each finger began to slowly grow, to sprout upward reaching an impossible length of more than three inches. They were a dark yellow color and reflected the light filtering in from the living room.

Angelo could see the nails appeared to be razor sharp. Then the hand seemed to twitch almost imperceptibly, and Angelo felt a searing pain in his right wrist, which was followed by a metallic clunk as his gun fell to the floor with a thud. Then in an instant of clarity, Angelo realized his right hand had accompanied the gun to the carpeted floor.

In agony, which he was helpless to express, Angelo looked into the now maniacal glowing black and red eyes of the woman and saw a smile appear on her face for the first time. It was a large hungry smile that exposed all of her large yellowed animal-like teeth, especially the two oversized canines, which were stained with crimson gore. It was at that moment Angelo understood everything. Those deadly teeth and razor sharp claws were the tools of this creature's trade. And that trade was savage slaughter, dismemberment and likely consumption of human beings.

Angelo watched powerlessly as her clawed hands rose slowly toward him, wrapping tightly around his throat. The very last thing he felt was his spine shattering as the creature gouged his neck and then twisted his head from his body.

The next day the police investigators arrived at the scene. They had been called by a neighbor, who had suspected something was not right at the Glickman house, and had peeked in the living room window seeing the bloodbath. The police had managed to identify all of the victims including Angelo, but neither they nor Angelo's wife would ever understand what had happened to them or what Angelo had been doing on the scene.

ZOMBIE PARTY

"I have a great idea, Cathy," Steve said.

Cathy waited with less than enthusiastic anticipation. Her husband always had ideas—loads of ideas, often more than she could handle and most of them tended to be far less than "great". In fact, she often thought of herself as the sanity filter in their marriage. She was the one who prevented many of Steve's "really great" ideas from ever coming to fruition. She understood if Steve and his wild imagination remained unchecked, God only knew what embarrassment or damage he might unintentionally inflict on himself or on her as well.

She braced herself for his suggestion. "What do you have in mind, dear?" She asked sweetly, all the while scrolling through her mental database of reasons why they wouldn't be able to do whatever crazy thing he was about to suggest.

"Well... You know how you wanted to have an unusual summer patio party this year?" he asked. "You said you wanted to do something different?"

"Here it comes," she thought, and then hesitantly replied, "Yes, I was looking to do something unique and different... but nothing too wild."

Steve was grinning, "Well. My idea is a little bit wild, but it's really cool too."

Cathy felt all of her muscles involuntarily tense up, getting ready for his suggestion. She loved her husband desperately, but sometimes his ideas could be too much for even her to tolerate. He was often like a little boy in a man's body.

"I was thinking..." Steve said cautiously, "Now don't say no right away... hear me out... I was thinking... maybe we could have a zombie-themed patio party."

"A what?" Cathy said immediately with perhaps more surprise in her voice than she had intended.

As Cathy stood staring at her husband, Steve was moving animatedly, as he always did when he was getting one of his inspirations. She knew the signs very well. His eyes tended to dart about and he seemed to be all arms and legs as he explained his ideas in a rapidly moving stream of conciseness.

Cathy understood how Steve's mind worked and was often envious of it. He would get a fundamental idea then he'd start talking. As he spoke, more of the idea would form and sometimes change and as it did, he continued to spout his ever-evolving ideas. His appearance was very much like an overly excited six-year-old, which was why Cathy had to take on the role of parent in order to try to keep his enthusiasm in check.

"A zombie party... listen... here's what I'm thinking." Steve said, "We could tell everyone to show up dressed as zombies... and, and... we could... we could serve Zombies, you know the cocktail... and our snacks and food could be prepared to look like... like body parts... you know... wow... this could be so cool!"

Steve was in full creative mode now and despite her better judgment, Cathy was actually beginning to like the idea. At first, she thought it might be something that worked better for Halloween and maybe not so much for mid-July. Then she remembered the popularity of the zombie craze for the past several years and knew no one else among their circle of friends had thought of doing this. So, why not be the first?

"I like it," Cathy said.

"But we could... What?" Steve replied, shocked. Cathy had never bought into one of his ideas right off the bat. He always had to try many different approaches to convince her. Then more often than not, the answer was an indefatigable no. "Did... did you say you liked it?"

"Yeah," She said. "I think I do. None of our friends have ever thought of doing anything like this before and zombies are pretty hot right now aren't they?"

"You bet," Steve said. "And I have so many great ideas."

Somehow, Cathy just knew he did.

***

The evening of the party, Cathy had struggle to keep Steve in control as he continued to come up with one creative last minute idea after another, many of which were way over the top—especially those involving food, drinks and snacks. She agreed with the ladyfinger cookies that looked like real fingers and she even bought into the Jello molded in the shape of brains. However, some of his ideas were just so gross no normal person would possibly be able to eat after seeing them.

For example, Steve owned a full-size latex zombie body in complete gory detail with the stomach removed, leaving an empty rubber cavity. His idea was to lay out the corpse on the serving table, line the cavity with plastic wrap and fill it with pulled pork or something equally revolting looking. There was something so disgusting about the idea of reaching down into the thing to get food that it actually made Cathy's stomach turn over. As a result, that idea, as well as many other equally as disgusting, went by the wayside.

Even up until the time the guests started arriving, Cathy had to reign in Steve's wild imagination. The turnout was a huge success with most of the fifty-some friends they invited showing up in various zombie costumes. Some of them simply wore torn shirts, pants and a little bit of greasepaint makeup but others were very detailed and quite impressive.

There was one character who arrived late who had a costume that both Cathy and Steve thought was worthy of a Hollywood film studio. It was incredible. She first saw him shambling into the back yard from around the side of their house, which was surrounded by woodlands. He dragged his right leg and his arms flopped about uncontrollably. His hair was greasy and unkempt, standing out in all different directions. The makeup on his face made him look as if he had been dead for weeks, especially the sunken cheeks and the eyes. He must have been wearing special contact lenses, because those eyes were filmed and gray. He also had some sort of dental appliance, which made him appear to have a mouth full of decayed, broken and missing choppers looking more like tombstones in an ancient burial ground than teeth.

Cathy couldn't believe the extent he went to for realism. Apparently, he had found some awful foul-smelling substance to smear on himself because he absolutely reeked. All in all the effect was very convincing. As he shambled into the yard, the crowds spread and avoided him and his awful odor as he growled and waved his arms spastically, playing the role for all he was worth.

Cathy was trying to figure out which of their friends he might be, but the makeup job was too good for her to tell. As if this wasn't enough for an award winning and convincing performance, Cathy realized he must have worked a plan out with one of the other guests, Bob Daley to act out a role-play of sorts.

The man shambled up to the bar where Bob was acting as bartender, busy making cocktails for the guests waiting in line. Every one of them cleared out of the way when the foul-smelling character approached.

Bob said jovially, "I can make you anything you want, but I'd most definitely recommend the Zombie—especially in your case." Then he threw back his head and let loose with a loud laugh.

That was when the unusual guest shuffled around the side of the bar and pulled Bob out to the front. Bob was doing a great job of playing the role of victim. He shouted curses at first and then pretended to try to punch the would-be zombie and pry the man's hands away from him, but to no avail. Bob stumbled to the ground. The crowd of partygoers was starting to watch and enjoy the show. Then the pair did something that was truly an amazing work of special effects choreography.

The one playing the zombie fell upon Bob, and tore open his already tattered shirt and appeared to dig his claw like fingers deep inside the flesh of Bob's stomach. The crowd was at the same time disgusted and astonished by the spectacle. Steve was watching intently and couldn't figure out how the pair had pulled it off. He assumed Bob must have been wearing some sort of prosthetic belly, which he had filled with red gelatin, fake blood and what looked like old sausage casings. The result was absolutely awesome.

The zombie attacker yanked out several feet of the simulated intestines as the fake blood and gelatin flew in every direction raining crimson down on Steve's plush green lawn. The monster brought the revolting looking material up to his lips and began chomping down on the stuff. All the while Bob was screaming in pretend agony and the crowd was going wild applauding, shouting cheers and taunts of encouragement for the incredible show.

Then suddenly Bob went silent, obviously pretending to be dead. The other character continued to pretend to eat Bob. After a time the onlookers must have assumed the show had run its course because they lost interest and returned to their chatting, eating and drinking. All the while, the zombie stayed in character simulating tearing apart the remains of Bob Dailey's lower body.

Finally, one guest who was ready for another drink walked up to the pair still on the ground and said, "OK guys. Fun is fun, but I'm parched and ready for another Zombie. How's about it Bob old boy?" Bob was sprawled on his back on the lawn surrounded by gore while the zombie remained bent over Bob's body eating his supposed insides. Neither of them gave any indication of hearing the guest, which frustrated him to no end.

He tapped the zombie character on the back perhaps a bit harder than he should have and said "Hey! Look Pal. I need a drink. Don't you think you and your buddy Bob have taken this gag far enough?"

With that, the zombie turned and buried his face in the crotch of the man's pants as the guest let out a gut-wrench howl, pounding his fists against the creature's head. The monster tore his head away and brought with it the front of the guest's pants along with his genitals as blood pumped from the gaping wound. In the grass, Bob began to stir slightly and soon he rolled over and began dragging his torso across the grass toward the same screaming guest. The entire lower half of Bob's body was gone, yet he was still moving.

No one cheered. No one shouted. Everyone stood in shocked silence staring at the unimaginable scene playing out before their unbelieving eyes. Then the howling guest went silent, fell to the ground and moments later began to arise once again to join the other two former humans, now flesh-craving zombies. In the distance, dozens more of the horrid creatures walked out from the surrounding woods. That was when the real screaming began.

AND THE SCALES FELL FROM MY EYES

A NOVELLA

*And straightway there fell from his eyes as it were
scales, and he received his sight; and he arose and
was baptized.* – Acts 9:18

*Therefore thus says the LORD, "Behold I am bringing
disaster on them which they will not be able to
escape; though they will cry to Me, yet I will not
listen to them."* – Jeremiah 11:11

*For He knows false men, And He sees iniquity
without investigating.* – Job 11:11

*So Moses said to the LORD, "Why have You been so
hard on Your servant? And why have I not found
favor in Your sight, that You have laid the burden of
all this people on me?* – Numbers 11:11

INTRODUCTION

I might as well get all of this out of the way right from
the very beginning. I am not crazy, no matter what you
might hear or no matter what you might think after
reading this account. I swear to you on a stack of bibles for
whatever that's worth, I'm as sane as the next guy, hell,
probably even more so. Also, I need to make something else

clear from the get-go; I'm not going to tell you my name. It's really not all that important to my story and my anonymity will allow me to be completely honest with you about... well, about everything. And, if I were to tell you my name chances are very good you'd recognize it and that might immediately prejudice you—so let's keep my identity a secret.

Another important bit if information. I decided to write this story through the co-writing services of another author I found. To be perfectly honest, I keep forgetting his entire name. I know his name is Anthony something or other. His surname is much too hard for me to recall. It always eludes me no matter how many times I hear it. I believe the name is something of Italian extraction. It probably starts with a D followed by an apostrophe as so many of them do; then it likely ends in a vowel, probably an "A" or an "O". But this is all of little consequence and honestly I really don't care if he is offended by that remark or not.

After all, the man is being handsomely paid to write whatever I tell him to write. He's has also signed a very strict non-disclosure contract forbidding him to ever reveal my identity under threat of severe legal and financial penalties. Besides, he's basically nobody in the literary world anyway. No one has any idea whatsoever who he is, especially when compared to my level of fame. Come to think of it, this little project might be exactly what his mediocre, floundering writing career needs, a stepping stone of sorts perhaps to some much needed recognition.

As I mentioned, I'm quite famous—at least my name is. Although, through a lot of hard work and due diligence on my part, I've managed to keep my face out of the public eye. I decided early on in my writing career that my life need not be the stuff of tabloid journalism. Unlike so many people in this world who crave notoriety I have no desire to see my face on TV or in grocery store magazines. In other words I'm no media whore.

Come to think of it, I'll have to be a bit careful as I embark on this narrative project; if I expose too much about my work an overly curious and resourceful reader might find some way to guess my true identity. I promise you I'm not saying this out of braggadocio or bluster, it's simply a fact. I suppose I'll have to rely on the skills of Mr. D'... whatever his name is... to help keep this knowledge from leaking out.

Allow me to preface this by saying co-writing this work is all very new and difficult for me. For starters, I don't generally play well with others. Also if you knew my name your first question might be how could the act of co-writing be such a challenge for someone who is a world-renowned thriller fiction author? Writing is what he does for a living. Isn't that what defines him? So why would he have so much indecision about the simple act of writing?

Oh dear. I suppose I may have just inadvertently given away a little bit about myself. I've just indicated that I'm a male with the use of the word "he" and I mentioned that I'm a well-known thriller writer. Well I suppose that information might be necessary anyway in order for me to tell you the rest of my story. And besides, I know there are hundreds of famous thriller writers out there. So I'm still fairly confident you won't be able to determine which one of the many I am. I'll have to make sure to tell my co-writer Anthony that it's OK to leave this portion of my story in place.

That being said, besides the fact that I have to work to protect my identity from you there are several other reasons for my discomfort in penning this tome. The most obvious is this type of writing is somewhat out of my element. Although this work will in essence be something of a thriller—actually a work of perhaps science fiction based horror—it's really not a work of fiction at all.

Take a moment to think about what I just said. This is a work of horror, yet not a work of fiction. As I'm sure you are well aware there's plenty of horror in our world and it doesn't always come in the forms of television, movies or literature. Sometimes it's just present in our everyday lives. And in this particular case the horror I'll speak about revolves around my own personal experiences. And I repeat; everything I tell you in this account will be completely true.

Secondly, when I do write I generally do so in a third person narrative style as oppose to the first person style, which we've chosen to use in this work. Although I find it a bit clunky, after a good deal of thought and discussion I reluctantly agreed with my cowriter that the first person accounting would be the best choice for this sort of story. I'll be the first to admit I'm not very comfortable with it. And although I know it's a major no-no to ask readers for forgiveness, especially in advance, I'm going to do so. You see, I'm a bit out of my element here as I'm sure my co-writer Anthony may be as well. He too usually writes in the third person. But hopefully between the two of us we'll manage to make this work and can produce a good and accurate record of my story.

Thirdly, the reason this is all so difficult for me is because it involves creatures—beings who many consider imaginary, but whom I've learned are very real. They've been spoken about by creative people since the beginning of recorded history, but as you'll soon learn, they aren't always the benevolent beings we've been led be believe they are. But I suppose that's enough about that for now. There'll be plenty of opportunity to discuss this further as my story unfolds.

Finally and perhaps most importantly, I have a genuine concern that upon completion of reading my story some people, perhaps most will assume I have gone completely stark-raving mad. And although there are times when I might even question my own sanity, I'm fairly confident I'm still of very sound mind and body as the expression goes.

If fact, I actually wish I were crazy; it might make everything I have to tell you that much easier. You see, it's the sanity of it all that's driving me crazy. I can just imagine coauthor Anthony's reaction when he reads that particular line. Regardless, with your approval please allow me to begin my tale. It's something of a long one and one that may at times annoy those readers who prefer a more fast-paced approach to story-telling, but I assure you, your patience will be rewarded.

1

As I inadvertently mentioned earlier I'm a bestselling author of thrillers. My numerous books are sold worldwide in print as well as digital and audio formats. They've been translated into a dozen languages for foreign distribution. A good number of them have been adapted to screen plays and have become major motion pictures. Royalties from all of these various forms of entertainment have made me a very wealthy man and more importantly, they've provided the financial security I need in order to continue to produce additional creative works.

This wealth aspect of my success is probably the part for which I am most grateful. The reason for this gratitude is because for most of my life I've struggled with finding adequate time to write. I've always enjoyed the act of putting words to paper and essentially creating something from nothing, but finding the time to do so was a constant challenge. Like most part-time writers I was forced in those early days to rely on the income from a variety of day-jobs, which I detested, in order to help support what I thought of as my true calling but what most people preferred to think of as my hobby.

In those days, trying to find someone, anyone to publish my work was incredibly difficult. No, let me rephrase that; it was downright impossible. The truth is there was a time when I couldn't find a single publisher to print my work. So as a result, I had collected a stack of rejection letters probably taller than the five-story tenement building where I used to rent a one-bedroom fleabag apartment. But at that time in my life, fleabag was the best I could afford. I should point out that, although I was not yet published, I had received a few offers from some obscure publications and magazines to print my work. However, the money being offered was either insulting or nonexistent.

I had read numerous articles by well-known authors who touted the importance of getting one's name out in front of the public for brand recognition purposes. That concept might be acceptable for a writer of shall we say average or below average skills, but I vowed to die with a house full of unpublished manuscripts before I would allow myself to give my works away for nothing. And as a result the only piles that were taller than my stacks of rejection slips were the heaps of aforementioned unpublished manuscripts.

I always envisioned these works someday being discovered maybe many years after I was dead and gone. And in my fantasy I imagined myself being posthumously recognized as the greatest thriller writer of all time. But back then I was forced to remain a great unknown.

I would consider using the cliché that I was so unknown I couldn't even get arrested, but sadly that expression would only hold true if you were to disregard that time when I actually did get arrested. It was an incident when I found myself handcuffed in the local police station after drunkenly smashing a beer bottle over the head of some loser who made a less than desirable comment about my writing abilities. Papa Hemmingway would have been proud of me that day.

The episode occurred at a get-together at a local bar following a meeting of our local writer's club. I'm not known for having a short fuse, but I had to admit I was more than a bit under the influence that night. And to be perfectly honest, the comment that character made was actually quite rude. Fortunately for me the man opted to drop the charges after encouragement from other club members, but my "permanent record" remains sullied to this day by that somewhat misguided yet justified offense.

It has often been suggested that I might have something of an attitude problem, a sense of superiority that, considering my past lack of journalistic success, was often thought of as unwarranted. But all I can say is I know and appreciate my own quality. But seriously, think about that for a moment. How difficult is it to appear superior to what we think of as the general public? If you look at what's out there walking among us, it doesn't take a rocket scientist to see that as a society, we've opted for quantity over quality. In my opinion, most of the people out there are barely human. All you need is a pulse to qualify as a member of the general public.

You might want to keep these opinions of mine in mind as you continue to read. Because the concepts of quantity over quality and what exactly constitutes humanity are paramount to what I've learned and to what truths I'll reveal to you later in this work. It explained a lot for me about why the world is the way is it is, and hopefully it will do the same for you.

2

I think the best way to start this tale is to tell you about something very strange, which began happening to me some time back around 2009 or 2010. This was back when I was still a great unknown, having not yet published my first work. At first, it all seemed innocent enough, something I just happened to notice occurring once in a while, nothing to get too upset about. Then it began happening more often, and then later on it began occurring much more often. That's when things started getting weird. And then a few months later it became such a regular occurrence that it began to annoy me and eventually even to concern me. Some of what I'm going to explain at this point may at first seem exciting but likely may start to become a bit mundane and perhaps for a while even a little bit boring. But trust me, all of it is essential in order for everyone to understand the path I had no choice but to follow and which has led me to where I am today: for better or worse.

What happened was this; I realized that for some unknown reason I had begun to I see the number 1111 appear in one form or another almost everywhere. For example, I might notice it on one of my many digital clocks, or my cell phone, or on a gas pump display or even from time to time on road signs or even on my automobile trip odometer. I was seeing 1111 virtually anywhere a numeric sequence might be seen. Then I started to notice other combinations of progressing or repeating numbers such as 1234, 4321, 2121, 1212, 1122 and other such groupings.

At first I simply blamed it on the fact that we now live in an age where numbers are displayed more prominently in digital format and more places than they have ever been before in history. So as a result I thought of it all as simply coincidental. For example, I might be driving in my car on my way home from work and I'd notice my digital clock reading 4:44. Or perhaps I'd wake up in the middle of the night and glance at my alarm clock and see it digitally displaying in bright red numbers 1:11. And sometimes while driving, I'd happen to look up and notice a mile marker along the highway and see it read 333.

There was also another strange phenomenon, which I began to notice in the very early morning or late at night. On occasions when I either drove or walked by certain streetlights they would go out. After I passed they would come on again. It seemed to always be a one-time occurrence. I couldn't get them to repeat the action no matter how many times I tried. And it wasn't always the same streetlights. It was all very unusual and when I combined that with the repeating numbers I was seeing, it was all becoming very bizarre for me. And I had an instinctual feeling that these two phenomena might somehow be related and tied to me for whatever reason.

Eventually the number sequences, as well as the dimming lights, began to occur more often; so much so that it started causing me great consternation. I couldn't understand why this was happening to me. It all seemed so unusual and maybe even a bit surrealistic. It was as if I was living in some sort of dream world. Deep in the pit of my stomach I knew there had to be some reason for this. I actually felt at times as if someone was trying to get my attention. But since that seemed ridiculous, like something out of one of my as yet unpublished novels or something a madman might suggest, I decided to keep those opinions to myself. After a while I eventually convinced myself this was all simply a matter of coincidence; the result of our new digital technology, and as such I did my best to ignore it.

But soon the sightings, which was how I thought of them, began happening even more often and had gone beyond the point of being a mere curiosity. It was very quickly becoming quite disturbing, perhaps even frightening for me. It seemed the more I tried to ignore this phenomena the more these numbers would appear. Then I began to wonder if maybe something really was wrong with me; you know, mentally. I'd never known anyone who had lost their mind before and there certainly was no history of insanity in my family, but surely the sort of things I was seeing were a far cry from normal.

Because the ever-increasing sightings were starting to work on my nerves I decided to do what any forward thinking individual in the twenty-first century would do; I searched the internet to see if anyone else was experiencing similar phenomena. I decided to take the broad-brush approach and simply search for the string "1111". I assumed if I got too many hits I could always fine-tune my search later. And to be perfectly honest, I really didn't expect to find much of anything.

Then to my surprise I was shocked to find over fifty-nine million hits from my simple string. OK. That was a surprise. It looked like my initial search had been way too general and I was going to have to narrow my description somewhat. But before I had a chance to type a different search string I saw a few links at the top of the listing, which seemed as though they might be exactly what I was looking for.

The first one I saw stated, "So you're seeing 11:11 everywhere. What does that mean?" Another included the word "guardians" while another spoke of "muses" and yet others mentioned some sort of beings called "lower angels."

After reviewing a few more of the hyperlink descriptions it became clear this was all heading in a direction that came dangerously close to what I thought of as "new age wacko philosophies". Needless to say I had absolutely no interest whatsoever in opening that particular can of worms, yet still I felt as though I needed to at least try to find an answer to my own digital dilemma.

After clicking on one of the links, I was astounded to learn that apparently a lot of people were apparently experiencing the same things I had been seeing. There was even a group that called themselves "The 11:11 Witnesses". They had their own web site as well as a blog and boasted over one hundred thousand worldwide members. It seemed as though thousands of other people were seeing the same kinds of things I had been seeing. Apparently this 11:11

stuff was still in its infancy and was on its way to becoming a sort of cult, maybe even a type of religion. I was intrigued to say the least.

At first I decided to read everything I could find on the web about it. However, I soon realized there was far more information available than I possibly had the time or desire to investigate. I needed to find a way to get more specific information: facts that related to my personal issues, not tons of generalized mumbo jumbo.

Then I thought it might be a good idea to reach out to a few of the most popular of these web sites to see what they might have to say to me on an individual level; you know, one-on-one. Using my writing skills, I devised a simple introductory note and using a special untraceable email address I sent the email to five or more of the top sites.

My initial email note read as follows: "*The number 1111 has been driving me crazy for the past year or so. It seems to be popping up everywhere. And lately it's actually starting to weird me out a bit. The same sort of thing is happening with other number combinations as well. I felt as if I was reaching the end of my rope when today I got the idea of searching the web for 1111. I was completely blown away by the number of sites I discovered that were dedicated to this subject. I had no idea that anyone else, let alone so many other people were experiencing this phenomenon. I still don't quite know what to make of it, but I'm glad to see I'm not alone. Is there anything you can tell me to help to put my mind at ease?*"

To my surprise, within a few minutes, the replies began to arrive. Apparently these new age disciples were very serious about spreading their gospel. Below is a segment of one of the first replies I received.

"*We certainly hope this information will be of great assistance to you. This will explain what we believe is the true meaning of what we call the 11:11 prompts which you have been seeing. Someone is definitely attempting to contact you. These beings that are sending you these visual prompts are what we like to refer to as guardians, muses and lesser angels.*"

"All righty then," I thought to myself, recalling those words from the link overview. And to think I was starting to wonder if maybe I was the crazy one. Needless to say, reading this wacky reply made me feel much better about my own state of mind, confused as it might have been. For one thing, it meant I was not alone in what I was seeing and at least I hadn't gone off the deep end about it as apparently these other weirdoes had.

Nevertheless I decided to read on. I figured, what could it hurt? The email continued, *"These beings are showing you the numbers to get your attention. They'll often vary the numbers to make you realize you're not just seeing random combinations, but in reality they're prompting you. You see, you're dealing with beings of an incredibly high level of intelligence; 'off the charts' as people say. These creatures also are indicating by singling you out that they want you to know they have important information they have to share with you. They are generally good beings and in some religions are thought of as gods."*

I thought again how this character actually believes that I and others were being contacted by some sort of God-like creatures who for some unknown reason have something very important to tell us and they apparently want me specifically to hear their story. I wondered at what point in the email I would be prompted to donate large sums of money, perhaps $1,111 to this new pew-jumping church of the holy guardians or whatever it might be called. But to my surprise and relief nowhere in the email was there any mention or request for a donation of any kind.

I closed this first email and opened another. It was very similar to the first even though it came from a completely different web site. At least I initially assumed these were all separate, individual web sites, but the more I thought about it the more I realized they could all just as easily be part of the same weirdo religion. This new writer explained how these "angels" were extremely loyal to humans and how they had been transformed into these celestial beings for the sole purpose of assisting us mere mortals in achieving a higher plane of spiritual existence.

He wrote, *"These creatures are all good beings. There are no longer any evil ones in existence. Some people, especially those of an enlightened mind will see this communication you are having as positive. While others of a narrower and less enlightened mind will fear their attempted intervention into our lives. But remember, we are entering the New Age. And the communication pathways to the higher spheres of enlightenment have largely been opened."*

It seemed the more I read, the less I understood what the hell all of this was about. Although part of me was glad to hear that if there were in fact, actually beings of some sort attempting to make contact with me, they were apparently benevolent in nature. Benevolence is generally good; hostility is usually not so good. According to this writer none of the bad creatures existed any longer. I found this somewhat odd since most religious people believe and think in terms of good and evil, Heaven and Hell and some form of God and the Devil. These 11:11 Witnesses seemed to think evil beings no longer existed. Obviously they had never walked along the same city streets late at night that I've walked. In my opinion, evil is alive and well.

I then decided to check out several other emails, which arrived during the next day or so. They were all very similar to these earlier ones.

One of them sounded surprisingly like they were paraphrasing FDR's inaugural address when they proclaimed, *"There is nothing to fear but fear itself."* They insisted, *"The Lucifer rebellion was finally put down during the mid-1980s, and Satan no longer exists."*

This verified what I originally had assumed. These new-agers believed there no longer was a Hell or Satan or any such concept. I thought the only important thing to die in the 1980s was disco.

Another email provided a list of things that I was supposedly able to do, now that I had become an enlightened individual. It explained:

"1. You are genetically capable of establishing two-way contact with the 11:11 beings if you choose to.

2. You are spiritually ready to be guided and to obtain information from these extremely intelligent beings whose IQ's are measured in the thousands."

Who measured these IQ's? It made me wonder. I imagined some celestial being taking an online Mensa exam or something. I chuckled to myself as I continued to read on.

"3. Whether you're aware of it or not, you are ascending in terms of spiritual growth.

4. The 11:11 beings will ask for something from you at some future time in exchange for the knowledge they provide to you."

This too made me stop and wonder for a moment. What sort of assistance might I be expected to render to these beings as compensation? I mean, I didn't ask for them to contact me and I certainly didn't ask for whatever knowledge they might choose to bestow upon me.

"5. It's even possible that a recently deceased member of your immediate family may have been the one who requested these beings contact you."

Again I had to wonder. Are they suggesting a dead relative's spirit was using the 11:11 beings to contact me? I didn't get the connection. I was thinking of these creatures as alive, perhaps extraterrestrials. But if that were the case, as strange as it may sound what, if anything did it have to do with the spirits of my dead relatives?

Then a thought suddenly came to me. My Uncle Wilbur, with whom I was very close, passed away a few months earlier and if what they were suggesting had any validity, perhaps Uncle Wilbur might have been the spirit who suggested the 11:11 beings contact me or maybe he might even be the actual entity trying to get my attention. Could that be possible? I decided it was more likely if these 11:11 beings actually were trying to contact me it was of their own volition and not as a favor to a dead uncle. But then again, that too seemed just as ridiculous.

"6. And, most importantly, your spirit guardians want you to get involved with these 11:11 beings. Your best opportunity to contact them would be through intense meditation."

Spirit guardians? Uncle Wilbur? Was any of this even worth considering? I wondered why I was allowing for such bizarre ideas to even be suggested. It was all so incredibly unbelievable.

I decided I had had enough for a while. I would have to think about everything I had read for a few days and see what, if any, other interesting emails would arrive to further "enlighten" me.

3

Several days later I received another note from one of the original e-mail responders. This time the guy was claiming to have actually seen some of these strange beings. He explained how, *"These creatures tend to be androgynous in appearance. They are a diverse collection of genderless individuals with numerous talents."*

OK. This was all starting to get a bit too bizarre. I mean, all of this talk of sexless angels and androgynous beings seemed to make no sense to me whatsoever. I mean honestly, why is it whenever anyone discusses seeing extraterrestrials or angelic beings the creatures they describe never seem to have any genitals? What the hell is that all about? Then on the other hand, why is it that paintings depicting demons, often show creatures with gigantic phalluses big enough to use for a jump rope? Seriously? In my opinion, this was all suddenly becoming a bit too cliché. In fact, the whole investigation was beginning to work on my nerves—almost as much as the digital sightings themselves.

I was becoming increasingly frustrated and I was just about to give up on the entire strange business when another email arrived that caught my attention and then suddenly things began to make a little more sense to me.

That message seemed to be less new-age-related and appeared to be at least somewhat more scientific in nature. It started out by saying, *"Numbers and numeric codes help us to define our very existence. Human DNA, which is often thought of as our genetic memory, is naturally encoded with the intent of being triggered by digital codes at specific times and frequencies. The purpose of these codes is to awaken the mind to a coming evolution of one's consciousness."*

"OK," I thought, "maybe not so wacky. So far, so good." I figured that maybe this guy was onto something, or was at least addressing the subject somewhat differently than the others had been doing.

"When you are seeing 11:11 it is one of those specific codes whose job it is to activate your DNA. You will also note that if you are seeing 11:11 often, it has a tendency to create synchronicities in your life."

I stopped reading for a moment and thought. "Synchronicities?" I had heard that word somewhere before, but wasn't really sure what it meant. I recalled how back in the 1980s the band "The Police" had released a recording of the same name. I planned on looking up the word after reading the email, but saw the author had already provided something of a definition for me.

"Synchronicities are nothing more than patterns that repeat in time. The concept of 'synchronicity' references the gears of time, although the actual existence of synchronicity cannot be scientifically proven. You can only experience synchronicities while they are occurring. The best you can do is to make note of them and then try to determine what you might have done to cause them to occur, with the hopes of triggering them again."

He explained, *"Synchronicities are people, places or events that your soul attracts like a magnet into your life in order to help you evolve into higher levels of consciousness. They also help to place additional emphasis on something going on in your life. The more you are 'consciously aware' of these synchronicities the more you become knowledgeable of how your soul is advancing in a positive way. Every day your life encounters meaningful coincidences, synchronicities that you have attracted. It's why you are here."*

Then the email further went on to clarify what these synchronicities might entail. It said, *"Here are a few examples of Synchronicity:*

"Let's say you're suffering with financial difficulties, yet somehow money for all your basic expenses such as rent, food, and utilities, always seems to become available. At

first when this happens you thank the universe or God for taking care of you. But then you realize it was you, yourself who actually created this good fortune.

"Here is another example of synchronicity. You've been out of work for quite some time and have been unable to find a job. You've just received your last check from the unemployment compensation bureau. You're worried sick about your future then suddenly a new job miraculously comes along.

"Or... you meet someone who you find interesting and who seems to touch your very soul. Then through the act of synchronicity you find that person coming into your life over and over again. You begin to develop a close friendship with that person.

"Another example is you feel depressed because you can't seem to find focus in your life. You feel like a rudderless ship adrift at sea. Then the next person you speak with inadvertently says something that suddenly points you in the right direction. These are all types of synchronicities."

I realized I could relate to quite a few of these synchronous events, as I'm sure many people might. I decided to pay closer attention to what this writer had to say.

He said, "Many believers consider seeing 11:11 to be a wake-up call. It can also be thought of as a key to unlocking the subconscious mind and accessing our genetic encoded memories. If you allow yourself to simply open up your mind, you will experience a sudden inner awakening after which your reality will never be the same. The thing is, once you open the door there's no closing it. There will be no going back. Once you see... you can never un-see."

This made me stop and think. That single statement about not being able to un-see what has been seen spoke volumes to me. It also made me a bit apprehensive as to whether or not I truly did want to become what they described and enlightened. Maybe ignorance truly was bliss. But I nonetheless read on.

"Your soul will quickly move you from one level of experience to another until you completely understand everything you are being shown. Also, because your

consciousness is expanding you'll learn faster and will experience greater comprehension. You'll become more aware of the meaning of various synchronicities and they will become more and more frequent. You will never reach the level of the 11:11 beings themselves but you'll quickly leave your fellow man eating your dust as you advance far beyond his mere mortal abilities.

I have to admit, this single paragraph really did intrigue me. I liked the idea of leaving my fellow man behind. I always felt I was intellectually superior to most of the people I met and I like the thought of taking what I considered my already greater intelligence to new levels of knowledge and awareness.

He wrote, *"Seeing these numbers will signal changes in the patterns of your life. You may also dream about the numbers or wake up at the exact same time every night with those same numbers displayed on your digital clock.*

This had already happened to me on many occasions. I would dream I saw a particular number on my digital alarm clock display. Then when I opened my eyes, the same number was right there is glowing red in front of me. This was incredible news! I thought about what this writer was telling me and to be honest, I was starting to warm up to some of what he was saying.

Now eager to learn more I read yet other emails that all had similar information as well as explanations. I won't bore you with the repetitive comments, as I'm sure you get the picture of what I was learning and where all of this might lead.

But then one email said something the others had not said so far. It read, *"Even if you go so far as to change the clocks in your car or house, it won't matter and you'll still see the numbers and continue to receive the prompts."*

"You can't stop it, because YOU aren't the one doing it. Once the 11:11 beings have gotten your attention, they'll be using other digital combinations to remind you of their presence. Even though you can't see them, they are there and they are very real."

And then he wrote something that really hit home for me. He said, *"Some people have also noticed street lights going out or on when they pass by. This is because the beings will use almost any electrically controlled device to try to get your attention.*"

"Wow!" I thought. That was exactly what had been happening to me. This was all starting to make real sense to me now.

Next he explained what I needed to do if I wanted to make contact with these mysterious beings. He said, "*When the 11:11 prompts appear to you, a direct channel opens up between you and these beings. When this happens, you should stop whatever you are doing and open up your mind to let them in.*"

Then he said, "*The revelations you receive may not come in the form of mental concepts or direct ideas. Rather, they could be an enhanced state of existence whereby you'll see everything as if with a pair of new all-seeing eyes. You'll have a deeper understanding of reality.*" A deeper understanding of reality? I wondered if this could possibly be true.

"*The appearance of 11:11 tells you it's time to take a good look around you and see what is real, and what might just be an illusion. You've been chosen, because you are ready to see. You can lead the way for others into a new way of living. The 11:11 is a pathway into the great unknown.*"

I believed I had learned at least enough to let me begin thinking seriously about what was going on with me and these so-called intelligent beings. The important thing was, although I might not have bought into everything these people were professing, I was no longer so bothered by what I had been seeing. Maybe it really was nothing to worry about. Maybe it was just all a coincidence and my fertile writer's imagination was simply getting the best of me for a while.

I decided to put it all out of my mind and give everything a chance to sink in and maybe stew for a bit. As such, I went on with my life as usual.

4

Regarding my 11:11 research, if I had understood what I had read in the emails, once a designated person received the signal, the numbers, all he had to do was open up his mind, clear out all of his thoughts and allow the message to be delivered. It apparently was that simple.

Because of my own misgivings about such an outlandish concept I continued to try to ignore the various prompts as much as possible. But it actually seemed like the more I tried to deny their existence, the more often these numbers would appear. It began to feel as if everywhere I looked the numbers were there. And try as I might I just couldn't get away from them. If there really was someone out there trying to get my attention, it was apparently working whether I wanted it to or not.

Finally one day while I was driving around and after having seen set after set of three and four-digit numbers I thought to myself, "What the hell; why not give it a try?" I mean what was the big deal anyway? Everything I read online said these beings weren't evil and they were supposed to exist for the sole purpose of helping humanity. If they were showing me these numbers to get my attention, why shouldn't I play along and see what this was all about? I was certain that just trying it one time wouldn't hurt anything.

Although I have to admit, even alone driving down the highway in my car, I felt extremely foolish when considering what I was about to do. Nevertheless I took a deep breath, let out a sigh and in the solitude of my car I said, "OK, whatever you are, angels, muses, guardians, here I am. I know you've got something you want to tell me.

So here's what I'm going to do. I'm going to open up my mind to you, just this once and just for a minute or so. I want you to show me whatever it is you seem to want me to see."

For a few moments there was nothing, no great epiphany, no miraculous transference of amazing knowledge, nothing. I remember how at the time I laughed to myself—at myself actually, feeling so completely foolish for having even tried such an idiotic experiment. I was grateful I had been alone in my car and no one else had heard me. If they had, they might have figured I'd finally lost it and they'd have likely called for the wacky wagon to haul me off to the funny farm. So then in a feeble attempt to take my mind away from the foolishness, I turned on the radio to listen to music. It helped to suppress my growing embarrassment.

After a few minutes I began to daydream and then out of nowhere the crux of an idea began to form in my mind. I recognized this as something I didn't want to ignore and I immediately turned off the radio so I wouldn't be distracted. Then before I had even realized what was happening the idea began to grow clearer. Within a few more minutes the idea took shape and I suddenly realized I had developed the complete concept for a novel: beginning, middle and end, everything. The whole thing came to me without a single bit of forethought, planning or even one iota of effort. And I instantly knew the idea was going to be a great one.

Over the course of the next several months I worked feverishly to convert this concept into written form and as cliché as it may sound, the resulting novel seemed to write itself. Then to my surprise and gratification the novel was picked up by a major publisher and not only became my first published work but became an international best seller as well.

It was all so incredibly crazy. In fact, it seemed completely impossible. But it was also very true. I had become an overnight sensation after years of constant rejection. My books seemed to fly off the shelves. The eBooks downloads were equally as impressive. Within no time at all I became well-known, well-respected author. Then the various movie deals began rolling in.

After that came my next best seller, then my next, and then the rest of them. Every single book I wrote became a blockbuster and the money just kept pouring in, faster than I could possibly hope to spend it. And every one of those winning ideas was the result of my watching for the digital alerts from whatever sort of mysterious muses were signaling me and then allowing them inside my head to plant their ideas.

Of course during my many interviews when I was inevitably asked what my inspiration was for that particular story I would humbly say I had no idea whatsoever and that the stories simply seemed to write themselves, which in essence was true. I honestly couldn't claim credit for any of the ideas. They weren't mine. They were given to me by whoever these strange unseen beings might have been. All I truly did was create a textual document detailing the ideas they provided me and the rest, as they say, was history. Granted, I did have to add my own special flair and writing style to each work. But that was to be expected. And strangely for dozens of years that exact same writing style brought me nothing but rejection. Now amazingly, I was making tons of money.

During the next several years I continued to watch for the signs, a clock, a road sign or billboard—anything with repeating triple and quadruple numbers. I also began to rely on these beings to help me make critical decisions in my personal life. If I was being offered a publishing contract or movie deal, one that sounded potentially lucrative, I would look around the meeting room for some digital device and see what it displayed. If it read, 11:11 or 12:34 or any of the previous strings that had brought good fortune I'd accept the deal. If not I wouldn't.

I knew the beings were watching out for me and guiding me to help me make the right choices. After all, that's how I managed to become so successful in my professional endeavors, so why not use the beings' great intellect and wisdom to help guide my personal life as well?

In my opinion it was the perfect win/win situation. I simply watched for the signs, opened my mind, listened to the voices in my head and wrote the stories as they were conveyed to me. Before long, I was world renowned for creating some of the best thriller fiction ever. And it was all because of these mysterious beings.

But then something changed. For some reason, they singled me out and chose me among all other humans to see something neither I, nor any other human being had the right to see. And this changed everything.

5

One day as I was driving back from a meeting with my publisher about yet another book and movie deal, I got a craving for something I hadn't had in a long time: a burger from a fast food joint. Any crummy fast food joint would do. I remembered a time when I survived on dollar menu cuisine, but since my success I had assumed I had put all of that garbage behind me. Lately I never ate anywhere but exclusive five-star restaurants. I could afford the best and I enjoyed the best. Yet here I was waxing nostalgic and craving a crappy burger. I figured why not? I can afford to do whatever I want so if I want a barf burger then so be it.

I pulled into the drive up line and ordered a double cheeseburger, large fries and a large Coke—no more dollar menu for me. Then I drove around to the first window to pay for my food. I looked up with my hand outstretched prepared to give the cashier my money, but what I saw almost caused me to drop the cash. The girl behind the window, which automatically slid open, was a young overweight thing, perhaps in her early twenties. She had large bulging brown eyes, a weak, almost nonexistent chin under which two other large masses of wobbling flesh merged to form what I assumed was supposed to be her neck.

Her nose was turned a bit upward with large round nostrils and I couldn't help but think to myself how much she resembled a toad. I mean, looking up at her from just a few feet away, the resemblance was astonishing. It made me wonder for a moment, at what point in the process of not taking care of ourselves or as they say, "letting ourselves go," do we actually stop being human, and was such a thing possible? I hesitated to think that way because I didn't want to come off sounding like some sort of Nazi with the whole sub-human concept. But being brutally honest, in terms of physical appearance alone, this girl hardly still qualified.

She turned to me and said in a rough voice, "That will be four dollars and seventy-nine cents sir." I was only half listening to her as I was still staring in amazement at the quivering mass of pseudo-reptilian throat flesh jiggling and dancing below her minimal chin. I was further surprised when the voice that came from her wide oversized mouth even sounded somewhat like the croaking of a frog.

I must have looked startled because she said, "Sorry about the voice, Sir. I have a mild case of laryngitis. It seems whenever I get a cold my voice is the first thing to go. I end up sounding like a toad." Then she chuckled deeply, which although I suppose the laugh was meant to put me at ease, it only served to increase my level of discomfort because of its frog-like quality.

Imagine how awkward I felt having this bizarre impression while simultaneously attempting to pay for my meal and appear like nothing was out of the ordinary. I smiled at her as politely as I could but I knew I simply couldn't stay there gawking at her any longer. I quickly handed her a ten dollar bill and told her to keep the change as I began to pull up to the pickup window.

As I did so I happened to glance into my left side mirror and was stunned to see the froggy-looking cashier was still watching me from her window giving me a strange wide-mouth reptilian grin. A moment later I was certain I must have been imagining things because there was no way I really could have seen what I actually thought I'd seen. A long tongue slithered from her mouth, flitted through the air, snatched a fly in mid-flight then snapped back inside along with its prize.

I slammed on my breaks just in time to avoid crashing into the rear of the car in line in front of me. I wondered what the hell was going on. Had I actually seen what I thought I had seen? Or was this all the result of my overactive writer's imagination? Surely it had to be a trick of the mid-day sun reflecting off of the window or something of that nature. No other explanation made any sense. There couldn't possibly be a frog woman working at this fast food restraint could there?

To say the event left me a bit shaken was most assuredly an understatement. But I soon learned this was just the beginning; there were many more unpleasant surprises to come. As I approached the pickup window I kept glancing every so often in my side mirror to see if the frog princess was still watching me. She must have retreated into her lair, likely to enjoy her flying morsel. Just the thought sent shivers down my spine and caused my stomach to lurch.

"Double cheese, large fries and large Coke?" a nasally voice asked from my left, calling down from the pickup window.

I looked up to see a tall, long-necked rail-thin young man with a beak-like nose holding a paper bag in one long-fingered hand and a paper cup in the other. His fingernails were what I considered far too long for a male to wear and they were painted black. To me they almost looked like the talons of a hawk. He had tiny, beady-looking eyes and his short spiky multi-colored hair stuck straight up around his head. Once again I found myself staring, mouth agape at the unusual individual standing before me. He looked exactly like a personified version of some species of bird.

It was all so strange. I shook my head to clear my thoughts and hopefully to make the horrible image go away. I looked at the dashboard and saw the digital clock, which read 11:01a.m. I knew exactly what that meant; it was a prompt. For some strange reason these beings wanted me to know something new. Not the plot for a book or a screenplay as they had been so generously giving me for years. No, I sensed whatever this was it would end up being something much bigger and much more important to these beings than mere fiction. I put my cup in the cup holder in my center console and placed the bag containing the burger and fries on the seat next to me. I opted not to look up at what I thought of as the bird boy again.

I suddenly realized two things. First, I was no longer in the least bit hungry and the second was that my hands were trembling, scarcely able to maintain a grip on the steering wheel. I decided it might be wise for me to pull into a parking space until I was able to regain my composure. I could smell the burger and fry scents permeating the inside of the car. I looked down at the food bag and it seemed to take all of my willpower not to open the bag and vomit inside. Instead, I held back my retch and put down all the windows while blasting the air-conditioned air straight at my face. I took several deep, relaxing breaths.

Behind me I heard strange grunting and what almost sounded like barking sounds and looked into my rear-view mirror to see a group of three teenage boys leaving the inside of the restaurant, dressed in low-slung baggy pants, sneakers, large baggy tee shirts and wide brimmed caps.

The boy in the middle was bigger than the other two in both height and girth. He seemed to look more like a gorilla to me than a human. I looked at his friend to his left and saw that he resembled a hyena with a huge nose and large, protruding teeth. His neck was long and his Adams apple bobbed up and down along its length. The fact that his face was adorned with patches and tufts of hair, an obvious attempt at a beard, did little to dissuade the hyena impression.

The third boy looked like some sort of lizard to me, having large bulging eyes similar to the cashier's and a sinister untrustworthy look of a predator about him. In fact, all three of the boys looked like a pack of wild predatory animals on the prowl. Then to my amazement, for a brief moment they ceased looking human at all and instead had become the very creatures I'd imagined them to resemble. An instant later, they reverted to their humanoid forms. The transition had been so brief I wasn't sure it actually had happened. I once again wondered what the hell was wrong with me. Had I actually seen that bizarre change or not? It all seemed like some sort of madness had befallen me. How could such a thing otherwise be possible?

I looked down at the clock on my dashboard and it now read 11:11a.m. Ten minutes had passed since I left the cashiers window. Suddenly I felt heat rising within my body and my flesh began to tingle. I had only ever passed out once in my life but it was a feeling I knew I would never forget. That feeling was suddenly encompassing me and there was nothing I could do to stop it as I felt the world around me fade to black.

6

I believe I had been unconscious for a time yet was somehow miraculously still aware. I began to feel as if I was leaving my body behind me and floating away. I briefly recalled accounts people had of near death experiences and wondered if perhaps I had experienced a sudden heart attack and maybe had even died. I looked down and saw my unconscious, hopefully not dead body in the car below me as I continued to float slowly upward.

Then I suddenly felt myself being pulled away from that spot at an unimaginable speed toward some unknown place far away. I assumed it had to be far away by the speed at which I was traveling. Everything around me was indistinguishable as landscapes flew by in a blur. What appeared to be billions of stars on a backdrop of blackness were shooting by me at incredible speeds, reminding me of a scene from an old Star Trek movie when the Starship Enterprise would jump to warp speed and zoom out into the blackness of the universe. Then I suddenly had an idea that perhaps I wasn't only being draw away in terms of distance but also in terms of space and yes, even time. Then that understanding became solidified and I knew I was somehow being transported back in time. I assumed the 11:11 beings were doing this for the purpose of showing me something I had never seen before. Perhaps it was something few if any human beings had ever seen.

Then just as abruptly as my journey had begun it ended. It seemed to take a few seconds for my brain to catch up with my body as I was momentarily disoriented. After a few moments I became aware once again of my surroundings and realized I was standing alone on a long sandy beach and it was nightfall. The air was thick with humidity and I looked down at my arms and could see the start of perspiration droplets forming on the surface of my flesh. There was a breeze coming in off of the ocean and when it touched the moisture on my arms it sent a slight chill throughout my body.

I could see the sun setting out over the wide expanse of an ocean. I wondered which ocean it might be. That depended on the time of day and whether or not I was still back east. Perhaps I was mistaken. If the sun was setting this would be the Pacific Ocean, but if the sun was rising it would be the Atlantic. And what if I had been transported to another location in the world? In that case it might not be either ocean.

I looked around smelling the salty scent of the water and hearing the distant high-pitched calling of ocean birds. The beach seemed to go on for miles to my left and right with not another soul anywhere in sight. It was as if I were the only human alive in the world. I later would discover there was something very prophetic about that particular thought.

I turned around and was startled to see a vast tropical forest spread out behind me traveling to both my left and my right along the beach for as far as I could see. Like the beach, the jungle seemed to go on for a great distance. Behind the dense barrier of jungle I could see large unfamiliar mountains rising high above the foliage, reaching far into the darkened sky, which was filled with more bright twinkling stars than I had ever seen in my life. Obviously, wherever and whenever I was, there was no civilization and therefore no light pollution to block the gorgeous view of the heavens above.

Instinctively, I began slowly walking toward the jungle, leaving the beach and the sunrise or perhaps sunset behind me. As I reached the edge of the dense foliage I saw what appeared to be the start of a well-worn path snaking its way deep into the jungle. I stepped onto the path and could suddenly hear the trees come alive with the calls and cries of whatever animals populated the area. For a moment I hesitated. I was a city boy and knew almost nothing of modern day nature let alone some wild and perhaps ancient tropical rainforest. I had no idea what might be awaiting me inside the thick undergrowth.

I heard another sound, buried somewhere deep within with myriad of animal noises—something unfamiliar yet still somehow slightly familiar. This sound didn't seem to be that of an animal or bird or even reptile but something else. It was like the mournful cry of some sad and pathetic creature coming from deep inside the jungle. I don't believe I had ever heard such a woeful wail before and the sound sent chills pulsating throughout my body.

These cries of what might be pain suddenly made the jungle even more disturbing and threatening than the original animal calls I had heard. Yet for some reason my body continued to walk deeper into the jungle as if I was no longer able to control its movement. I was aware of walking but unaware of my commanding the action. It was very surrealistic and for a moment I wondered if I might be dreaming, but the sensations of sight, sound, smell, touch and even taste were so acute I knew this unbelievably had to be real.

I passed through the jungle along the winding path without being accosted in any way and eventually exited the massive wall of tall trees to find myself at the base of the large mountain range. These were the same mountains I had seen from the beach, but now as I stood at their base I could see they were even grander than I had imagined. Like the jungle they seemed to stretch out in both directions for as far as I could see.

In the distance at the base of the nearest mountain I saw something that caught my eye. There was a large opening to what I assumed to be a cave. In the near darkness around me I would have likely missed this feature had it not been for the eerie florescent blue glow emanating from inside, causing the opening to look like a giant pale blue eye against the blackness of the mountain face.

I found myself walking purposefully toward the opening having no more idea why I was doing so than I had when I walked through the jungle. Behind me I could once again hear that unidentifiable mournful cry, which seemed to have been joined by a chorus of other similar cries. I felt as if these moans were trying to tell me something—perhaps trying to warn me against going inside the cave.

But I knew nothing would be able to stop me, since I was apparently not doing any of this of my own accord. I felt as if I were being drawn into the cave by an almost magnetic force. Strangely, I didn't feel any reluctance about entering the cave as the glowing blue light seemed to calm me in a way I cannot begin to explain. Yet the closer I got to the iridescent opening the louder the warning cries from deep in the jungle seemed to become.

As I got within a few feet of the entrance, I turned and took a final look at the dark jungle behind me. I could see what appeared to be hundreds of pairs of silvery red eyes glimmering in the blackness. They were watching me and I had a definite sensation they were still trying to warn me as well. Any apprehension I may have felt was overpowered by my inquisitiveness to learn what it was that awaited me inside the strange glowing cave.

Throwing all caution to the wind, I took a deep breath and slowly began to pass through the cavernous entrance, both uncertain yet incredibly curious about what might await me inside. Oddly, I didn't feel the slightest fear for my own safety. It was as if I understood I had been brought to this strange tropical place in some long-ago time for the sole purpose of learning. Then learn I would. I entered the cave.

7

Upon entering the cavern, I was bathed in a wash of blinding blue-white light. I suddenly felt a tingling sensation on the surface of my skin as if my flesh was somehow being electrostatically cleansed of all germs and offensive particulates. I felt cleaner than I had ever felt in my entire life. Even the inside of my mouth and my teeth felt as if I had just returned from having them professionally cleaned at a dentist, only even more so.

Looking downward I suddenly realized I was naked. I had no idea where my clothing had gone or how I had ended up in this state. Oddly, for some reason I was neither embarrassed nor concerned about being in this most natural condition. It was as if it was not only right but was also the only appropriate way for me to be presented in such a place. And I was far too overwhelmed by the sensations I was experiencing to pay any attention to my attire or lack of which.

It was as if every single nerve on the surface of my skin was tingling, like every hair was standing on end. And all the while the blue-white aura surrounded me, I had a sudden understanding that this primitive jungle habitat really was a place that existed millions of years earlier, just before the dawn of mankind. This was simply part of the knowing, which I suspected the 11:11 beings must have wanted to pass on to me.

I stepped forward out of the brightest of the light and then within the space of a few seconds I saw everything. I took everything in as if time itself had ceased to exist. Like the biblical convert Saul had expressed of his own experience on the road to Damascus, the scales likewise fell from my eyes and I was able to see everything anew and could begin to understand the truth.

The cave was not just a cave but appeared to be some sort of modern day laboratory or hospital. It was not what one might think of as a typical laboratory but something more organic in nature. It was unlike anything I had ever seen before.

Directly in front of me I saw what appeared to be an operating table of some sort, but it was not made of shining stainless steel or covered in a white sheet as one would expect to see in a twenty-first century hospital. Although the shape and functionality seemed to be similar to that of an operating table it appeared to be constructed of something almost flesh-like in nature. One very disturbing feature about the table was when I looked closely at its surface it seemed to actually be alive and even appeared to pulsate. Somehow I understood this thing was not a sentient being, although it was alive in the same sense as a plant or tree is alive. This was obviously some sort of living fleshy tissue, which could be molded into whatever shape might be required. These skin-like tables were not anchored to the cavern floor but seemed to hover just a few inches above the ground.

Next to the table was a cart of sorts apparently made up of the same flesh-like tissue, which held a variety of what looked to be operating tools such as forceps, clamps and scalpels, as well as an assortment of syringes. Unlike modern day instruments, these implements were not made of glass or stainless steel but some yellowish-white material resembling bone, which had been formed into the required shapes. Beneath the tools was what I at first thought to be a cloth table covering, but which I realized was composed of some translucent sparkling red membrane.

Behind what I thought of as the operating table was an array of cages constructed of a similar fleshy material while the round elements forming the bars of the cages were composed of the same bone-like composite as the tools seemed to have been made. I looked up and out into as much of the cave as was currently illuminated and saw the entire periphery of the cavern was covered with dozens of these cages of various sizes. Likewise similar tables stretched out for as far as I could see, also numbering in the dozens.

Every cage contained an animal of some type, likely retrieved from the surrounding jungle. There were birds, lizards, monkeys, gorillas, cougars, tigers and representatives of virtually every species I had ever heard of, as well as some I didn't recognize. A number of the cages contained creatures that looked so foreign to me as to have come from another galaxy. For some reason that thought seemed to ring true for me.

However, I discovered the cages were not the only things that were occupied; the operating tables contained... animals... or maybe humans... or perhaps they were... something... else. I looked again at the closest table and saw what resembled a chimpanzee strapped to the undulating surface of the table. Upon closer examination I'd have had to say it only partially looked like a chimpanzee. In fact, it looked more like some sort of ape/human hybrid.

There appeared to be countless tubes of some sort sticking out from the creature's body, leading to a square fleshy box mounted on top of one of the nearby utility carts. The tubes appeared to be made of a plant-like translucent substance. The creature turned its eyes toward me as much as it was able to with its head held securely in place by a restraining device composed of some vine-like substance. I momentarily was caught off guard by the level of intelligence I saw in the creature's pleading eyes. I had seen primates many times in various city zoos around the country and although they had a natural curiosity about them I had never seen any of them look at me with such outright and obvious intelligence. Flowing through the translucent tubes was a variety of brightly colored luminescent liquids ranging from red to blue to yellow and green. I was immediately reminded of what I imagined a dialysis machine might look like while treating kidney patients, although I had never actually seen one. If that was true, then this had to be a type of dialysis to the extreme.

Upon closer examination I realized the strange tubes were actually some sort of living organism reminiscent of a sea creature or perhaps worm-like thing and the liquid was being forced through them by the undulating and pulsating actions of the tubular organisms themselves. At the ends of the tubes where they attached to the creature's flesh, the tube spread out like a series of webbed fingers that buried themselves under the creature's skin. The webbing appeared to create a leak-proof seal at the end of the tubes.

I looked over at the next table and a similar scenario was playing out, but this time it was with a large bird-like creature whose feathers had been completely removed, leaving it a barren fleshy carcass. It too looked at me with a level of understanding I had never before witnessed in any bird; not that I had any more experience with birds than I had with primates. But I did know a look of intelligence when I saw one. I couldn't understand what was happening to these poor wretched creatures but it appeared to be some sort of unimaginable, torturous experimentation.

I looked out over the vast glowing expanse of the cavernous laboratory saw dozens of these living tables all occupied with strange creatures in various stages of treatment all being fed by these horrible biological machines. I had a feeling that this was not the entire cavern, but only a small portion. I suspected if I were to continue to walk deeper into the darker recesses of the cave they would light up as well revealing similar tables. I suddenly knew there were likely hundreds if not thousands of these inhumane experiments taking place in this cavern of horror.

"Inhumane... in human... un human," I thought suddenly with the slightest hint of some possible understanding not quite present but trying to work its way to the surface.

8

A moment later, I felt as though someone was watching me. I turned to see several dozen creatures entering the illuminated section of the cave through a darkened side passageway. They glowed with the same effervescence, which presently permeated the cave. These creatures were tall, well over six feet in height and were extremely thin. They were reminiscent of those creatures known as "Grays" depicted in the numerous alien and space invader movies, except much, much taller.

Their arms, legs and necks were long, awkward looking and spindly. Likewise their necks were twice as long as a typical human's and miraculously managed to hold up heads that were large and bulbous in nature. Their eyes were two enormous black oval orbs tilted slightly at an angle. Their faces had two small holes where I would have suspected their noses should have been and their mouths, from this distance seemed to be nothing more than small slits.

They began to fan out in various directions within the cave without speaking, yet their motions seemed to have been choreographed. It was then I realized there were not actually walking but were floating a few inches above the ground. They systematically moved from table to table, taking samples, adjusting tubes and apparently monitoring the status of the strange mutated creatures on the tables. They appeared to be ignoring me or else they simply felt I was of no consequence to them.

I suddenly felt a presence behind me and turned to stare up into the flat, nose-less face and large soulless eyes of one of the creatures. Its glowing effervescent skin, if it could be called skin, was extremely smooth in appearance. It stood well over six or seven feet tall as it looked down at me with an expression, or lack of which, that I took for curiosity. Its lip-less slit of a mouth never opened yet I could still hear its thoughts as if it were speaking to me in a calm soothing voice. No, I should correct that statement because it wasn't so much communicating to me with actual words as it was projecting pictures, movies, images, emotions and in some cases entire concepts into my mind at a speed I had never before imagined.

Although I realized no more than a few seconds had passed, in those few seconds my eyes were open as never before and I was immersed in a sea of knowledge. I instantly understood that no other living human being on the planet had ever been privileged to receive this information before.

What I was seeing here was the very origins of mankind itself. I was looking into the face of what our ancient ancestors must have thought of as gods. These beings, these other-worldly creatures were taking members of the wild animal population of earth and were infusing them with their own genetic material and creating an entirely new species: homo-sapiens, mankind, us. It was an extraterrestrial version of the old movie "The Island Of Dr. Moreau". These animals were being transformed. These beings were creating the human race from animals.

Then suddenly everything began to make sense to me regarding what I had seen in the parking lot of the fast food place. I knew why the 11:11 beings had allowed me to see how the cashier had resembled a frog and why the one who handed me my food looked like a bird. Then there were the three juvenile delinquents, each of whom had their own unique animal-like appearances. For that brief moment in time I had been given the gift of sight beyond sight; a tease, the ability to see the human species for what it really was, as it had originally existed.

It all became clear. I thought back to how many times during my life I had met people and immediately noticed how much they resembled animals. Some had long horse-like faces with huge teeth. Others were built like apes; while still others look like either birds or reptiles. I'm sure if you think hard about it you too will recall having incidents where people actually looked like animals to you.

I think this fact also helps to explain why cartoonists such as Walt Disney had been so successful at personifying their cartoon animals to resemble humans. Whether they were aware of it or not they had seen something very close to what I had just been shown. Perhaps the 11:11 beings had given them a bit of insight into the reality I now understood.

I now knew the truth. I had looked into the faces of our creators. I had been given the most secret and perhaps most sacred of all knowledge: the very origin of mankind. Man was created from a genetic hybrid process, joining the essence of the animals of Earth and the genetic components of these early 11:11 beings. This also helped me to better understand the aggression, which exists naturally inside every human being; and why it seems so hard at times to tame our inner animal. Again, I was reminded of the Island of Dr. Moreau and the rules he had to teach his creatures to force them to quell their animal instincts. I recalled what they referred to in the movie as the House Of Pain.

In nature, there are predators and prey. Likewise, within humankind, there are aggressors and there are victims. I suddenly had a vision appear inside my mind. It was the image of my face, as it existed in its human form. Then as I looked on, the image began to morph into something, which resembled a cross between a human and a panther, or perhaps a cougar. Whatever the exact nature of the beast was, it was most definitely a member of the big game cat family. These beings were telling me that I had descended from one of these creatures: a predatory cat.

I now understood the reason for why man tended to behave as violently as he did. These 11:11 beings made us that way. They apparently could create a new race of beings in their own image, but they could not successfully manage to remove the savage animal essence completely from us. They assumed millions of years of evolution might take care of this, but they were mistaken. Religion couldn't do it, nor could man's laws or even the threat of execution stop the violent animal within man.

But the question, which still remained was why had I been chosen me to be their messenger? And was being a messenger actually what they wanted from me? What was it about me that made me so special? Then the creature must have planted the idea inside my mind because I suddenly realized exactly what their reason was. It was my creativity, my writing skills. I was probably the only human alive who the 11:11 beings felt they could trust to pass on such vital information.

I would be expected to write their story and pass it on to the rest of the world in a concise way that everyone could understand. In my earlier contact with these beings, they had provided me with the stories, which resulted in my subsequent wealth and fame. They had had been deliberately providing me with the resources, which would put me in a position where I could do exactly what they wanted me to not do. I could use my notoriety to spread their word, to be in essence a disciple of their new doctrine. And that was exactly what I planned to do. I would spread their word. At least I had planned on doing just that. I wanted to but it somehow got sidetracked. I began I suppose to succumb to my inner beast—my true self. And that's when things began to go horribly wrong.

9

I woke up the next morning to the sound of someone banging on my front door. For the record, although I most definitely could afford a maid or a manservant, I prefer my privacy. As such, I live alone, which is just the way I like it. I tried ignoring the knocking, but it persisted. Since I was the only one available to answer it and since the knocking was obviously not going to stop, I stumbled out of bed as tired and miserable as I usually am first thing in the morning, perhaps even more so. I glanced over at the clock on the nightstand and saw it was 11:01, which was technically still morning as far as I was concerned. And yes, I did notice the significance of the digits. It was apparent that the 11:11 beings had something else for me to learn, but whatever that might be would have to wait until I got rid of whoever was beating down my front door.

I should point out here that part of the reason I had been sleeping so late was because I had been recovering from a major drinking binge from the previous night. Who could really fault me for tying one on after all I had been through and after everything I had learned the previous day? I was stressed out to say the least. Because of that, as well as my hangover and exhaustion, I approached the door as angry as the proverbial hibernating bear that had been poked with a sharp stick.

I yanked open the door ready to let whomever was on the other side know exactly what I thought of their disturbing me when I suddenly stopped, surprised. Standing on my doorstep was a very slight man, just slightly over five feet tall and rail-thin. He looked as though it might weigh one hundred and thirty pounds sopping wet. He had a long large muzzle of a nose and equally long and thin neck. He carried a suitcase of sorts with him and he appeared to be a door-to-door salesman. I didn't think there were any of those types around anymore. He wore brown shoes, brown pants, a white shirt and a red bowtie. My first thought was to tell him to go away and to slam the door in his face, but there was something I couldn't quite identify that told me not to be so brash, but instead to wait and see what transpired. I recalled the 11:01 sighting in my bedroom. Yes, perhaps the beings wanted me to see this thing through for a bit.

Before I was even able to ask him what it was he wanted, the funny little man announced he was selling some sort of "organic vegetarian food delivery service plan". On the pocket of his shirt was a logo consisting of a cluster of carrots and the name "Naturally Natural Organic Vegetable Service". I should point out at this time that for the most part I've always hated just about all vegetables. I'm a carnivore and having learned what I had learned the previous day, all of this meat eating suddenly made perfect sense to me. If I truly were descended from panthers, jaguars, lions or cougars, why would I care about anything but meat?

"It was only natural," I thought to myself with an internal chuckle. Then ironically, I thought, "Naturally natural."

I was next stunned to discover I was suddenly, almost uncontrollably hungry for fresh meat, for any fresh meat. It was as if a craving had come out of nowhere; and the desire was not just for fresh meat or rare meat but raw meat dripping with blood. I've always enjoyed my steak on the rare side but never anything too much in the realm of say steak tartare. But suddenly I felt a longing for raw, completely uncooked meat. I looked down at the little man and then suddenly all of my senses became heightened to a level I had never experienced before and had never anticipated. I was dumbstruck. I was not only looking at this man but I was looking through him and sensing his presence in ways, that were all new and disturbingly realistic to me. I could smell his slightly mint-tinged mouthwash breath and his body cologne with a slight trace of perspiration even from several feet away. And what was much worse was that the smell of his sweat and the general scent of him combined were making my mouth involuntarily water. My lord, I was actually salivating. I could hear the man's blood pulsating as it coursed through his veins and unbelievably, I swear I could smell and almost taste it. All of these sensations were driving me absolutely mad with hunger.

I couldn't believe what was happening to me. It took every ounce of willpower I had to keep me from bending down and tearing off his large nose and swallowing it whole. I stared at him for a moment in utter amazement afraid to move, fearful of what I might do if I did move.

The man's ears were large pointing upward and his big eyes were spaced widely apart. He had a pencil thin mustache, which stood out like whiskers on both sides of his lip and he displayed some sort of nervous tick, which made the tip of his nose occasionally twitch when he spoke. At first, I thought it was no wonder he represented an organic vegetable service; he looked more like a timid little bunny rabbit than a man. Then as I watched, his countenance began to transform right before my eyes. His face became that of a rabbit and the visage of the man was gone. Then a moment later, the man's face returned.

I looked up at the digital clock on my living room video recorder and realized it was 11:11a.m. I instantly knew what I had to do. I understood the reasons for the cravings and these heightened senses. The 11:11 people had shown me my place at the top of the food chain and they were telling me it was time for me to be what I rightfully needed to be. I needed to accept my true self. I was born to be a predator and a hunter.

I stepped away from the door and invited the little unsuspecting creature into my home. I told him to sit on the sofa while I went and got myself a cup of coffee. I asked him if he would like some coffee as well but he declined asking for organic vegetable juice instead. That didn't come as any surprise to me. I told him I had none but could bring him a cold bottle of water. He looked displeased but I really didn't care. I had something to do and "Bunny

Man's" fragile sensitivities were the least of my concerns. Yes, that was how I began to think of him—as Bunny Man.

After returning with my coffee and the bottle of water, I sat down next to him and took a sip from my drink, waiting for him to open his water. After a few seconds, he unscrewed the cap, took a few sips and said he would like to show me the products he had to offer. It was quite disturbing watching his face changing back and forth from human to rabbit, but I knew that soon none of that would matter. God I was starving! As he reached to place the water on the coffee table, I took a large plastic bag I had hidden behind my back and pulled it down over his rabbit head.

The little creature began to kick and scream and struggle but he was weak and I was strong; he was prey and I was the predator. After a few minutes, his bunny eyes began to bug out and redden with spidery crimson veins as the last of his oxygen ran out and he died. This filled me with a sense of euphoria the likes of which I have never before experienced. I looked at the clock and it read 11:22a.m. Exactly eleven minutes from the time this prey entered my den until he was dead. "Not bad for my first kill," I thought. I felt as if I was making my species proud.

Then I dragged the little man down into my basement. It was large but almost completely empty except for a few items I had placed there over the previous months. At the time I purchased the things and made modifications to the basement, I had no real idea why I was doing so. It just seemed like a good idea. Apparently, the 11:11 people were guiding me in this direction even back then. There was a large stainless steel two-door freezer, an indoor slop sink and an eight by three foot stainless steel table. Nearby there was a smaller stainless steel cart with a variety of electric carpentry tools. I had made sure the room was well equipped with electrical outlets. There was a wall faucet with a long hose attached and the floor sloped downward from all sides to a drain in the center of the room directly below the table. My mouth was now practically drooling with anticipation.

After a bit of contemplation, I went over to the table where I had placed a hacksaw along with the other tools. I went up to the kitchen and grabbed a box of large freezer bags and a permanent marker bringing them with me down to the basement.

I had no idea how difficult it was going to be to dismember a corpse using just a hacksaw. I realized it would probably be much better to use the circular saw I had purchased, as it would be more efficient way of removing appendages than dragging the hand saw back and forth over flesh, sinew and bone, until the blade was dull and my arms ached with pain. And I learned my assumption was most certainly correct; the circular saw did a much better job of quickly dismembering the frail corpse although the splatter resulting from the high-speed blade was a lot messier. I had a hose at the ready to wash down the area when I was finished. My formerly beautiful white basement was soaked with gore. Fortunately, I had chosen to use a high gloss paint, which cleaned up very easily. Again, I found it curious how I had made the decision to use that type of paint over a month earlier, not realizing how important it would be.

I'm sure by now you are wondering what I might have done next. I realized my first order of business had to be satisfying my rising blood lust. I did so immediately by tearing off a few sections of the creature's flesh and muscle then eating them raw. This single act created a sensation that could only be described as somewhere beyond ecstasy. When I again regained control of my emotions, I used the freezer bags I had brought down to conveniently store the remaining body parts and meat sections for freezing. I labeled them with things like "Bunny Man Hand" or "Bunny Man Foot" and so on along with the day's date. One must always keep freshness in mind when freezing meat.

Now I'm sure a lot of you out there are probably thinking there must be something wrong with me for me to commit what society might see as not only a heinous crime, but a taboo act as well, but you are sadly mistaken. I was not then nor am I now insane. On the contrary, I saw my true self and had embraced my origins. I was born to be a hunter and a killer; I just hadn't realized it until the 11:11 people showed me the truth. Once the scales were removed from my eyes, I saw the truth. And the truth was not insanity; it was simply reality.

10

"Bunny Man" may have been my first, but as you probably have guessed by now, he was not to be my last. Several days later, having grown tired of the taste of rabbit, I decided I should once again go on the hunt for some other inferior species. As it worked out, I discovered I had a craving for fowl.

I waited until dark then drove down to the seedier part of town in search of the appropriate solution to my particular longing. I didn't use any of my higher-end vehicles for this excursion. Instead, I used an old beater car I had picked up months earlier for a song. This was another of those things I did without understanding why. Then I swapped out the license plates with a car parked along the street several miles from my home.

When I drove past the corners where prostitutes were known to pedal their wears, I discovered the streetwalkers were out early that evening. It looked like it would be good fortune for me and not so good for them. I noticed several of them flagging down cars and offering themselves brazenly right out in the open as it they were untouchable by the law. Perhaps that was true. Maybe someone had paid off the police or maybe a city official to look the other way. I didn't know nor did I care. As I was well aware, there are many forms of justice in this world. One in particular came immediately to mind and that was the law of the jungle: survival of the fittest.

That night there was a wide assortment of human animals occupying the street corners including apes, rabbits, reptiles and many others. I wasn't surprised to have not seen any cats among the throng. We are far too proud and noble a breed to associate with such rabble—unless we are on the prowl for food. I suspected there might actually be some females of my breed participating in the prostitution profession, but these would likely be high-end pricey call-girl types who catered to the upper echelon of society, perhaps even exclusively to other male cat descendants.

A particularly thin boney creature approached my car as I stopped and rolled down the window. She very much resembled a large lanky member of some bird family although I couldn't identify which one. She had a long thin neck, a small mouth, a beak-like nose and beady little eyes. He hair was done up high and was multi-colored adding to the effect.

"You lookin' for a date big guy?" She said with as alluring a tone as she could manage with her raspy smoker's voice. The stench of her last cigarette and body odor along with the overpowering reek of her cheap perfume permeating the car was almost enough to make me retch. As if to make things worse, she leaned over looking in through the passenger window. The neckline of her blouse hung so far down and I could see her small exposed breasts dangling from her boney chest, which was covered with inflamed and oozing soars. If she knew what I knew about our ancestors she would have turned and fled in terror from the predator before her, but she remained ignorantly bent over gawking into my car with her squinty eyes and miniscule-pustule covered breasts.

Although I personally wanted nothing to do with this particular whore, I glanced at the digital clock on the dashboard to make sure I was reading the situation correctly and noticed it read 9:05p.m. That wasn't a proper number combination to indicate this was something I should consider. Thank goodness for that. Although I had no desire to make this trollop my next meal I was having a hard time controlling the urge to nevertheless grab her by her scrawny slut-neck and snap it like a twig.

Instead, I made the nobler choice. I simply waved her off and far too politely than was required said, "No... no I don't think so... not tonight thank you." Ignoring her stream of vulgar cackles, which faded as the window rolled up and I got further away, I then drove around the corner hoping for something much more delectable and was not as disappointing as that bag of bones. Then, there she was, standing squat under the fading amber glow of a failing streetlight was a plump meaty trollop who very much resembled an overstuffed Cornish game hen. My mouth immediately began to salivate.

I pulled over to the curb. The tramp waddled over to the door as I looked down at the digital clock, which now read 9:09p.m. Yes. This must be the one. Not wasting any time with small talk, I opened the door and she flopped clumsily inside, her breath wheezing as she struggled to get comfortable. She pulled the door closed and I suppose she was about to explain her fees for various services but before she had the opportunity, I punched her in the face slamming her head against the side window and knocking her out cold.

I drove home careful to obey all the speed limits and traffic signs. The last thing I needed was some cop to pull me over with a deliciously plump unconscious game hen hooker in my car. I knew I had every right to have her and to do whatever I wanted with her. However, I also understood the laws that were created and enforced by humans wouldn't take into account the truth of my origins. These humans most certainly would not understand or approve of my hunting. They might even want to punish me for my skill and prowess. Some might treat me as if I were mad when in fact; it was they, who had lost touch with their ancestral ways.

Slowly driving up my driveway, I pressed the automatic garage door opener and slid my car silently into the darkness of the garage, then closed the door quickly behind me. It took all of my strength to drag the unconscious hen out of the car and over to the top of the basement steps. As I got there, she started to come to and began muttering a string of barely audible obscenities at me. All it took was one good strategically placed kick, and the corpulent capon went flying down the stairs, flopping head over heels and landing on the concrete floor with a sharp crack as her pudgy neck snapped, killing her instantly.

For the record, once washed then properly sliced and diced she was absolutely delicious. I had no idea I had been missing such amazing delicacies for so long. The 11:11 beings had truly opened my eyes to an amazing reality the likes of which no other human could appreciate. I was happier than I had ever been in my entire life.

Over the course of the next several months, I entertained any and every single one of my gastronomic cravings. There were so many different creatures, which I had hunted, killed and devoured that I lost track of exactly how many there had been. I was in paradise. I was king of my jungle. I wanted this to feeling to last forever.

11

As is often the case in life, it seems all good things must come to an end. My own situation, I unfortunately learned was to be no exception. No matter how much I was enjoying my newfound place at the top of the food chain, it apparently had to end. In hindsight, had I done what I originally believed the beings had wanted me to do and written a book about what they had taught me of the origins of humanity, perhaps they would have found a way to protect me, perhaps not. I can't help but wonder if my getting hung up on the hunt and the taste of the flesh of lesser creatures somehow angered these 11:11 beings. Maybe they allowed things to go bad for me to punish me for my indiscretions. I suppose I may never know. Based on what has happened since then, I suppose it really doesn't matter anyway.

Here is how events took place, at least to the best of my recollection. It had been almost a year since my encounter with the 11:11 beings, since that time on the strange island with the cave and the experiments. It's very hard for me to nail down dates because time seems to have little meaning for me anymore. Regardless, here is what transpired. One day when I was once again sleeping late as all good big game hunting cats do after a successful kill, a loud and demanding knock came to my front door. The knock was much louder and much more deliberate than the frail knocking "Bunny Man" had made on that fateful day so many months earlier when I scored my first meal. Still not completely awake I stumbled to the front door angry and practically growling. I yanked it open harshly, determined to tear the throat out of whoever had disturbed my rest.

I stood in both shocked amazement and confusion looking up at the two huge burly looking dog-faced police officers who were waiting on the other side of the door. One of them bore an amazing resemblance to a British bulldog while the other looked more like a bloodhound. Behind them were several other cops and further back there were apparently still more whom I couldn't see as clearly. I could make out glimpses of one, which resembled a large ape and another who might have looked like a bear. I had to chuckle to myself as these all seemed appropriate animals for the role of police officers to me. The bloodhound-looking cop held out a piece of paper in his paw/hand, thrusting it forward and telling me it was a warrant for my arrest for murder.

I was speechless to say the least. Murder? What was this idiot talking about? I hadn't murdered anyone. Murder was a crime reserved for one human being killing another. Didn't they realize what a ridiculous accusation this was? Their stupid human laws no longer applied to me or to my kind. Couldn't they see that? Of course, I hadn't murdered anyone; all I did was hunt for my food as any good stalking cat would—and quite successfully, I might add. That was well within the accepted laws of nature. Surely, even a bunch of stupid dogs, apes and bears must be able to understand that.

Breaking out of my shocked stupor, I started to protest but before I could get a word out I found my hands being roughly pulled behind my back and could feel the cold of steel and the pinch of handcuffs locking around my wrists. Didn't these Beasts know whom they were dealing with? Then I realized they likely did not. I suspected there wasn't a single reader among the herd of them. But surely they had seen my movies. Then again I recalled how most people pay little attention to the credits and knew nothing about who had written the screenplays for the movies, no matter how successful.

"This is all some sort of big unfortunate misunderstanding," I said but was quickly stopped from speaking by a large horse-faced officer who came up from my left and proceeded to read me my Miranda rights while another officer, a big hairy ape looked on angrily. Normally these creatures wouldn't have concerned me, despite their size. I was descended from hunting cats and I could have handled myself if need be. However, now with my wrists manacled, I was helpless to fight back.

Within a few minutes what seemed like a small army of cops all resembling a variety of dogs, horses, bears and a few more apes all poured into my home and began tearing the place apart. An officer dragged me out to a waiting police cruiser then unceremoniously dumped me into the back seat slamming the door tightly behind me. If I could have slipped out of my cuffs, I would have started killing them one by one. Although I'm certain I would have been killed in the struggle, I might have at least had the opportunity to take some of them with me. Now in hindsight, perhaps death would have been a better alternative than what actually happened.

The police very quickly found my special food preparation and storage area in the basement, as well as my butchering table and all of my cutting tools. As it turned out, they were all apparently quite upset by the discovery. It made me chuckle actually. Several of the officers, young pups by the looks of them, had the audacity to rush out of the house vomit all over my precisely manicured front lawn. The nerve of them! What was wrong with these creatures? Didn't they understand? Didn't they also have the need to eat meat? They weren't all vegetarians were they? I supposed in their small still-undeveloped animal brains, they simply couldn't comprehend the same ideals, which those of us at the top of the food chain understood. Why was that my fault? Why should they treat me so poorly because of their lack of understanding?

They drove me to a local precinct and dropped me off at a small interrogation room where I sat alone for several hours. After that, several detectives came into the room and the questions began. I refused to answer a single one until I first had an opportunity to consult with my attorney. I told them I had been read my rights and I wanted to invoke those rights at that time. I wanted to call my lawyer. The truth was I didn't know any criminal lawyers but I figured I could have my publisher contact someone from his legal department and have him find me the best mouthpiece money could buy. But no matter how I protested, my words fell on deaf ears. It didn't seem to matter at all to the officers, who continued to refuse to give me an opportunity to call anyone. What the hell was going on? Wasn't I still in America?

To my shock and displeasure, I learned just moments before my arraignment that my case had been handed over to a court appointed attorney. This whole thing had gone beyond the point of ridiculous. I protested repeatedly that I could afford the very best and demanded to hire the most successful defense attorney in town. However, they would have none of that. Moreover, here is the really bizarre part of the story. Every single person of authority I encountered insisted that I was destitute and couldn't afford a lawyer. Hence, the reason for the court appointed attorney. They said that no matter what my financial situation I still had the right to proper courtroom representation. Were they insane? I was a world famous author with not only books and screenplays to my name but movies as well. I was rolling in money. How could everyone keep insisting that I was penniless? I was starting to wonder if the 11:11 people might have transported me to some other planet or dimension.

During my subsequent arraignment, I tried to explain my dissatisfaction with my legal representation to the judge, a delicious looking owl-like female creature who if she would give me half a chance I would have gladly made my next meal. However, bound and shackled as I was there was little opportunity for such pleasure. The judge told me if I was unhappy with my current representation, she would find me another but sooner or later I had to accept one of them. She too insisted I had no money to pay my own lawyer. I had to wonder what sort of conspiracy was being concocted against me.

Then after some time I figured it all out; a conspiracy was exactly what had occurred. Someone or more likely multiple people, probably the very same people who were now prosecuting me, had seized this opportunity to somehow hijack my bank accounts and had stolen all of my money. That owl-faced bitch of a judge was probably in on it as well—maybe a few of the cops and some other law enforcement types. That was the only explanation for why someone as wealthy as myself could suddenly find himself in such a financial quandary. They had all conspired to steal my fortune.

I quickly turned and whispered my conspiracy theory to my court appointed attorney who didn't seem to be taking my complaints seriously. In fact, he seemed to be leaning back away from me as if I was producing a foul smell or something. I was aghast. Was this really the person appointed to look out for my wellbeing? It was obvious he had no interest in helping me whatsoever. I was starting to realize that he also might even have been involved in the whole conspiracy.

Then instead of helping me get bail or even speaking up on my behalf, all he did was insist that I have a session in front of a court psychiatrist who, by the way, I now also believe was part of the plot to discredit me and steal my money. I must admit, in the beginning I originally trusted the good doctor even though he looked a bit like a fox with his long pointed snout and smallish eyes. However, he too did little to help my cause; in fact, it was this doctor who had the audacity to label me as a delusional, psychotic, schizophrenic, homicidal maniac.

Even after I took the time to tell him all about the 11:11 beings and how they told me about my proper place in life, it did little to appease him. I then gave him a detailed explanation about the origins of mankind and how I was not a murderer but was simply hunting for my food, which my race has been doing since the dawn of time. I mean, how much simpler could I have explained things to him? He too seemed to back away from me every time I spoke. Now that I think about it, everyone I met was acting the same way. It was crazy the way they were treating me. Yet, like the others, this doctor had the nerve to look at me as if I were the one who was insane.

If there was anything even slightly good the doctor did for me it was to have me declared incompetent to stand trial. I suppose as ludicrous as that may sound, it did at least keep me from both going on trial for murder and from being thrown in prison. I doubt I would have lasted very long among the general population. I might be fine one-on-one but in a cluster of several dozen creatures more savage than I could ever hope to be, I suspected I would not have survived. Instead, they put me somewhere else. I'm not exactly sure where I am now, but I do know that I'm alone in my small room and have had no contact with others except for my weekly sessions with yet another psychiatrist.

The food isn't too bad and they don't seem to mind when I skip most of the vegetables. They've even been nice enough to serve my meat very rare, not as raw as I would prefer it but it's acceptable. I have no close relatives whom I might contact to assist me, even if I could get the people in charge of this place to give me access to a telephone, which they won't. I continually ask to speak to my publisher, but they insist I have none. This is all very frustrating at times.

A few months ago they told me about some unknown writer who wanted to interview me and write a book or novella about my story. I figured I had nothing to lose. At least I might have the opportunity to bring some attention not only to my own plight but it would also be an opportunity to get the 11:11 peoples' message out there. I was even hoping that maybe if they saw I was doing something to spread their word, they might find some way to help me and get me out of this strange place. However, nothing else has seemed to work so I suppose this story might be my last shot at freedom.

Well, now you all know what I know. I hope that my co-author Anthony D'whater-his-name is has been able to tell my story and explain the injustice perpetrated against me. He has promised to allow me to see the final product and to edit it as I see fit. However, I can only hope he is true to his word, because as long as I am locked in here, there is little I can do to prevent him from treating me badly in print if he should choose to do so. Now that I think about it, I'm not even sure how to go about enforcing the confidentiality document, which I had him sign. So I suppose I am as much at his mercy as I am with my captors. This is not the sort of life someone descended from such noble beasts should have to endure. Unfortunately, it's the only life I now have.

COAUTHOR'S EPILOGUE

This is Anthony T. D'Angelo, the so-called coauthor of this account. My purpose for this epilogue is to clarify a few things for you. I felt it necessary that you understand the truth behind the story you have just read. First, let me state that there is no coauthor arrangement going on here between myself, and the unnamed subject of this account. I am the sole author of this work.

The anonymous character in this story, the narrator is a real person; however, he was not involved in the actual writing of this piece. When I set out to write it, I did so with the intention of making it sound as if it had come directly from the subject, and as such, I chose to write it in the first person. Had I allowed the subject to write or even co-write the work you would have never been able to follow the story line, because there would have been none; at least, not one you could have even attempted to understand. You see, he has a tendency to ramble and speak in a non-linear and illogical fashion, which only he can comprehend; at least, I think he can.

Most normal people who want to present a story do so in a chronological progression. They usually start at the beginning with step one, then the remaining steps will generally follow in a logical evolution and then finally there is the end. Granted in some stories there are flashbacks to other times in history but that too is usually also done in a coherent fashion. However, the subject of the previous story has no perception of space and time or no comprehension of the logical flow of information. From what I can tell, he hasn't had such an understanding for quite some time. Creating this work required me painstakingly to sift through the jumbles of information, which he dictated to me over the course of several months' worth of interviews. Next, I had to try to make sense of it all before attempting to turn it into a story—one that most normal, sane people would be able to understand.

As I mentioned, in this narrative I was writing as if I were the subject of the story and as such, I had this character tell you some things which in reality were untrue but in his mind were completely real. This also helped with the evolution of the story. For example, I had him tell you that he paid me a handsome sum of money to "co-write" the work and that he forced me in turn to sign a non-disclosure agreement in order to prevent me from divulging his name.

Although again he does believe this to be the case, it is not true either. It was what he, in his deluded mind, needed to believe in order for the work to progress, but it was all a complete fabrication. The truth is I took extensive notes while he sat across the room from me flapping his gums relentlessly, waving his arms maniacally and spewing out one insane monologue after another consisting of nothing more than rambling streams of consciousness. As such, my job was to take all of this rubbish and attempt to reorganize it so it flowed in at least some semblance of logical order. I also felt if I could make it sound as if the narrator was a normal, intelligent and sane person, it might make the ending of the account even more powerful. I hope that I have succeeded.

There was no need for the so-called non-disclosure agreement. I received no money for my time and work in creating this story. It was something I just chose to do because it seemed like a viable project, at least initially. In hindsight, maybe it wasn't such a good idea after all. God knows it left me feeling as if I wanted to run away screaming or bang my head against the wall on more than one occasion. There wasn't a shower in the world that could make me feel clean enough after listening to him carry on for hours. That sort of emotional filth never seems to come clean.

In reality, my so-called "partner" in this endeavor is not a famous author, nor is he rich. The truth is the man is destitute, practically homeless and most definitely insane. Although it's true that he has written mountains of manuscripts, they are all in my opinion, rubbish consisting of typical rambling incoherent half-thoughts. It's no wonder he has never managed to get even a single one of his works published. As I described in the story his stacks of rejection slips actually do rival his stacks of unpublished manuscripts.

If I did tell you his name, you might recognize it, however not for his being famous as for his being infamous. You may recall it from national news stories from several years ago, or you might not. As is typical, his sort of notoriety tends to be short-lived and quickly forgotten. You likely may recognize and recall his misdeeds, but his name is destined to fade into oblivion, which is perfectly fine with me. I have chosen not to identify him because in my opinion, although his story is quite interesting in a sick and twisted way, he doesn't deserve any additional notoriety for his sordid crimes.

As I said earlier, he is quite mad and currently resides at the Danesville home for the criminally insane, in Schuylkill County, Pennsylvania where he will likely spend the remainder of his miserable life. That is to say unless he is somehow miraculously cured of his illness. If that were to happen, he would likely be tried, convicted then moved to death row at some maximum-security prison where he would await his execution. However, after spending several months listening to his manic ramblings, I suspect in my unprofessional assessment, the chances of his ever recovering are non-existent.

We don't get too many criminals of his ilk in this part of the country, so when I heard about his murderous and cannibalistic spree I followed his arrest and incarceration, which for a time was the primary focus of the local media. After his commitment to the mental institution, I decided he might be an interesting subject for a book or at least a novella. It took several years and hundreds of phone calls, letters and emails to various officials before I could arrange to meet with him. You might wonder why I would go to such trouble. The bottom line was I felt someone needed to attempt to comprehend and present what this lunatic was thinking, what motivated him to do what he had done. The result of that endeavor was the story you have just read.

Think about it for a moment. This character was a failed writer who couldn't get anything published. He spent his entire life living in poverty, starving for his art as they say. Although to some this might seem like a noble endeavor, there is nothing noble about poverty, starvation and mental instability. My subject was certain that any day someone would discover him and would subsequently become rich and famous. Yet that day never arrived. I suspect, in order to cope with his failure and the waste of his entire life he began to fantasize about a life he never had. He probably believed some force was holding him back from success. Like many paranoids who feel someone or something other than themselves is responsible for their failures, he had to believe that as well. Otherwise anyone with what he believed was his level of genius surely would have been successful many years earlier.

From our conversations, I determined he had rationalized that if one unknown force was holding him back, perhaps there was another force in the universe, which might exist to help him. He simply had to find it. That was exactly what he did with the creation of his imaginary 11:11 beings. Maybe he really did begin to notice the numbers 11:11 and others similar numbers showing up from time to time. Who hasn't? I know I have. It's all pure coincidence, the result of our living in a digital age. Since most numerical values are nowadays presented to us in digital format, it's only natural that we might begin seeing repetitive numbers.

He actually did research his numeric sightings on the internet, on a free computer at the local public library, and those emails presented in the story are paraphrases with artistic license of some of those he had told me he had received. Just to verify this, I too did a similar search and sent out a similar email to that which he had sent to the various sites. To my surprise, I started to receive return emails very much like many of the same results he claimed to have received; so at least that part of his story held water. There are groups of people out there who actually do believe in these 11:11 beings. Unfortunately for him, their belief also served to fuel his delusional fantasy.

Then from what I could determine somehow in his twisted and broken mind he took the idea of a race of super-beings, the 11:11 people from these emails and decided they were trying to contact him personally. Why such a group of beings would have any interest in him is beyond my comprehension and probably beyond yours as well. But in his mind he was one of the greatest undiscovered authors on the planet. Therefore it only made sense to him that he would be the one human with whom they would share their secret.

Based on our interviews with people who had known him during his earlier days, before the insanity had gotten so severe, I had the impression he not only thought of himself in terms of being superior to most of his fellow man, but he also was something of a racist and a bigot. Looking at him from that perspective, the idea of him seeing people who he considered inferior to himself as something less than human was a natural state of mind for him. Some of these earlier associates had stated that he would often compare people with animals stating that one person looked like a lizard or another looked like a horse or a bird or an ape. Obviously, the seeds for his delusion were planted early on in life, which grew and flourished into the madness he experienced.

Then somehow he managed to take his life-long feeling of superiority as well as thinking of others as sub-human and combine that with the propaganda he received from the internet. Next, he dumped it all into the garbage blender, which served as his mind and set the control knob for puree. When all was said and done he had apparently convinced himself that a race of superior beings had been trying to contact him to deliver a special message for the masses. What message could be better than tangible proof about the origin of mankind itself? Can you say delusions of grandeur cubed?

Then at some point in time, he must have passed out, likely from hunger since he seldom ate regularly and then hallucinated about the entire episode of his encounter with the extraterrestrials in the cave. The result was exactly

what he wanted the result to be; he now believed that
humanity was descended from wild animals, which were
genetically altered by aliens. And he, of course, was
descended from the top of the food chain.

Therefore, he deduced that whatever he chose to do
was good because like the linage of kings and rulers
through the ages he believed his bloodline was superior to
everyone else's. He truly believed he was a god among men
and therefore he had a right if not an obligation to do
whatever he chose to do. From there his life, which was
already essentially in the toilet, began to plummet into an
even more severe downhill spiral.

Everything else discussed in the story and claimed by
the subject—the fame, the money, the big house and all
those other material things—were nothing more than
figments of his imagination. In his mind, that was his life.
In reality he was homeless and destitute. He was a
squatter, living in an abandoned factory building in one of
the worst parts of the city. The only possessions he
managed to hang onto were the boxes of his unpublished
books and stories, and of course, his rejection slips.

He did however have a somewhat similar combination
torture chamber butcher shop in one of the basement
levels of the abandoned factory, but it was neither as clean
nor as well-equipped as he chose to describe in his
account. I've seen police photos of the crime scene and it
was beyond revolting. Imagine a dirt floor, cement block
basement with no electricity, no water, no windows and
absolutely no ventilation. Now imagine months and
months' worth of splattered blood, rotting human remains,
severed limbs and sections of raw meat all in various
stages of decomposition. That was what his so-called
workshop was really like.

In this story I've spared you quite a bit of the gore,
which was the reality of his crimes. My goal was simply
provided you with just an overview of a few accounts of his
heinous acts. There were actually so many murders, one
more unspeakable than the next. It nauseates me just to
think about them. I've seen some of the pictures and I've
read the police reports. Many of these killings were

confirmed and the victims identified but many others that he confessed to remained unverified.

Since he primarily preyed on the lowest level of society, the fact that these people went missing may have gone largely unnoticed. If what he has told me is true however, the numbers could go into the hundreds. But as I said, he is a madman and has no idea what's real and what's fantasy. So neither he, nor I nor anyone else will likely ever really know just how bad his murderous spree of wanton slaughter and cannibalism actually was.

I'm certain someday, if most of the horrifying murders are documented, there will be enough stories of madness and mayhem to fill a thousand-page novel. When that day comes, I suspect I'll just leave that particular work to someone else. The fact is I've simply had enough of his madness for one lifetime. Although you may have found reading these few accounts in this story a bit disturbing, learning all the gory details and hearing about them from his own lips, with that inhuman look in his eyes staring wildly at me was more chilling than you could possibly imagine.

So that's my story and I hope you appreciated it. I won't ask if you enjoyed it because if you did, perhaps society should worry about you as well. But feel free to read it again if it suits you and think about it the next time you happen to look at the digital clock on your microwave oven or digital video recorder and you notice the numbers 11:11 or 4:44 or maybe even 12:34. Who knows? Maybe someone is trying to get your attention. I most certainly hope to God they are not.